HOMETOWN HEARTS

SHIPMENT 1

Stranger in Town by Brenda Novak
Baby's First Homecoming by Cathy McDavid
Her Surprise Hero by Abby Gaines
A Mother's Homecoming by Tanya Michaels
A Firefighter in the Family by Trish Milburn
Tempted by a Texan by Mindy Neff

SHIPMENT 2

It Takes a Family by Victoria Pade
The Sheriff of Heartbreak County by Kathleen Creighton
A Hometown Boy by Janice Kay Johnson
The Renegade Cowboy Returns by Tina Leonard
Unexpected Bride by Lisa Childs
Accidental Hero by Loralee Lillibridge

SHIPMENT 3

An Unlikely Mommy by Tanya Michaels
Single Dad Sheriff by Lisa Childs
In Protective Custody by Beth Cornelison
Cowboy to the Rescue by Trish Milburn
The Ranch She Left Behind by Kathleen O'Brien
Most Wanted Woman by Maggie Price
A Weaver Wedding by Allison Leigh

SHIPMENT 4

A Better Man by Emilie Rose
Daddy Protector by Jacqueline Diamond
The Road to Bayou Bridge by Liz Talley
Fully Engaged by Catherine Mann
The Cowboy's Secret Son by Trish Milburn
A Husband's Watch by Karen Templeton

SHIPMENT 5

His Best Friend's Baby by Molly O'Keefe
Caleb's Bride by Wendy Warren
Her Sister's Secret Life by Pamela Toth
Lori's Little Secret by Christine Rimmer
High-Stakes Bride by Fiona Brand
Hometown Honey by Kara Lennox

SHIPMENT 6

Reining in the Rancher by Karen Templeton
A Man to Rely On by Cindi Myers
Your Ranch or Mine? by Cindy Kirk
Mother in Training by Marie Ferrarella
A Baby for the Bachelor by Victoria Pade
The One She Left Behind by Kristi Gold
Her Son's Hero by Vicki Essex

SHIPMENT 7

Once and Again by Brenda Harlen
Her Sister's Fiancé by Teresa Hill
Family at Stake by Molly O'Keefe
Adding Up to Marriage by Karen Templeton
Bachelor Dad by Roxann Delaney
It's That Time of Year by Christine Wenger

SHIPMENT 8

The Rancher's Christmas Princess by Christine Rimmer
Their Baby Miracle by Lillian Darcy
Mad About Max by Penny McCusker
No Ordinary Joe by Michelle Celmer
The Soldier's Baby Bargain by Beth Kery
The Maverick's Christmas Baby by Victoria Pade

HOMETOWN HEARTS

A Better Man

USA TODAY Bestselling Author

EMILIE ROSE

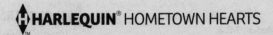

Recycling programs
for this product may
not exist in your area.

ISBN-13: 978-0-373-21470-9

A Better Man

Printed in U.S.A.

www.Harlequin.com

USA TODAY bestselling author and two-time RITA® Award finalist **Emilie Rose** lives in North Carolina with her own romance hero. Writing is her third career. She's managed a medical office and a home day care—neither offered half as much satisfaction as plotting happy endings. Her hobbies include gardening, fishing, cooking and traveling to find her next book setting. Visit her website, emilierose.com, or email her at EmilieRoseAuthor@aol.com.

To the men and women who serve our country, allowing us the freedom to read and write what we choose.

Chapter One

Roth Sterling had sworn he'd never set foot in the godforsaken hellhole of Quincey, North Carolina, again. But twelve years after his escape, here he stood, eating those bitter words.

The town held too many memories. Most of them bad. But what choice did he have with his murderous bastard of a father due to be paroled from prison in two months?

He opened the door of his new apartment, stepped inside and shoved the key into his pocket. He had limited time to convince his mother not to allow the animal who'd beaten her for fifteen years back into her life. Better yet, Roth would persuade her to divorce the man and take out a restraining order. But even if she did, could the town's five-officer team enforce it?

Maybe. Maybe not.

Restraining orders tended to be useless if the one being restrained chose to ignore them. He'd seen enough domestic abuse cases end badly during his time with the Charlotte Police Department to know the statistics. They weren't good.

He'd spoken to his father only twice in the past seventeen years, most recently when his father had announced that he and Roth's mother were going to move into their old house in Quincey.

Roth's father had filled his ears with a load of rehabilitated, remorseful, I've-been-saved crap, and Roth hadn't believed one word of it. The old man still had an evil glint in his eyes—the same glint Roth had often seen as a kid right before dear ole dad knocked him senseless. But Roth's pleas to the parole board to keep his father behind bars had fallen on deaf ears, and he'd had to change tactics.

His parents' return to Quincey was forcing Roth to do the same. Temporarily. Quincey's advertisement for a police chief had provided a perfect cover. As the newly appointed chief,

Roth would be in a position to insure that if his father laid a hand on Roth's mother—or anyone else—he'd pay. Roth hadn't been able to protect her when he'd been a kid, but he could now. He rested his right hand on the butt of his Glock. With lethal force, if necessary.

History wasn't going to repeat itself. Not on his watch.

He rolled his shoulders, trying to ease out the stiffness, then strolled through the den, kitchen and each of the two bedrooms, noting the age and wear of Quincey's only apartment building.

A fresh coat of off-white paint on the walls couldn't compensate for the scarred hardwood floors, worn linoleum and old cabinetry. The place was clean, but it was a far cry from his condominium in the gated complex in Charlotte, with its clubhouse, gym, pool and hot tub, but these digs would suffice.

He wasn't crazy about being on the ground floor. It made unlawful entry too easy. The sliding glass door onto the small patio could be a problem. He registered the inadequate locks on the doors and windows and the nooks and crannies where a perp could hide. He'd have to hit the hardware store before it closed if he wanted to beef up his security.

Quincey used to roll up the sidewalks at dark. Did they still?

He returned to the living room and glanced out at his loaded-down Chevy truck and the rented U-Haul trailer parked by the curb. In the olden days his buddies would have shown up before his tires cooled to help him unload, but he'd seen no sign of Chuck, Joe or Billy since arriving an hour ago. At three on a Thursday afternoon they might be at work. He hadn't notified them of his arrival. He'd counted on the Quincey rumor mill doing the job for him. No doubt the phone lines had started humming the minute he'd signed his contract last month.

He was looking forward to seeing the guys and catching up—if they still lived here. The letters between him, Joe and Billy had been sporadic, first because none of them had been the letter-writing type, and second, because Roth's unit had often been deployed to places where mail delivery wasn't high on the list of survival needs. By the time he'd settled in Charlotte the correspondence had ceased altogether. Maybe the guys had finally escaped. Twelve years ago that's all any of them had wanted.

Any of them, except Piper Hamilton.

A hint of regret weighted his shoulders.

Piper's roots had run deep in the community, and she'd never planned to leave. He raked a palm over his freshly trimmed hair and tried to push away the memories, but he couldn't force the image of her trusting blue eyes and long, sunlit hair from his head. He'd loved her. More than he'd ever loved anyone. And he'd hurt her. Deliberately. Not with his fists—his father's modus operandi—but with his actions, his words.

They'd been little more than kids, too young to take on the commitment they'd been racing toward. The split couldn't have been anything but good for them. But it hadn't been easy. And he'd handled it badly. It had worked out for him. The Marines had given him his first taste of freedom from living in his father's dark shadow and success and a career he loved. Had it worked out as well for Piper? Had she married and raised a family the way she'd wanted?

He had a few ghosts to lay to rest and apologizing to Piper was at the top of the list.

In a town this size, he'd bump into her sooner or later, but he preferred to set his own timetable instead of waiting. He'd make it happen. The sooner the better.

A knock on the door preceded Doyle, the apartment manager. "Suit ya?"

"It'll do."

"Sure you want to pay month to month? Save ya fifty bucks a month if you sign a year's lease."

Roth had no intention of being here that long. "Month to month is fine."

"Alrighty then. Y'all have a good day." Doyle waddled down the cracked sidewalk toward his office.

Roth stepped outside. His furniture wasn't going to unload itself. He headed toward his truck, aware as his boots pounded the concrete of the watchful eyes and shadows shifting at windows. But no doors opened, and no one came out to say hello or offer assistance as he rolled up the trailer's door and lowered the ramp.

He'd expected more of a welcome, for curiosity's sake if nothing else. After all, it wasn't every day one of the town's delinquents returned to head up the local law enforcement team.

He scanned the empty streets. An invisible noose tightened around his neck and claustrophobia closed in, slowly crushing out a lungful of the smog-free air.

Temporary.

Folks in a tight-knit community liked to stick their noses in your business, often acting as judge and jury, their opinions shaped by hearsay rather than fact. They usually helped out when you needed 'em—if for no other reason than to root for tidbits to tattle.

But apparently not today.

He checked to make sure his leather jacket concealed his weapon. The pistol could be scaring off people. He wouldn't officially pick up his badge until Monday morning, but surely the citizens expected the new chief of police to carry a weapon in or out of uniform?

The temperature was mild for the end of March, but he'd work up a sweat. Regardless, he'd keep on the jacket. He unstrapped the hand truck and muscled his gun safe onto the two-wheeled unit. Getting the hazards out of the way and securing them was his first order of business. He manhandled the heavy piece up the walk. After he situated the steel box in the spare bedroom closet, he returned to the trailer and lugged boxes inside, stacking them in the rooms labeled on each box.

A couple of teenagers whizzed past on skateboards, staring hard but not slowing. Ditto the beige station wagon, navy sedan and silver pickup with a dented rear quarter panel and low rear tire.

Hell, he was starting to think folks didn't want him here. You'd think they'd be pleased that he'd finally gotten his act together.

An hour later he had emptied the truck bed and had everything out of the trailer except the sofa, dresser and his king-size mattress, and still no one had offered assistance. That wasn't like the town he remembered. Screw it. He'd hit the hardware store, buy better locks and try to round up a strong back to help him finish the job.

He locked up, hoofed it across the asphalt and turned down Main Street. This morning when he'd driven in he'd been surprised to find that little had changed in the past twelve years. There were a few more shops—he'd investigate another day.

He pushed open the door and automatically noted two customers, white males, sixties, and Hal Smith behind the cash register in what looked like the same blue apron he'd always worn. The store owner, with his wispy white hair in a bad comb-over that couldn't hide his pale, spotted scalp, had to be eighty by now.

"Mr. Smith, good to see you again."

The owner sized him up. Roth offered his

hand and the man hesitated before returning the gesture. The shake was brief. "Sterling. Heard you was coming back. What can I do for you?"

The cool tone was hard to miss. Damn strange, considering Quincey needed a chief, and Roth was, if anything, overqualified, and he'd taken one hell of a pay cut for this job. What was the problem? "I need window and door locks."

"Doyle's apartment not secure enough for you?"

"No, sir. A credit card would jimmy anyone in."

"Locks are on aisle three." But Hal didn't move to help. Maybe age had slowed him down.

"I also need help unloading a few bulky items. Know anyone interested in earning a few bucks?"

Smith glanced toward the other customers then at Roth. "Can't say as I do."

Roth nodded his thanks and turned for aisle three. Guess it would take a while for folks to figure out he wasn't a hell-raising kid anymore. He wouldn't be in town longer than absolutely necessary, but he'd be here long enough to show this apple had fallen far from his daddy's rotten tree. He wasn't white trash anymore.

* * *

Roth Sterling was back.

Piper Hamilton fought a rising tide of panic as she reversed out of her parking space as fast as she dared. Her fingers cramped on the steering wheel and her palms grew slick.

She'd heard the first whisper of impending doom when Mrs. Peabody had brought her geriatric cat into the veterinary clinic after lunch. Then it seemed each successive client had made a point of sharing the latest Roth sighting with Piper.

Roth had bought locks at the hardware store. Roth had hired a couple of high school kids to help him unload furniture. Roth had visited the market, but he hadn't driven his big black pickup over to the old home place yet....

Roth this. Roth that. As if she wanted a play-by-play on the man she used to love— the one who'd dumped her and left her pregnant.

Most of the afternoon's clients had also made sure Piper knew they wouldn't welcome the man who'd usurped her father as chief with the community's usual open arms and Southern charm. While she appreciated their loyalty, their animosity only added to her worries. If the town gathered their figurative wagons around her, Roth might think she had something to hide. And she did.

The only stoplight turned red as she approached the intersection at Main Street even though there wasn't any oncoming traffic. She muttered a curse and braked hard. It had been one of those days when nothing went right.

She checked her mother's real estate office parking lot. Empty. Hopefully Mom was at home guarding the fort and the treasure.

Piper ripped the clip from her hair and massaged her scalp, then tapped the wheel, urging the light to change. When it finally did she had to resist the impulse to race home. Not even being the chief's—*former* chief's—daughter made her immune to getting pulled over for a lecture. If anything, her father's deputies had become a little overzealous in their honorary "uncle" roles since her father's stroke six months ago.

Her father. She sighed. Eight weeks ago the town council had strong-armed him into resigning and told him they'd already begun searching for his replacement.

His bitterness over being stripped of the job that defined him for thirty years festered inside him like an abscess. He'd spread his infectious pus of discontent over anyone within hearing distance.

But why had the town council hired Roth Sterling? Surely there had been better candidates than a troublemaker who'd left town and not once come back to visit?

Her street finally came into view. She saw her mother's sedan in the driveway of the home they shared and exhaled in relief. If her mother was at home, then maybe Josh would be, too. Piper prayed her son would be in his room, doing his imitation of an uncommunicative adolescent.

She threw the car into Park and raced up the walk. Her mother opened the door before Piper could reach for the knob. "I take it you've heard?"

Piper didn't ask for clarification. "Yes. Where's Josh?"

"Upstairs. I bought him a new game to keep him occupied until we come up with a plan."

"Good idea." Usually Piper didn't allow her son to veg out on video games until after he'd finished his homework, but today she'd settle for anything that kept him out of sight.

"Piper, what are we going to do?"

The house smelled delicious, a testament to her mother's stress level. Mom always baked when she was agitated. Piper put down her purse and hung up her jacket then checked to make sure Josh wasn't nearby. To be on the safe side, she pointed to the kitchen and held her tongue even though her thoughts were tripping all over themselves. They reached the room on the opposite side of the house from his bedroom.

"We'll do whatever it takes to protect him, but we'll have to stick with the same story you told everyone before Josh and I came home."

"Do you think Roth will buy it?"

"I hope so. I can't believe he came back. He always wanted more than Quincey had to offer."

More than *she* had to offer.

Strain lined her mother's immaculately made-up face. As the town's only real estate agent, her mother never looked less than magazine-advertisement perfect even when she was baking.

Her mother pulled a cookie sheet from the oven. "I cannot believe the town council kept their choice for chief a secret. They even conducted the interviews out of town. No one said a word about who they'd hired until Roth arrived today. And now everybody's talking."

Piper pressed a finger against the tension headache chiseling between her eyebrows. This spelled disaster in so many ways. "Does Daddy know?"

"Who do you think told me? Your father was there when 'Sterling strutted into the g'damned station like he owned the place.'" She did a pretty good imitation of her husband's rough drawl. "I thought Lou would have another stroke before I could get him off the phone."

"I thought the council was being considerate of Daddy by not flaunting the interview process in his face. Now I'm not so sure."

"It wasn't considerate, Piper. It was underhanded. They started advertising for his position even before Lou resigned. I should have put the puzzle pieces together when Eloise Sterling canceled the lease on the tenants of her family's home place. She only gave them thirty days to vacate."

"How is Daddy taking this?"

"Not well. He immediately started predicting gloom and doom about you know who." Ann Marie tilted her head toward Josh's room. "Your father wants to come over and discuss our options."

Piper grimaced. Great. She'd have to play referee between her parents again. Any time they got together it tended to result in a verbal skirmish with Piper stuck in the middle while they took shots at each other. All because of the choices Piper had made twelve years ago. Guilt weighed on her.

But if she'd given in to her father's browbeating and gone through with the abortion or her mother's pleas to give up the baby for adoption, then Piper wouldn't have Josh, and he was the best thing that had ever happened to her. The negative result was that her decision had started a feud between her parents that hadn't ended.

They'd tried to keep that secret. Piper hadn't learned until she'd returned to Quincey after her four-year exile that her pregnancy had ended her parents' marriage. Well, not ended *technically,* since they were still legally married, but they lived on opposite sides of town with separate bank accounts, separate lives, and no amount of coaxing on her part had managed to get them to bury the hatchet.

"I'll talk to Dad."

"What good will that do? He's too pig-headed to listen to any opinion except his own. But your father is right about one thing. Roth will find out about Josh."

Piper's stomach churned. She should start dinner—and not just to keep her hands and mind occupied. When Josh ventured from his room he'd eat anything that didn't run from him, and it would be better if his feast didn't consist of six-dozen cookies.

"Mom, we can't undo the lies. We have our story, and we're sticking to it."

"All Roth will have to do is demand a paternity test."

Piper had chewed off a couple of fingernails over that prospect this afternoon. "Please don't borrow trouble. We have enough to worry about already. He didn't want our child twelve years ago. Let's hope that hasn't changed."

Piper hoped it would be enough. Otherwise catastrophe could strike, and she could lose the most important thing in her life. Her son.

The front door opened Friday as Piper was preparing to close for lunch. She looked up, expecting to see a frantic pet owner with an emergency.

Roth Sterling filled the doorway—an entirely different kind of crisis. Even without the shoulder-length chestnut waves she'd once loved to run her fingers through there was no mistaking that rugged face, those seductive brown eyes or the mesmerizing mouth that had taught her so much about pleasure.

A lead weight crash-landed in her stomach. The hum of the computer and the yap of the dogs in the kennel in the rear of the building faded into a whir of white noise.

He looked the same. But different. Harder somehow, as if his youth had been chiseled away by age and experience that his spiky short hair only accentuated. His face was leaner, his cheekbones more pronounced. Shallow lines fanned from the corners of his eyes. Beneath a battered brown leather jacket his shoulders had filled out since the last time she'd seen him, held him, made love with him. Watched him walk away.

"Hello, Piper." Like his body, his voice had morphed into something steelier. Sexier.

But despite all the changes, his effect on her hadn't altered one iota. Her knees softened like butter in the sun and her breaths shortened. It took effort to force air through her vocal cords. "Hello, Roth."

He crossed the waiting room, a confident

stride replacing his old cocky swagger. Thick thigh muscles strained the fabric of his faded jeans. He'd been lean and rangy at twenty. At thirty-two he looked sinewy and dangerous. "You're looking good."

A hot flush started deep inside her, licking through her chest, up her neck and across her cheeks. She cursed the telling reaction.

She'd checked the mirror two minutes ago when she'd washed up after their last patient. Her slipping ponytail, baggy lavender scrubs and walking shoes were nothing to brag about. But at least she'd applied makeup this morning, because she'd known that eventually she would bump into him. And most of it was still on despite doggie licks and sweat.

"Liar."

His grin, as devilish and dangerous as she remembered, rocked her equilibrium. "I always call 'em like I see 'em."

Get a grip. Remember what he did to you?

She straightened, trying to find her backbone and the anger that had driven her for years. Both appeared to be AWOL. "Did you need something?"

"To say hello away from the prying eyes of Quincey."

"Those same prying eyes very likely tracked

your path to the clinic. But thanks for stopping by. Now if you'll excuse me, I need to lock up for lunch." She hoped her cool, unemotional tone sounded as convincing to him.

His smile broadened. "That's why I'm here. I came to take you to lunch."

Alarm erupted inside her like a Fourth of July fireworks display. She couldn't risk a trip—or a slip—down memory lane. "I already have plans."

Piper reached for her keys and her knuckles bumped Josh's school picture. One look at that photograph and Roth would know the truth. And he didn't deserve to know. Not after what he'd done. Although he had no reason to come behind the high counter she wasn't taking any chances. She scooted the frame behind her monitor.

The light on the two-line phone went out, indicating Madison had ended her call. The sound of her boss's desk drawer opening and closing filled Piper with urgency. She wanted Roth gone before Madison came out. Even though Madison had become more friend than employer over the past five years, Piper had never shared the intimate details of her history with Roth. She didn't intend to start now.

She circled the desk, opened the door and

tipped her head to face her nemesis. She'd forgotten how tall he was.

"Don't let me keep you. Have a nice day." She added a saccharine smile.

"What? No welcome back?"

"Did you really expect one?"

Roth folded his arms and rocked back on his heels. "We need to talk about what happened, Piper."

"No, we don't. The past is over. No need to rehash it."

"We left things…unsettled."

He had no idea what an understatement that was. Piper checked over her shoulder to make sure Madison hadn't left her office yet. "No, Roth. You made your feelings perfectly clear when you shoved a fistful of money at me and told me to visit the clinic and take care of *my* problem. But that was twelve years ago. I'm over it and over you."

"Did you?"

She blinked and swallowed, trying to ease the knot forming in her throat. From the moment she'd heard of his return she'd known this question would come up. She should have been prepared. But she wasn't. And she'd never been a good liar.

"Did I what?"

"Visit the clinic." His eyes searched her face.

Her heart pounded and her palms moistened. The door handle slipped from her fingers. *Stick with the facts.*

"Dad drove me to one in Raleigh. It's far enough away that nobody here would know..." She bit her lip, unable to finish because that's where the truth he needed to hear stopped. Anything she added would have to be a lie.

"Piper," Madison called as her footsteps squeaked down the long tile hall, filling Piper with a mixture of relief over the interruption and dread over the upcoming meeting. "Mrs. Lee's Chihuahua is in labor and it's not going well. I have to cancel our lunch and make a house call. If the labor drags on or I have to bring Pebbles in for a C-section, I'll call your cell."

Madison reached the archway between the treatment rooms and the waiting area and spotted Roth. "Oh, I'm sorry. I didn't realize we had company."

Her ex-lover and her boss stared at each other. Then Madison hiked an expectant eyebrow at Piper. Piper reluctantly accepted that she couldn't avoid making introductions. "Madison, this is Roth Sterling, Quincey's new police chief. Roth, Dr. Madison Monroe."

Madison smiled and extended her hand. She, unlike Quincey natives, tended to avoid the gossip and intrigue of small-town living. But her interest in the new male specimen couldn't be missed. Piper lost her appetite.

"Nice to meet you, Chief Sterling, and some other time I'd love to hear what brought you here. But I have to run."

"Good to meet you, too, Doc," Roth replied. "And the answer is simple. I came home."

Piper didn't like the sound of that. *Home* implied a certain…permanence.

Madison's eyes widened. "Home? You're a local?"

"Yes."

Madison shot Piper a look that promised an inquisition when she returned, then with a wave she grabbed her med-kit, and rushed out the door.

Roth's dark eyes zeroed in on her, making her feel antsy and uncomfortable. "You're not the veterinarian?"

She couldn't believe he remembered her long-ago dream. "I'm Madison's assistant."

"What happened to vet school?"

She wiggled her toes in her shoes. "Plans change."

He flashed one of his lethal grins and her abdomen quivered. "And because yours have, you're now free for lunch. Let's go."

No. No. No. "I need to set up the surgical room in case Madison needs it."

"I'll wait."

She did not want to spend any more time with him. "Look, Roth, while I appreciate your invitation, I really don't have time for a long lunch break."

"Then I'll get a takeout from the diner and we'll eat here."

Alone behind a locked door? She searched for another excuse to avoid this encounter and couldn't find one. "The gossips would be the ones feasting if you did that."

"Sounds like Quincey hasn't changed." He shoved his hands into his pockets. "We're sharing a meal, Piper. If not lunch, then dinner. I'm not on duty until Monday. I can park it right here—" he pointed at a waiting room chair "—and wait until you're available."

Not what she wanted to hear. She wasn't going to be able to avoid him. Resignation settled over her.

"When you put it like that, how can I refuse?" If she did, she'd only arouse his curiosity, and the last thing she wanted was Roth Sterling snooping around in her personal life.

"Exactly."

Chapter Two

"Let's go. I'll prep the room when I get back. We'll have to hurry in case Madison needs me." Piper snatched her purse and headed out, eager to get this encounter behind her.

Then maybe Roth would go away and forget her. Again.

"Your enthusiasm underwhelms me." She heard the teasing note in his voice and didn't need to look to know he was smiling. His smiles used to turn her to mush. But she couldn't let them have that effect now.

After locking up she followed him into the parking lot.

He scanned the busy-for-Quincey streets. "Traffic's picked up from what I remember."

"Over the past few years we've had several mom-and-pop antiques stores open up. That makes Quincey a mecca for weekend shoppers." She hoped that meant the shopkeepers would be too busy with their customers to notice her comings and goings or her lunch partner. "The diner will be packed. There's a barbecue place ten miles south of here."

"Afraid to be seen in town with me?"

She couldn't risk someone stopping by their table to ask about her son. "I don't have the time to wait for a table or be constantly interrupted by people welcoming you."

"I don't think the welcomes will be a problem. I'll drive." He led her toward a big black truck.

She caught herself admiring the way he filled out his jeans and couldn't force her gaze away any more than she could stop a freight train with her pinkie finger. Roth still looked damned good. Better than any of the slim pickings in town, for sure.

An old familiar hunger trickled through her—one she hadn't experienced in so long that she almost didn't recognize the budding tension in her belly. When she did she tried to pop the bubble by focusing on the wreckage he'd made of her life when he'd said goodbye.

She clung to the hurt and anger like a shield, but no matter how much his betrayal stung, she didn't—*couldn't*—hate Roth, because he'd given her the most precious part of her life. Josh.

He opened the door and she climbed into the high cab. When he slid into the driver's seat she fastened her seat belt and took shallow breaths through her mouth to avoid the tantalizing aroma of his scent. It didn't work.

He put the truck in gear and hit the highway. "If you didn't go to vet school, what have you been doing since I last saw you?"

Raising your son. She held her tongue and searched for an acceptable answer.

"Right after you left, my father's great-aunt fell and broke her hip. She needed live-in help while she recuperated. I was available."

"I don't remember your aunt."

"She moved to Florida when I was a baby."

That earned her a quick look. "Florida? *You* left Quincey?"

His disbelieving tone raised her hackles. "I was going away for college."

One corner of his mouth lifted. "You were going to commute. The chief wasn't about to let his baby girl live in a dorm with all those wild college girls."

True. She couldn't deny she'd been sheltered and her father had been—and still was—overprotective, which explained the sad state of her social life. She might be thirty, but he still treated her like a child.

Scratching at a spot on her scrubs, she searched for a way to give Roth enough information to satisfy his curiosity without revealing too much. "I was ready for a change of scenery anyway after…"

"Our breakup?"

"Yes."

"Why didn't you go to school after you finished playing nurse?"

"It took Aunt Agnes longer to recover than expected. By then I'd lost my financial aid and reapplying for everything was too much of a hassle. I went to community college for a veterinary assistant degree instead. As long as I'm able to work with animals, it doesn't really matter in what capacity."

"There's a substantial difference in salary."

"I was never about the money, Roth. You know that."

For a moment his somber gaze held hers, then he focused on the road. "That's what you always said, but you weren't used to doing without or eating wild game or macaroni every night. You were the chief's little princess."

"And you only asked me out to get under my father's skin in retaliation for him riding your back."

"Best bet I ever accepted. Then I fell for you, Piper. Fell hard." He shook his head. "But we were so damned young."

The memories made her chest ache. "I heard your mother's moving back. I'll bet she's happy you're going to be here."

"I wouldn't know."

Surprise rippled over her. "But she knows you've been appointed chief, right?"

"If she does, she didn't hear it from me."

"Why not?"

He hesitated, a muscle bunching in his jaw. "We…had a difference of opinion."

"About?"

"Several things. And after I joined the Marines communication was never easy."

"You're a Marine?" Her eyes raked him again. Military service could explain the short hair, chiseled physique and perfect posture.

"Was."

"How long have you been out?"

"Four years."

She waited for him to elaborate. Most men liked to talk about themselves. Why couldn't he be one of them? Instead, getting information out of him resembled an inquisition. "What have you been doing?"

"Working with the Charlotte-Mecklenburg P.D. SWAT team."

Her pulse stuttered. All this time he'd been only a few hours away. "You never mentioned an interest in the military or law enforcement when we were together."

"Never considered either."

"Then why enlist?"

His dark gaze stabbed her again. "Your father didn't tell you?"

"Tell me what?"

The hum of his radial tires on the blacktop filled the cab for so long she thought he might not answer. "After he arrested me for jacking Gus's car the chief gave me a choice. Enlist or jail. Either way, if I ever came near you again, he promised my mother would pay."

Her breath caught at the unjust accusation. Her father had known how much she loved Roth. He wouldn't deliberately hurt her by sending Roth away. "Daddy would never have made such a threat."

"Wrong." Roth clenched the wheel. "He put me in the back of his patrol car and took me to visit my father in prison. Then he drove me to the recruitment office and stood over me while I signed the papers."

Denial ripped through her. "I don't believe you. My father is a stickler for rules. He wouldn't bend them let alone break them. Besides, your mother moved away soon after you did. My father wouldn't have had any influence over her."

A disgusted sound erupted from his throat. "I didn't expect her to take the money I sent her each month and move closer to the prison holding the bastard who beat her and convinced her she deserved it."

She gasped. He'd never spoken so plainly about his past when they were together. If anything, he'd tried to shield her from it. Sure, she'd heard the stories compliments of her father and the Quincey grapevine, but having Roth confirm them rattled her.

"None of that would have happened if you hadn't confessed to a crime you didn't commit. Daddy could never have proven you'd stolen Gus's Corvette."

"My prints were all over that car, and your

father claimed he had witnesses and enough proof to lock me away."

"There couldn't have been witnesses or proof if you didn't do it. And your prints were on the car because you'd worked on it that morning."

Roth's father had been a mechanic before going to prison, and Roth had taken over his daddy's business while still in high school. Even though she'd had no interest in cars she'd spent countless hours standing beside open hoods watching him work to be with him.

"Your dad had most of the county's legal system in his pocket. He could have railroaded a conviction through."

"Of course he had influential friends. How could he not after all those years as chief? But having connections is not a crime. Lying to the police is. I tried to tell him the truth but he wouldn't listen to me. You should have told Daddy Chuck took the car for a joyride. Instead, you chose to lie for your buddy over telling the truth and staying with me."

The old anger, frustration, hurt and resentment poured like acid from her mouth. "Admit it, Roth. You wanted to cut your ties to me and Quincey, and Chuck provided the perfect opportunity. Maybe you and he pre-arranged it."

Roth exhaled roughly. He swung sharply into the gravel parking lot of Pig In a Blanket, stomped on the brake and silenced the engine, then twisted to face her. "We did no such thing. I was bad news, Piper. You deserved better. And so did Chuck."

"Chuck was a thief. Why did he deserve your loyalty more than me?" She hated the hurt in her tone, but this conversation exposed so many memories. The sharp edges of the bills stabbing her palm when he'd folded her fingers around his money roll. The cold resolution in his eyes when he'd told her he was leaving. The fear, hollowness and helplessness of watching him walk away without a backward glance.

He'd left her, eighteen, alone and pregnant and terrified of what her father would do when he found out.

"Let's eat. You're short of time. Remember?"

She blinked away the past. She was too upset to eat, but the chance to finally put her questions to rest sent her bustling into the unpretentious restaurant.

Roth surveyed the interior and the other

customers. Piper searched for familiar faces as the hostess led them to the only open booth, and relaxed a bit when she recognized no one from Quincey.

Roth took the seat facing the door, the way her father always did. It had to be a cop thing.

The waitress delivered a fragrant basket of hush puppies, took their orders and departed.

"Would you really have gone to jail for Chuck?"

"Yes," he answered without hesitation.

"Why, Roth? Why would you sacrifice your freedom for him?"

He held her gaze. "Chuck was the closest thing to a brother I had. An arrest would have cost him his football scholarship to State and his chance to get out of here."

Did he really not know what had happened to his best friend? "Have you kept in touch with Chuck?"

"No. He wasn't much on writing."

"He was kicked out of college his first year for cheating and he lost his scholarship. He's been in and out of jail ever since, mostly for petty stuff, but still… You sacrificed us for nothing."

Roth sat back so quickly his ladder-back chair creaked. "You're kidding."

"You'll have plenty of time to catch up with him now. He'll be one of your most frequent overnight guests at the station."

She fidgeted with the corner of the paper place mat. "Why come back now?"

Now when she'd finally gotten her life together.

"The job opened up."

"My father's job."

"Your father retired."

"Not by choice."

His eyes narrowed. "If not by choice, then how?"

"The town council forced him out."

Frown lines grooved his forehead. "That could explain the hostility I've encountered. The chief was well liked. Why force his retirement?"

"Six months ago Dad had a mild stroke followed by quadruple bypass surgery. His recovery hasn't gone as smoothly as we'd hoped."

"He looked fine when I saw him at the station."

"He's getting better, but he still has some… deficiencies." Her father went into the office every day even though the council wouldn't let him do more than visit. He claimed his staff was his family and the station his second home. "If he had a bit more time, he'd be able to work again, but the council isn't made up of Dad's cronies anymore. We've had an influx of new blood. I guess they ran out of patience. They certainly hired you on the sly."

The waitress placed their meals on the table and batted her eyelashes at Roth. Rather than watch to see if Roth returned the flirtation, Piper stared at her plate and gathered the courage to ask the one question burning a hole in her brain.

"How long are you staying?"

"Why? Does my return disturb you, Piper?"

She would never let him know how much. "I can't imagine you being happy here. You always hated busybodies. Quincey is still full of them. Nothing has changed."

"I spent nearly eight years on active duty, most of it deployed to the world's hellholes, where I didn't know who or what was waiting around the corner to take out me or a member of my team. I can handle gossips whose only weapons are words."

The idea of him in harm's way disturbed her, but she brushed it aside. His well-being was no longer her concern. "That's not what you used to say when those gossips reported your every move to my father."

"Times and perspectives change. The townsfolk will soon see they underestimated me."

Relieved to finally learn the reason Roth had returned, Piper's stiff spine eased. "Once you've proved that, then what?"

And how long would it take to make his point?

"Your father spent thirty years on the Quincey police force. What makes you think I won't do the same?"

Panic pulsed thorough her. "You'll hate it here. The way you always did. We're forty miles from anywhere interesting. You'll be bored out of your mind. No one comes back once they leave."

"You did."

"I—I—that's different. My family's here." She'd returned for Josh. She wanted her son to have his grandparents' love and support—even if it could be a bit smothering.

"And mine will be," he replied, his tone and face grim.

Roth reached across the table and covered her hand with his. She tried to jerk away, but he held fast. The heat of his touch flooded through her, making her heart race.

"Piper, I invited you to lunch because I owe you an apology. I never intended to hurt you. Twelve years ago we were too young to handle the situation we found ourselves in."

"You mean *you* weren't ready for the responsibility of a wife and child."

His cheeks darkened. "You're right. I'm not proud to admit I freaked out when you told me you were pregnant. I suddenly saw myself as my father's son. I'd spent my life listening to that bastard accuse my mother of ruining his life by getting pregnant—as if he'd had no part in it—right before he knocked the hell out of her." His grip tightened. "I couldn't do it, Piper. I couldn't take the chance that I'd turn into a monster like him, and I couldn't watch the love in your eyes turn to hate."

"You wouldn't have and I would never—"

"You don't know that. And you deserved better than a mechanic who barely scraped through high school. Hell, you were a straight-A student with years of college ahead of you. If you'd married me, your parents would have disowned you. I couldn't afford college tuition on what little I made from the garage. I would have held you back and you would have grown to resent me."

The sincerity in his eyes told her he believed what he said, but it didn't change the facts. His presence could cause problems for her and Josh. She yanked her hand free.

"Is that how you made peace with your decision, Roth? You weren't there for me when I needed you. You left me to face my parents *alone*. I won't ever forget that."

He stiffened. "I've admitted I made mistakes. I thought we could be friends."

Friends? With the man who could destroy her world?

"I prefer friends I can count on. And don't think I've been sitting around pining for your return. I've moved on with my life." She gestured to the untouched food in front of her. "Do we have to do this?"

"If you don't eat your lunch, I'm going to think there's a reason you can't handle a little conversation with me." His challenging tone reminded her of the old Roth.

She fisted her hands beneath the table and fought for calm. He wanted to play games? Fine, she could play games. But instead of him grilling her, she'd let him feel the heat.

"Your becoming a cop is ironic, isn't it? You and your posse were pains in the Quincey Police Department's behind."

"We were. What about you? Did you stir up

any trouble while you were out of the chief's surveillance?"

Her heart bounded. "I had better things to do than cause problems for other people." Except her parents, apparently.

"And what brought you home?"

"Aunt Agnes sold her house and moved into a retirement community." One that hadn't allowed children. "Then Dr. Jones, Quincey's old vet, needed help."

"He retired?"

"He died soon after I went to work for him. His heirs sold the practice to Madison. Lucky for me, she kept me on."

"Ever married?"

Every muscle in her body snapped taut. She should have seen that one coming. "No. You?"

The idea of him with another woman and other children gave her indigestion.

"Not even close. I can't believe nobody snapped you up. There were plenty of guys wanting what I had."

"Oh, please. The men in town were terrified of my father and you know it. That's why I'd never had a date before you asked me out."

A tender, reminiscent smile curved his lips and her toes. "Eighteen and never been kissed. You know I won twenty bucks off my *posse* for asking you out. But you avoided my question. Any close calls?"

Stalling for time, she shoved a bite of the pork into her mouth and chewed without tasting. Then she swallowed and sipped her tea while hunting for the words and the guts to perpetuate the lie she'd been living. She'd told this story a dozen times. Why was it so much harder to repeat it to him? "I was…engaged."

His fist clenched on the table. "Was? You dumped him?"

She blinked once, twice, and fought the urge to squirm under Roth's unwavering gaze. She could not afford to mess up. Josh's future depended on her making this convincing.

"No. He…passed away."

"I'm sorry for your loss. Who was he? A local?"

Breathe. "Someone I—I met when I lived in Florida."

"Did the chief approve of him?"

Another unexpected question—one her mother's fib had never addressed. "Yes." *Change the subject.* "What did you do in the Marines?"

A moment stretched between them and from the determined look in his eyes, she feared he wouldn't let her shift the conversation away from the dicey subject of her make-believe past. "I was a member of the Scout Sniper Battalion."

"You were a sniper? You killed people?" Cold crept through her veins.

Her raised voice had heads turning. She winced.

"The entire restaurant doesn't need to know. But yes, I was a sniper when my unit needed me to be. But that was only a small part of my job."

A range of emotions rolled through her like a rock slide, fear and revulsion leading the pack. "How many kills?"

"Piper—"

"I've spent hours watching the military channel with my father while he recuperated. I know snipers keep some kind of journal or score card."

"The number is irrelevant. My targets were murderers and insurgents or hostage takers. Every one I eliminated was a purposeful effort to save others' lives."

Like father, like son, the townsfolk had always said, but she'd never believed Roth had any violent tendencies. "You swore you'd never turn into your father."

Revulsion filled his face. "I didn't. My father was a mean, murdering bastard."

"He killed my uncle in the heat of passion. You kill with cold, calculated precision."

How many more of his father's bad traits had he inherited?

A muscle ticked in his jaw, but otherwise he remained utterly still. "Becoming a sniper wasn't about killing. It was about gaining total control of my body and emotions—something my father never had."

"But you got up every day, cleaned your rifle and waited for orders to shoot someone."

"Not every day."

"How many Roth?"

His eyes turned cold. "That's classified information."

"And with the SWAT team, were you a sniper there, too?"

"Yes. Finish your lunch. It's time to take you back to the office."

She knew in her head that wars were violent and snipers were sometimes the most expedient method. The same could be said for hostage situations. But her heart looked across the table and saw a man who had killed. More than once.

For Josh's safety she had to keep her son as far away from Roth as possible.

Chapter Three

Lunch hadn't gone well. Roth punched the accelerator as soon as the office door closed behind Piper. She'd put him on the defensive. But he'd made his apology. Objective accomplished, albeit with some collateral damage.

The first land mine being that she still got to him. If anything, she was more beautiful than before. It had been impossible to sit across from her and not remember the way her dimples used to flash, the love that had once shone from her blue eyes or the taste of her lips and the feel of her soft curves pressed against him.

The follow-up strike had been Piper's accusation that he'd been looking for a way out of their relationship. As much as he hated to admit it, there was some truth in her words. Leaving her twelve years ago had been one of the hardest things he'd ever done, and his pride had been eviscerated when she'd sworn she'd never have the baby of white trash like him and thrown his money in his face.

But part of him had been relieved. He'd decided long before he met Piper that he'd never have children. If he didn't have kids, he couldn't fail them—or hurt them—the way his father had him. His opinion hadn't changed over the years. Marriage wasn't high on his to-do list, either. Cop marriages didn't last.

What really burned like a chemical weapon was her accusing him of being like his father. He'd left Quincey behind and racked up numerous commendations to wipe that connection from his life. Yet less than twenty-four hours back and the one person who'd never judged him by his father's actions was the one throwing that at him.

The fear and revulsion in her eyes when she'd grilled him about his job had gouged deep. Uneasiness wasn't an uncommon reaction to finding out his specialty, and it was the primary reason he didn't blab about his missions. But he wasn't ashamed of his skills, his success or his service, and he wasn't going to lie about the role he'd played. He'd saved a hell of a lot of lives. That was all that mattered. Why did he care what anyone— *Piper*—thought?

But something about the afternoon nagged him as he drove down Main Street checking out the new storefronts, and he'd learned not to ignore his instincts. Piper's body language had been off. There'd been a slight tremor of her hands and her gaze had bounced away repeatedly. That, combined with the deep breaths she'd taken before answering his questions led him down an unexpected path.

His training automatically identified those as traits of someone with something to hide. But in a town like Quincey where your business was everybody's business and secrets were impossible to keep, what could Piper be concealing? Probably nothing. More than likely their past was the issue. But he would find out.

He stopped at the light and weighed his options. He could see his apartment from here, but the idea of returning to his claustrophobic rooms held no appeal. Determined to lay one more ghost to rest, he steered the truck toward the old home place.

He passed one of the deputies driving the opposite direction and waved. The gesture wasn't returned. Maybe the man didn't recognize Roth's truck. But given what Piper had said about her father being forced out of office, the lack of acknowledgment could be because the deputies were loyal to the old chief. Roth would have to deal with that Monday.

A few new houses had sprung up along the rural route. He slowed as he approached the hairpin turn that had changed his life. Chuck had hit the curve at full speed in Gus Benson's Corvette, lost control and nailed a hundred-year-old oak. The oak still stood with a scar in its trunk. Miraculously, Chuck had walked away without a scratch, as drunks often do, but he'd totaled the car.

If not for that wreck, Gus and the chief would never have known about the joyride. What would have happened then? Roth had asked himself a hundred times during those early years when he'd been fighting to forget Piper. Would they have married? Would their baby have been a boy or girl? Would he have turned into an abusive ass like his father and ended up in jail as so many people had predicted? Or would he have, as Piper had insisted today, found another way to escape?

He detoured down a back road leading to the bridge spanning Deer Hunter's Creek. He'd slept under the old wooden trestles too many nights to count—most of the time to hunt at sunrise, but sometimes to escape the sound of his mother's crying.

More than once after his father had beat her then passed out in his recliner, Roth had contemplated ending his mother's suffering by using his hunting rifle on his father. But that would have made him as much of an animal as his old man. Leaving had been the only way to avoid temptation.

Something about the dense woods bordering the creek snagged Roth's attention as his tires rumbled over the boards. One thing drilled into him as a sniper was that if something didn't fit he'd better check it out. He pulled onto the shoulder, climbed from the cab and studied the landscape. Not one broken branch or pinecone littered the ground. Too clean.

Resting his hand on his holstered Glock, he carefully made his way down the steep, leaf-covered bank, cataloguing the signs of habitation. Someone had tucked an old metal chair and small table into a hollow. The tracks along the bank looked a few days old. A recent rain had caved in the edges, making it impossible to identify the type or size of shoe or the original depth of the impression.

The prints led to a rock-ringed fire pit. He squatted and touched the carefully positioned stones. Cold and damp. Somebody had been camping here. But not recently.

On the far side of the bridge a neatly stacked pile of branches acted as a screen and/or fuel supply. A metal can hung from a bungee cord suspended between two bridge supports. Pretty smart to hang it out of wildlife's reach. He took down the can and pried off the lid with his pocketknife. Matches. Beef jerky. Packages of sunflower seeds and peanuts. A resealable plastic bag with two cookies. A small pocketknife.

No drug paraphernalia. No booze.

He returned the bucket and scanned the makeshift camp again, looking for any clue to who'd been here. Probably not a hunter judging by the lack of spent shotgun shells or rifle casings. And not likely pot-smoking teens, who tended to leave snack wrappers lying around. He hadn't noticed any beggars in Quincey. Did the town have homeless peo-

ple? Charlotte's street corners had been littered with them.

He scanned the area one last time. Today,
who camped here wasn't his concern, but
come Monday morning, once he'd donned
his badge, it would be. He'd check for crimes
in the vicinity and ID the squatter. A known
hazard was easier to control.

Determined to get the next item checked
off his list, he returned to his truck. The pine
forest gave way to fields. He braked involuntarily when he spotted a white clapboard
house that shouldn't be there. This was his
family's land, wasn't it? Or had he been away
so long he'd lost his orientation?

He checked the side mirror. Sure enough,
there at the base of the oak tree he'd carved
his and Piper's initials in stood the hundred-
year-old cement post marking the beginning
of Roth land. His mother's family had owned
this property, and she'd given him her maiden
name in good ole Southern tradition.

He rolled forward again, finding two more
houses in what had been soybean fields. Not
that his father had ever farmed. After his
grandfather died Roth's parents had leased
the land to supplement the meager income
his father made from the garage.

Roth had hunted the fields to put meat on the table. Deer. Rabbit. Turkey. Quail. Wild boar. If you could eat it, he could shoot it.

Had his mother sold the property? Or had it been repossessed for nonpayment of taxes? She hadn't mentioned either when she'd called to tell him about his father's pending release three months ago.

He'd never been able to understand why she hadn't divorced her good-for-nothing husband. Her name was the only one on the property deed she'd inherited, and she had the income from the acreage to support herself. Eloise had always claimed it was because she loved Seth, and no matter how hard Roth had tried, he'd never been able to convince his mama that love didn't blacken eyes or break bones.

It was a shame a deputy had to die before the cops did anything about his father's actions, and for that he blamed Lou Hamilton. Hamilton's department had been useless whenever Roth called them as a kid because Roth's mother had refused to press charges. Seeing his father hauled off to prison had been a tremendous relief.

Roth's muscles tensed and his grip on the wheel tightened as he crested the hill leading to the home place. He focused on tactical breathing, exhaling slowly and forcing each kinked muscle to relax the way he had before taking a shot.

He emerged from the copse of dense oaks and holly trees. A new mailbox and post marked the property. Lush green grass carpeted what had once been a muddy, weed-choked, car-parts-strewn yard. He drove up the gravel driveway and the house came into view. For a moment he sat in the truck trying to make sense of it all. The place looked nothing like he remembered. Even the old garage had been spruced up.

He'd expected to find the structure rotting from almost twelve years of neglect. Instead, the house looked better than it ever had when Roth had lived here. Pale yellow paint coated what had once been peeling white boards, and the black shutters hung parallel to the windows instead of dangling at a weird angle or sitting on the ground propped against the foundation. Somebody had put a lot of money and work into the place. Who?

The brightly colored toys dotting the lawn looked as out of place as an iceberg at the equator. A child's squeal rent the air then a medium-size mutt raced around the corner of the house with a hip-high redhead on its heels. The girl skidded to a halt beside Roth's truck, her tail-waving, tongue-lagging friend beside her.

"Hey, mister."

Opening his door, he climbed out. His experience with children was limited to encounters with fellow officers' offspring. "Hey, kid. You live here?"

"Yessir."

The front door opened. A woman in her late twenties with dark red hair and freckles to match the girl's came out. She descended the stairs quickly and put a hand on the child's shoulder. "Can I help you?"

"I'm Roth Sterling. I lived here. A long time ago."

The stiffness left her frame. "Oh. Are you the owner? I thought I remembered the agent saying a woman was moving in."

"My mother."

"We're going to miss this place. It's a wonderful house."

She didn't have the memories attached to the place that he did. "It's in great shape. Did you fix it up?"

"Oh, no. It was in perfect condition when we moved in and the rental company has folks who come out whenever something needs fixing."

Who was paying for this? He and his mother would have to have a talk. "Have you been here long?"

"Almost eight years. Quincey is a lovely community. Close enough to Raleigh for convenience, but far enough away for privacy and safety. We don't want to leave the area. Ann Marie is looking for another house for us nearby."

"Ann Marie Hamilton?"

"Yes. Do you know her?"

Piper's mother. "I did. I've been gone a while."

"She's Quincey's only real estate agent. If you're looking for a place near your mama, maybe Ann Marie can help you find one."

He might not be planning to stay, but no one else needed to know that. He could use a fictitious house search to find out what Piper was hiding. "I appreciate the tip. I'll give her a call."

Time for a little recon.

"Spill it," Madison said as she set down her med-kit.

Piper tried to gather her scattered thoughts and pretended to be busy shuffling the charts on her desk. "How's Pebbles?"

"Routine delivery. Mrs. Lee exaggerated as usual." Her boss/friend hitched a hip on the counter, parking a butt cheek on the files and effectively ending the shuffling. "And don't ignore the question. Who is Roth Sterling? How do you know him? And what is he to you?"

Piper had exceeded her fib quota for the year with Roth. She could not look Madison in the eye and lie. "We dated when I was eighteen. It was a long time ago."

"Will you be dating him again?"

"No." Piper winced at her sharp tone, and sure enough, Madison's hiked eyebrows said she'd picked up on it.

"So you're saying he's available?"

Ba-boom, ba-boom, ba-boom. Piper's heart slammed against her rib cage then lodged in her throat. "He says he's single."

"That's not what I asked, Piper. I don't have to tell you how limited the selection of eligible men is around here. At least your father parades potential dates in front of you."

Her father. Roth's story had Piper so conflicted. There was no way her rule-following father could have done as Roth said. Her father would never deliberately hurt her or break the law. She believed that with every fiber of her being.

But Roth had sounded so convincing. She ached to confide in Madison and ask her opinion. But Piper said nothing. She couldn't risk it. The person she needed to talk to was her father.

"Each of the men Dad brings home has been screened more thoroughly than an FBI candidate. They're so squeaky clean they don't even have dirty thoughts."

"Hmm. Sounds like you have a penchant for bad boys. And I think Chief Sterling might be one. He has an edge that's kind of sexy."

Piper remained mute. The less she said the better. Roth had definitely been a bad boy and he'd abandoned her.

But was he a liar? He had to be.

Madison sighed. "I remember the last time I had sex. Do you?"

"Do I remember the last time you had sex?"

"Funny girl. I know you too well for playing dumb to fool me. I'm saying we're both overdue for someone to satisfy our biological urges. I don't think you've hooked up with anyone in the five years I've known you."

"Neither have you."

"No, I haven't." The sad tinge of her voice

reminded Piper how little she knew about Madison's life before Quincey. She knew her friend had been married and suffered a miscarriage. But that was it. Madison didn't like to talk about the reasons she'd relocated from a busy suburb of Atlanta to a sleepy Southern town. But that was okay because then Piper could keep her secrets without feeling guilty.

Madison rose. "I might be ready for something...temporary. Scorching hot and brief. That's what I need. How about you? Is Roth going to be the one who breaks your drought?"

Adrenaline shot through Piper's veins. "Absolutely not."

"Why? Is he a jerk? Did he cheat on you with another woman? Another man?"

Piper nearly choked on a shocked laugh. "You are awful. He didn't cheat on me." *He did something worse. He made me love him then he left us.* "If you want him, he's yours."

"Hmm. I'll think about it. He definitely has the tall, dark and handsome thing going for him."

Piper's stomach churned and she realized this would be one of those sour grapes situations from the fables she'd read to Josh. She didn't want Roth, but she couldn't handle a ringside seat watching him sweep another woman off her feet either.

Piper made a beeline for her father's immediately after work. She had to know who had lied. Roth or Lou. She was almost certain it was the former, but that twinge of doubt had nagged her all afternoon and turned her into such a clumsy idiot that even Madison had started looking at her funny.

Piper whipped the Jeep into the driveway of the house where she'd grown up and leaped from the vehicle.

Her father stepped onto the porch. "Piper, this is a surprise."

He didn't look like a man with dark secrets.

She stalked up the sidewalk. "I had lunch with Roth Sterling today."

He stiffened and his welcoming smile faded. But that didn't prove anything. He'd always hated Roth.

"He didn't waste any time looking you up."

"Did you coerce him into joining the Marines?"

His hesitation made goose bumps rise on Piper's skin. *No. Please no.*

"Now, baby—"

"I'm not a baby. I'm thirty years old. And

I deserve the truth. Did you threaten to send him to jail if he didn't enlist, then drive him to the recruitment office and stand over him until he signed the forms?"

"He had a choice."

"Did you pressure him with threats against his mother?"

"I did it for your own good, Piper. That boy was headed to the same place as his daddy— prison."

Oh. My. God. Roth hadn't lied. A tremor started deep inside and worked its way to her extremities as the magnitude of his confession overwhelmed her.

"You knew he didn't steal and wreck Gus's car, didn't you?"

"I need a beer. Want one?" He disappeared through the front door. The screen door slapped behind him like a gunshot making her jump.

Piper's feet seemed glued to the porch. She forced them into action and followed him, anger and betrayal vying for supremacy. "You knew, didn't you?"

Her father yanked open the refrigerator, pulled out a beer and popped the top. He took a long drink then lowered the can and wiped his mouth. "No matter what you claimed, evidence indicated him and he didn't deny it."

Her thoughts and emotions churned like floodwaters oversetting everything she thought she'd known, everything she'd believed to be fact. She'd believed Roth had betrayed her. But so had her father, the man she loved and trusted more than anyone.

What else had he lied about? Did she dare trust anything he'd told her? It was too much to take in.

"What happened to innocent until proved guilty?"

"Now, Piper—"

"What happened to the truth and your sworn duty to uphold the law?"

"That boy needed discipline. I knew the military would set him straight."

"What if he'd refused to sign? Would you have prosecuted an innocent man?"

"Piper—"

"Just how far over the line were you willing to go, Daddy?"

"It wasn't like that. I knew he'd sign the contract to protect his mama. She couldn't survive without the money he'd send her if he drew a military paycheck. Land poor, that's what she was. All that Roth land and she couldn't sell it for dirt. Market's changed now. We have new folk coming into town and property's worth something, but back then…" He shook his head.

Piper wanted to slap his beer out of his hand, and violence had never been her thing. "Don't change the subject. The real estate market has nothing to do with your lies. To me. To Roth. To the rest of the force. To Quincey. You betrayed your badge."

He blanched and a spark of concern skipped through her. She probably shouldn't upset him, given his heart condition. But damn it, he'd deliberately driven away the man she loved, the father of her baby.

"Let me tell you something, little lady. I have never done anything detrimental to this town or this badge. I gave Sterling a chance to break the mold and become something better than his no-good daddy. And apparently he has if the sonofabitch has stolen my job."

His selfishness blew her away. How could he honestly believe he'd done the right thing? No wonder her mother had left him.

Did her mother know? Was she in on this, too?

Piper's eyes and chest burned. "Do not try

to make out like you had his best interest at heart. I don't buy it for one minute."

"You gonna stand there and tell me you wouldn't lie to protect Josh? Because I know better. You've lived a lie for the past eight years."

She flinched. He was right. Her life since returning had been one big lie. She'd forgiven her father for sending her away. Now it appeared that hadn't been his only sin.

"I wouldn't send an innocent, hardworking man to jail."

"You're making a fuss over nothing. Sterling would have turned on that boy before going to court. They were tight, but they weren't kin."

His continued justification of his misdeed infuriated her. "If you think he would have betrayed Chuck, then you don't know Roth very well."

"Turned on you, didn't he? Left you in a bad way." Rage rumbled in his voice.

"So did you, Daddy. But what you did was worse. At least Roth had the guts to tell me to my face that he didn't want me. You, the man I loved and trusted with all my heart, stabbed me in the back. And when you found out I was pregnant you threw me out of your house for falling in love when your sin was so much worse. No wonder Mom left you. You're a hypocrite and a liar."

Her voice broke.

"You are not the man I thought you were, and I don't know if I can ever forgive you. I do know I will never trust you again."

Josh closed his math textbook. "I'm going to bed."

Finally! Piper hadn't had a moment alone with her mother since arriving home.

She forced herself to smile, rise and kiss Josh on the top of his head as if nothing were wrong, despite her tumbled thoughts. And then she hugged him. He tolerated the embrace. He never hugged back anymore.

"You'll get the math. Hang in there. Sleep tight. Love you."

"Yeah."

She missed the return "I love you." Those had ended within the past few months, but everyone assured her he'd be her affectionate son again sometime between eighteen and thirty. She might have to lose the closeness to him because of his age and maturing process, but she wouldn't let Roth come between them.

But that was another worry. Tonight she

had a more important concern. She had to know if her mother had been a part of her father's deceit. If Ann Marie had been in on the lies, Piper would never trust either parent again. With anything. Especially Josh.

She listened until Josh's bedroom door clicked shut then went to look for her mother. Piper found her curled in her usual spot on the sofa reading her favorite cooking magazine.

Piper's tongue felt thick. Her pulse accelerated. She and her mother had become very close since Piper's return from Florida. Had their relationship all been based on a lie?

"Mom, did you know Daddy forced Roth to join the Marines by threatening to make life difficult for Eloise if he didn't?"

Her mother's shock and dismay looked real. "Lou would never—"

"He admitted to me today that he did. He implicated Roth for stealing and wrecking Gus's car even though he suspected Chuck, then Dad threatened Roth with jail if he didn't enlist. He even drove him to the recruitment office."

Her mother's mouth opened, closed. She shook her head, her bewilderment too genuine to be faked. "I can't believe your father would— He lives for that badge." And then the horror on her face transformed into understanding.

Understanding?

"Your father would do anything to protect you. You know that, don't you?"

"But to send an innocent man to jail?"

"Piper, I hate that your father did what he did, and I certainly don't condone it. But I know how much it used to upset him when he couldn't do anything for Roth's mama. He begged Eloise to press charges. And she refused. Time and time again.

"I remember one night after another visit to the Sterling house he came home and made me promise that if he ever lifted a hand to me, that I'd wait until he was asleep then take his pistol and put a bullet in his head."

Revulsion rolled through Piper.

"If Lou did what you claim, then it was to keep you from walking in Eloise's shoes. That woman loved her man. Too much. More than she loved herself or her son. Promise me that won't ever be you."

Her mother's words didn't excuse Piper's father's betrayal. But they did explain his motivation. Piper wasn't ready to forgive him. But she was a step closer to understanding his actions.

Chapter Four

Josh slammed into the kitchen Saturday morning, startling Piper into splashing liquid over the rim of the hummingbird feeder. But then Josh slammed everywhere these days. He seemed to always be in a hurry. And she was preoccupied.

"Good morning, Josh," she said over her shoulder, feigning calm she was far from feeling. Anger at her father had kept her up most the night. She didn't want him anywhere near her or her son. But how could she keep them apart? Josh worshipped his grandfather—a man whose soul had been blackened by dishonesty. Not a good role model.

"You aren't ready," Josh said with eleven-year-old angst and flung himself against the counter.

The bicycle helmet on his head sent her stomach plummeting. She and Josh rode every Saturday she didn't have to work unless it was pouring rain. Why couldn't it have rained today?

Her mind raced. They could hardly tool around town and then calmly have breakfast at the diner with her father the way they had in the past. Not without her pretending everything was normal, and not without running the risk of bumping into Roth. She wasn't eager to see either man at the moment.

Searching her brain for an excuse that Josh would accept, she capped the feeder and rinsed the sticky solution from her hands.

"Grandma asked me to set up the hummingbird feeders. The birds usually come back around the first of April. After I finish I thought we'd drive into Raleigh for a movie."

"There's nothing good playing, and I told Will I'd go with him to check the trotlines later. If we catch any catfish, can I eat dinner with him? His mom's fried catfish is the best!"

"Last week you said your grandfather's

fried catfish was the best. And you've been begging for new shoes."

"Oh, man. Do we have to do that today?"

"I have time today. Next weekend the clinic's open on Saturday. I'll have to work."

"What about breakfast with Grandpa?"

"He can eat without us."

And tomorrow she'd have to figure out somewhere else she and Josh could go where they'd be unlikely to encounter either of the men on her Dislike list.

Josh stubbed the toe of his sneaker into the tile floor. "Okay."

"Call Will and tell him about your change of plans."

"Will has a cell phone."

She welcomed the old argument—anything to keep her mind off the ache in her heart. "You're eleven. You don't need a phone. Besides, you know I can't afford one for you right now."

He shuffled out of the room, his slouching shoulders revealing his lack of enthusiasm over spending a day with his mother. She'd try to make it up to him by letting him have lunch in the mall food court. There were no fast-food joints in Quincey.

One potential disaster averted. For now.

That left tomorrow to rearrange. She wasn't sure how long she could cocoon Josh before he figured out something was wrong. But what choice did she have? She wanted to avoid Roth as long as possible.

Avoiding him could prove expensive if she had to keep carting Josh out of town for extracurricular activities. But if she was lucky, Roth would run out of patience with Quincey before she ran out of money and ways to dodge him.

The bell tinkled with obnoxious cheer above Roth's head as he let himself into Ann Marie Hamilton's real estate office on Saturday morning. Her assistant, the same woman from twelve years ago, sat behind the desk acting as gatekeeper. He couldn't recall her name.

Her automatic smile slipped when she recognized him. "May I help you?"

"I need to talk to Mrs. Hamilton."

"May I tell her what it's about?"

Fishing for gossip. Typical. "I can do that myself."

The woman bristled, her round face turning red to the dark roots of her dyed blond hair, and Roth realized he'd better try harder to cover his irritation with busybodies if he wanted the populace to be cooperative and to look out for his mother after he left.

"I'm interested in rental houses."

"Doyle's apartment not good enough for you?"

Snide witch. "It's fine. Short term. But if a man wants to put down roots, he needs something more permanent."

He was blowing smoke out his ass since he had no intention of staying in this godforsaken town one day longer than necessary, but he'd have to do plenty of evasive double-talk during his dealings with Ann Marie if he wanted to pump her for information about Piper.

"A rental's still a rental."

Enough. "Is Ann Marie available?"

"I'll check." The woman rose, slowly strolling the three steps to the open office door then paused. "Roth Sterling would like to speak to you about rental homes. Do you have a moment?"

As if Piper's mother hadn't overheard the entire conversation and the parking spaces outside her building weren't empty. Moments later Ann Marie appeared. She looked exactly as he expected Piper to look in twenty years or so. Only unlike her daughter, Ann Marie was dressed for success, her face and chin-length hair immaculate. Piper had always dressed for comfort and preferred to keep her hair out of the way.

Twelve years ago he'd stolen countless hair-clips so he could run his fingers through Piper's golden strands—especially when they'd made love. Those long locks had felt damned good dragging across his skin. The memory sent a rush of heat through him. When he'd packed his bag for boot camp he'd left all the clips and bands behind. What had his mother done with the stolen treasures?

"Good morning, Mr. Sterling."

Mr. Sterling? He'd find more warmth in a polar icecap than her voice, and her forced smile didn't fool him for a second. "Mrs. Hamilton. I see you're still the only real estate agent in town."

"I am. Come in. Have a seat and tell me what you need."

Her office was girlie, decorated with flowers, pale colors and delicate furniture that made him wonder if the pieces could hold his weight. He gingerly lowered himself into one of the fragile-looking chairs.

"I'm interested in leasing a house preferably with an option to buy in a neighborhood with people my age, like Piper."

"Piper lives with me. Our neighborhood is quite diverse, but there are no rental properties."

"She's back at the old home place?" And back under Daddy's heavy thumb?

"No."

That raised a few questions. "You and the chief moved?"

"I moved. Lou did not."

Piper's parents had split? More questions wrestled for priority. Not wanting to put Ann Marie on the defensive, he reined them in. "I noticed a few new houses when I drove around town—on Roth land."

"Your mother sold parcels, I'm assuming to support herself? But I can't be certain."

He linked his fingers in his lap and kept his mouth shut since he didn't know the answers to her questions. He'd learned in the course of his career that a silent stare often loosened lips.

"You moved into your apartment two days ago. What about your lease?"

"I'm renting month to month until something better comes along." Like an opportunity to return to Charlotte.

"I heard your mother was moving back. You could stay with her."

"No." He almost barked the word, then took a moment to gather his composure. "My father will be with her."

Mrs. Hamilton's face paled ever so slightly. "Seth is getting out?"

So the people of Quincy hadn't heard. Hadn't they been following the release logs as religiously as Roth had? Weren't they concerned about keeping that evil spawn out of town?

"Scheduled for parole the last day of May. Released early for good behavior." What a load of garbage.

"I see. Well…" She pulled a flowered pad of paper forward and clicked her pink pen. Three times. "How many bedrooms would you like?"

He shrugged. "Doesn't really matter."

"Will someone be helping you choose your next residence?"

Smooth, Mrs. H. "No. Just me. For now."

He deliberately tacked on the last to keep her guessing.

"And what do you think a house will give you that an apartment won't? You have a pool now. None of the houses around Quincey have pools. And there's the extra work of yard upkeep, lawn mowers and whatnot to buy."

"Swimming in the river's fine with me,

and I've never minded hard work. I'm looking for space. A place to cook out on the grill with my friends and my coworkers. I believe in team building."

The corners of her lips turned down, reminding him his team had once been her husband's, and she'd been the one to cook for them. "Will you have friends staying over? Is that why you need the extra space?"

He had to fight a smile at her not-so-subtle inquisition. "Not sure yet. But it's best to be prepared. It was good seeing Piper yesterday. She mentioned her fiancé."

Ann Marie blinked. Twice. "Yes. Tragic, how their love was cut short."

"Did you and the chief like him?"

Six pendulum swings of the grandmother clock in the corner marked her hesitation. "We unfortunately never had the opportunity to meet him before his…accident. They lived so far away and Lou doesn't fly."

Roth's antennae sparked. Piper had said her father approved of the guy. So one of them was lying. But who? He'd guess Piper. What would Ann Marie gain by saying she'd never met her future son-in-law?

"Piper didn't mention what kind of accident, and I didn't want to pry and upset her about…what was his name?"

Click. Click. "Rick. And it was a motorcycle accident. You know Florida doesn't have helmet laws?" She straightened her pen and paper. "Roth, Piper doesn't need you…toying with her affections again. She's made a good life here for herself and her son."

Her words shocked him like a Taser. "Piper has a son?"

Ann Marie nodded stiffly. "Rick was killed just days before their wedding, leaving Piper pregnant. They were so in love and in such a rush to start their lives together that they jumped the gun a bit."

"That so?" Jealousy burned like a gas main break in his gut. He wanted to punch something, to shoot something, to annihilate something. He struggled to rein in his reaction. He'd vowed he'd never be the kind of man who could be ruled by his emotions.

Obviously her fiancé hadn't been the white trash she'd accused Roth of being since she hadn't aborted Rick's kid.

Click. Click. "So please, don't try to resurrect anything."

He tried to focus on Ann Marie's last statement rather than the bombshell she'd dropped. "Reuniting with Piper is not part of my plan."

As Piper had said, the past was over. There would be no attempt at reconciliation. Loving and losing her had sent him to a very dangerous place mentally—one where he hadn't cared whether he lived or died. And it had taken him a long time to crawl out of that dark hole.

Ann Marie searched his face then nodded. "All right. There are not a lot of rental units available despite the market downturn. But I can make up a list of the houses that are available."

Roth had learned far more than he'd bargained for and he needed to leave to process it. He rose on legs that felt as stiff as telephone poles. "Do that, and I'll give them a drive-by. If any of them grabs my interest, then I'll be in touch."

He left the office determined to find Piper. At least now he knew what she was trying to hide.

Piper had moved on. She'd had another man's child.

So where was the relief he should be experiencing?

* * *

"You did what!" The plate slipped from Piper's hands and splashed into the sink filled with soapy water, shattering the peace of their Saturday-night after-dinner washing-up ritual.

Her mother actually looked quite smug. "I told Roth our story."

"Why?"

"Because Quincey has limited places to hide. He was going to find out about Josh sooner or later. It's best to send him down the wrong path before he jumps to conclusions and finds the right one. And I wanted to warn him off."

Piper didn't like the sound of that. Roth had never been one to back down from a challenge. "Warn him off how exactly?"

"He needs to know you haven't been pining away for him."

But she had. Despite the anger and hurt, for years she'd waited for him to find her and tell her he'd made a mistake. That he loved her. Wanted to marry her and raise their child together. Eventually that love had turned to disappointment then to anger and finally to determination. She didn't need him to make a good life for herself and Josh.

"Mom, I wish you wouldn't volunteer information. The less we say the better. Roth has always been a genius at figuring out puzzles. That's what made him such a good mechanic. If we don't sync our stories perfectly, he'll root out the inconsistencies."

"We've discussed this too many times to make mistakes, and to be on the safe side, I told Roth your father and I had never met Rick. That way our descriptions of him won't contradict each other."

Piper's stomach sank as if she'd swallowed lead. "Roth asked me if Dad approved of Rick. I said yes. *Yes* implies you'd met him. Our story is already getting tangled."

Had Roth caught that small contradiction? Was it enough to spark his curiosity? Would he even care? She hoped not. Otherwise, she could be in big trouble.

"I'll have to think of a story to cover that."

"Mom, telling more lies is not the answer."

"Then what is, Piper? I don't put much faith in your belief that Roth won't be interested in his own son."

"He wasn't when I told him I was pregnant. Why would that have changed? If he confronts me, I'll make it clear I want nothing from him. Him or Dad. In fact, I'd be happy not to lay eyes on either of the traitors again."

"If only life were as easy as ignoring what we don't want to see. But it isn't, sweetie. And we learn the most from our toughest obstacles. Avoiding your father is not the answer. He's upset that you stood him up for breakfast today."

"*He's* upset? After what he did? I don't want him anywhere near us."

"Piper, I'll be the first to admit he's a bullheaded idiot sometimes. But he is your father and he loves you."

"He proved that well—by running off the man I wanted to marry."

"Lou did what he thought he had to do to protect you."

"He could have given Roth and me a chance to work things out." She regretted voicing the old hurt the moment the words left her lips.

"Oh, baby, do you honestly think time would have made a difference? If Roth had wanted to contact you, he could have found a way—even with you in Florida. You had friends who would have forwarded a letter or given him your number. But he didn't call and he didn't write."

"Neither did Daddy—until you threatened to move to Florida to be with Josh and me."

"Whether you choose to forgive your father

or not, we need him in our corner right now. He still has legal connections we might need if Roth isn't as disinterested as you think."

"You expect me to forgive and forget Daddy's betrayal just like that?"

"No. But please don't shut your father out. You may not need him. But Lou has lost everything that matters to him. He needs you and Josh. He has nothing else to live for."

The words landed like an avalanche of guilt on Piper's shoulders. "You don't think he'd hurt himself?"

"I don't know. I've never seen him like this, and I'm worried."

Piper might not ever forgive her father. But she would never forgive herself if he did something stupid because she shut him out of hers and Josh's lives.

"Okay. I'll call him. And I'll let him spend time with Josh. But I won't trust him."

"Why is everybody acting so weird?"

Josh's plaintive question stalled Piper's heart. "What do you mean *weird*?"

"You're all antsy. You can't sit still. Like Will when he hasn't taken his ADD medication. And Grandpa keeps looking down the road like he's expecting somebody to run us off. And why are we fishing here anyway? This isn't our lucky spot."

Her son was too perceptive. Piper looked at her father, silently pleading for help. She could hardly tell Josh they'd chosen the isolated spot because they were hiding from the new chief or that she'd tagged along on what was usually a male-only fishing trip because she was ticked at her father.

Lou snapped to attention. "I heard a rumor of a big catfish wallering in the mud under that downed tree. You plan on standing here chattering all day or are we gonna bait up and cast a line to see who catches him first?"

The distraction worked like a charm. Josh hustled to his grandfather's side. Her father glanced her way and Piper nodded her thanks.

As a result of his stroke her father had lost dexterity in his left hand, and while he'd regained a lot of control, some of his fine motor skills were still lacking. Piper bit her lip and resisted the urge to help.

Luckily, Josh took over, grabbing the beef liver as soon as her father cut it and threading the chunks onto the barbed hooks. "I don't know why we can't just set trotlines like Will."

"Trotlines are lazy-man's fishing. You set 'em and come back the next day. Where's the sport in that? Catching a big'un with a rod and reel takes skill and patience. You have to outsmart that bottom dweller and muscle him into your frying pan. Now *that's* fishing. Not fetching."

"If I catch him, what will you give me?" Josh taunted.

Piper's father smiled, the left side of his mouth turning up slightly less than the right. "The best fried catfish dinner you ever had. Will's mama has nothing on my secret recipe, and you can tell her I said so."

Their banter thawed Piper's heart slightly. There was no doubting her father's love for his only grandchild. Josh desperately needed a male influence and without her father she wasn't sure where he'd get it. Was she making a mistake in trying to keep Josh and Roth apart?

No. For a lot of reasons, involvement with Roth wouldn't be good for Josh. That meant she'd have to contain her anger and disappointment and let him spend as much time with his grandfather as he needed.

They strolled toward the riverbank with their rods in hand. Piper caught her breath when she recognized Josh's stride. He walked like his father. In the twelve years Roth had been out of her life, she'd forgotten his walk—it was one of the few details she'd been able to wipe from her mind. Until now.

Her father put his hand on Josh's shoulder. "Listen up, Josh, starting tomorrow my deputies will be adjusting to the new chief and learning his ways. Don't know how he feels about 'em giving civilians a ride. So take the bus home from school. Don't be hitchin' a ride, ya hear?"

"I hate the bus. And why do we have to have a new chief?"

"'Cuz I'm not one hundred percent healed yet. And Quincey needs someone to run the department until I am."

"You don't like being retired?"

"It's like summer vacation. You know how you get bored by the end? I can't fish every day. There are more important matters to tend to, an' I can't do 'em sitting in my recliner."

Piper heard the frustration in his voice that his reassuring smile couldn't hide, and her heart ached for him. No matter how furious she was, she didn't wish him ill. And yes, she supposed a part of her still loved him and wanted the old chief back.

She especially wanted the new chief gone. The sooner the better. She just didn't know how to convince Roth there was nothing here for him now.

But if there was a way, she'd find it. And she needed to do it soon.

Roth stood outside the squat brick building housing the Quincey P.D. early Monday morning, eager to get this show on the road. The sooner he took control and assessed his officers the sooner he'd know who he could trust—and who he couldn't.

Quincey's mayor climbed from his Tahoe and joined Roth on the sidewalk.

"Snodgrass, you might have warned me that you'd forced Chief Hamilton to resign."

"Former Chief Hamilton has been a figurehead since his stroke. He's been unable to perform his duties, and his prolonged visits to the station keep the deputies who sit on their behinds entertaining him from doing theirs. The council's decision was the best one for Quincey."

Two of the town council members joined them, then shadowed them on their trek up the sidewalk. The mayor paused outside the door. "We've had an increase in petty crime of late, primarily vandalism and some spray painting."

"Gangs?"

"Doubtful. It's not gang signs. But if the officers are here playing cards with the former chief, they are not out looking for our troublemakers."

"You are aware that I was once one of Quincey's troublemakers."

Snodgrass's expression turned wily. "That should give you an advantage in ferreting out ours."

"Still, I would have appreciated a heads-up about the hostility."

"You're a Marine. You can handle hostile natives, can't you?"

Oohrah. "Absolutely."

"And it is only the natives who will require…let's call it an adjustment period. The newer citizens aren't as backwoods or close-minded."

Had the man read his résumé? "I am one of the backwoods natives."

"You were. We are hoping your combination of native know-how and military and police experience will have widened your view and will help us run things more efficiently. Quincey's police force has become…complacent.

"As for your deputies, the only one to watch is Butch White. He has seniority and has been acting unofficially as interim chief. He wanted this job and was convinced he was entitled to it."

Snodgrass nodded and one of his minions jumped to open the door, then the mayor motioned for Roth to precede him. The trio of new blood followed Roth in like fish in a school.

"Good morning." Roth greeted his deputies, and like Thursday when he'd dropped by to introduce himself and pick up his uniforms, the happy-to-meet-you vibes were noticeably absent.

Jones, the lone female, and Morris muttered replies. White and Aycock remained mute. Roth drilled Aycock with what one of Roth's boot camp drill instructors had called the "dead stare."

Aycock folded. "Morning. Sir."

Roth locked gazes with White. The older man's expression turned obstinate. Why had he been passed over for promotion? He'd been with the department since Roth's time in Quincey. Roth could easily ask around, but he'd learned a long time ago to distrust gossip. He would have to watch White and figure out what his issues were.

Snodgrass cleared his throat. "Deputy

White, would you retrieve the chief's badge and gun and the appropriate forms, please?"

White's surly attitude and snail's pace as he fetched the items from a glass-enclosed office—Roth's new office—confirmed his passive-aggressive resistance. He returned and slammed the items on the scarred desk in front of Snodgrass.

Roth picked up the pistol and checked the chamber and clip. "HK. Nice weapon and able to withstand abuse." Like being slammed into a solid surface.

The mayor nodded. "We upgraded our weapons last year. The HK 9mm is supposed to be what European officers carry. Deputy White, as the senior officer present, you may have the honor of swearing in the new chief."

White folded his beefy arms. "You're the mayor. You carry more clout in this town. You do it."

Oh, yeah, Roth and his second-in-command would have to work out their differences. White wouldn't like taking orders from a man twenty-plus years his junior. But doling out discipline was a skill Roth had mastered in the Corps. He could handle anything the deputy tossed at him.

The mayor offered a Bible. Roth experienced a slight twinge of conscience when he rested his hand on the book and repeated the oath, knowing he'd be counting the days until he could surrender his badge.

Then it was done. Roth was committed to protect the town that had done nothing to protect him or his mother. But he'd survived worse.

He pinned his badge to his blue uniform shirt and holstered the gun. The mayor offered him a pen. Chest tightening, Roth slashed his signature on the contract's relevant lines.

Snodgrass pointed to the last form. "This one needs a witness. Who—"

"Deputy White will be my witness," Roth commanded, and challenged the man to decline. Refusing a direct order from his superior would be grounds for dismissal.

White got the message and after a noticeable hesitation he scratched illegibly across the form. His scowl made it clear he considered the battle lines drawn.

The deputy would learn quickly that this Marine didn't retreat just because the job looked tough.

Chapter Five

"Why didn't you tell me?" Madison asked as she sat at her kitchen table across from Piper.

Piper hoped Madison wasn't talking about what every single person who'd walked through the clinic's door this morning had brought up. "Tell you what?"

"Piper Hamilton, don't give me that innocent look. You know what I'm talking about. I can't believe I had to hear about your juicy past with Chief Sterling from my clients instead of you."

"There's nothing to tell. We dated. Briefly. It ended badly."

"You did more than date. I can't believe

you would have let me bake a cake for the new chief like every other eligible woman in Quincey."

"You don't bake."

Madison rolled her eyes. "That's not the point. Is he Josh's father?"

Piper nearly dropped her sandwich. "Wh-why ask such a crazy question?"

"Josh looks like him."

"My son is a blond, like me."

"Yes, but he has his daddy's brown eyes. Those eyes will talk a lot of girls out of their panties in a few years. You should be worried. Does Roth know?"

Piper miraculously managed to follow Madison's train of thought. She seriously considered lying for all of thirty seconds. "No. And I don't want to bring it to Roth's attention, so please keep quiet."

"Sweetie, that's a hard secret to keep with them practically living on top of each other. If Sterling has half a brain cell in his gorgeous body, all he has to do is a little math. It's not like you to deny the obvious."

Piper shoved her sandwich away. Never mind that Madison made the best chicken salad in the world, at the moment Piper would choke if she tried to eat another bite. "I usually like Monday lunches at your house. You're killing that pleasure for me today."

"What happened?" Madison ignored her complaint.

What was the point in evading the truth? "I got pregnant. I thought we'd get married. Instead, when I told Roth he offered me money for an abortion and then he left town."

"Sonofabit—"

"It's not entirely his fault. I recently discovered my father threatened Roth and coerced him into joining the Marines. And… I told Roth I'd never give birth to the child of white trash like him."

"Not nice, and so not like you to be a vindictive bitch."

"No. I hate conflict. But I was hurt and scared, and I struck back the only way I knew how."

"Becoming old and wise requires us to go through the young and stupid stage. Don't beat yourself up over it. What can I do to help?"

"I wish I knew. But mostly, I wish Roth had never come back."

"Wishing is a waste of time. Trust me on that. You need a plan, and you need to consider telling Roth about Josh and letting the man contribute to your son's upkeep."

"I don't want anything from Roth."

"Maybe *you* don't. But doesn't Josh deserve to know his father?"

The question cut deep—right to the heart of Piper's insecurities. When Josh was younger she'd been enough. And when they'd moved home her father had pitched in. But lately... Josh had been moody, acting as if something bothered him. When she asked what was wrong he said, "Nothing." Her mom claimed it was puberty. Piper wasn't so sure.

Whatever the problem was, Roth wasn't the answer.

"I'm convinced Roth won't hang around long. He's always hated Quincey. I don't want Josh to get attached and then get abandoned."

"Like you did."

Piper picked at the crust on her bread. "Yes."

Madison grasped Piper's hand. "Even in the best, the strongest relationships, there's no guarantee that you won't get left behind."

The raw pain and sadness in Madison's eyes tugged at Piper's heart. "Roth was a Marine sniper. He killed people for a living. And before he came here he was a sniper with the Charlotte SWAT team."

"I can see how that might bother you, but, sweetie, that was his job."

"But how could he kill people in cold blood? I've seen the sniper shows with my father. They plot and plan, sometimes for months, to kill someone."

"He'd do it the same way I euthanize pets— by focusing on the good you're doing. In my case I try to end an animal's suffering. In his, I'm guessing there's a very good reason for him to follow an order to take someone out. That doesn't make either of us a killer."

That was eerily similar to what Roth had said.

"Madison, I'm scared of that dark side of him. And I can't risk losing my son to some- one like that. Roth could try to take Josh away. At the very least he would get joint custody. Or Josh could hate me for lying to him about his father. Either way, I lose."

The front door of Ann Marie's office slammed open. Only one person dared to enter her carefully restored, on-the-historical- register, former-train-station office that way.

Lou Hamilton.

If he'd put a fresh dent in the plaster behind the door, she would ring his neck. After he repaired it. The man was still good for some things.

"Ann Marie!"

She rose, smoothing her palms down her skirt, and met him in the doorway. "Good afternoon, Lou. Doris, why don't you take your lunch break now?"

"But—"

"I'll go when you get back. I'm waiting for a call and don't want to leave the phone uncovered." As well as she and her secretary worked together, Doris was one of the biggest gossips, and their corner office on Main and Maple Streets gave her the perfect vantage point to see everybody's business.

Doris looked predictably disappointed. Lou only stormed in when he had something interesting to grouse about. He never dropped by to chat the way he'd done before Piper became pregnant and he'd taken the stance that Ann Marie couldn't forgive or forget.

Ann Marie waited until her assistant had gathered her purse and shuffled out the door before marching over to inspect her wall. Her fingertip trailed over a telltale dent. "You're going to fix that."

"Course I will. Do you know what that sonofabitch has done?"

"To which fine citizen are you referring?" But she knew. Lou had only one man in his sights at the moment.

"Sterling sent Morris and Jones home and told them to come back this evening. Then he said, 'We're not going to sit on our asses and collect our paychecks. We'll be working twelve-hour shifts and patrolling when we're not doing paperwork.' Then he left Butch in the office to run Dispatch, with orders to clean the equipment while he waited for calls to come in."

"Don't other towns' officers work shifts?"

"I don't care about other towns. That's not how we operate. We've never worked shifts and we're all available 'round the clock when calls come in. That damned Snodgrass and his peons have been bending Sterling's ear."

She didn't bother reminding Lou he was no longer part of the "we." In his mind he would always be Chief.

"You're angry because you've lost your daily poker game. And you shouldn't be getting this worked up over something that's not your problem. You have your checkup this afternoon and you don't want your blood pressure to be too high."

"I will not let that jackass ruin my department."

That did it. There were times you just couldn't ignore pigheadedness. "It's not your department anymore, Lou."

She said it as gently as possible, but he paled as if she'd slapped him.

"Sterling has to go. Have you even thought about what will happen if he finds out about Josh? He might sue for joint custody, and if he does, then Josh will spend time with him. What grandma ignores her grandson? Which means Josh will be keeping company with Roth's mother, and where Eloise goes, Seth goes. I will not allow the murdering bastard who killed my brother anywhere near my grandson."

Fear fisted in Ann Marie's stomach. She collapsed into her chair. "I've thought of nothing else since Roth told me his daddy was getting out, and I'm worried sick. But Lou, if you don't control your anger, Roth will start asking questions about what has you so riled. And if he asks the right ones, then we might face exactly what we fear the most."

"Over my dead body."

She hoped that was an empty threat.

"None of us wants that. Piper needs us now

more than ever, so please, try to put her well-being first instead of forcing your edicts on everyone else."

He flinched at the low blow. It wasn't often that she brought up the decision he'd made that had destroyed their marriage. But he had to focus on Piper and not his pride, or they could lose everything they held dear.

And Ann Marie would not, by God, lose her daughter again.

A quick flash of red amongst the pines caught Roth's attention. He slowed the patrol car and scanned the woods, but whoever was out there had gone to ground.

He stopped the car, silenced the radio, lowered the windows two inches and killed the engine. Then he waited. Listening. Watching. Snipers learned patience early in their careers. Or they died. Five minutes passed before the top of a blond head preceded a pale face from behind a trunk. A boy. Too young to be out of school. Dark eyes. Medium build. Five and a half feet tall.

Roth blipped the siren with one hand and reached for the door handle with the other. He fully expected his quarry to flee. Instead, the boy strolled toward the car. He stopped abruptly when Roth emerged. And then he considered running. Roth could read it in the sudden tensing of the kid's muscles and the slight flexing of his knees.

"No point in taking off now. I've seen you well enough to have a good description. Plus having to chase you would really piss me off."

Roth did a visual for weapons or accomplices and saw neither. The crunch of the gravel beneath his feet gave way to the crackle of dead leaves. "Good weather for a hike, but shouldn't you be in school?"

"I got out early." A touch of defiant attitude, but not enough to be in-your-face disrespectful.

"Got out or left? You don't look old enough to be in the high school job release program."

The boy rolled a shoulder.

"That your stuff under the bridge?"

A slight dip of the chin was his only answer.

"This used to be one of my favorite hides when I was your age. The deer cross this gulch about a hundred yards that way." He pointed. "I nailed a number of twelve-point bucks from that high spot right there." He indicated a rise in the land without taking his eyes off the kid.

"Twelve points is decent," the boy offered grudgingly.

"Fed us for a while. You hunting?" Roth hadn't spotted a rifle or shotgun, but there were always hiding places if you knew where to look.

"Nah. My mom won't let me have a rifle." The kid stubbed his toe.

"Just cutting class then."

Another shrug. "I didn't want to ride the bus."

"Because the buses are crowded and smelly or because you're having problems with somebody on the bus?"

The bowed head popped up. Bingo.

"Anything I can do to help?"

"Like what?"

"I'm not offering to arrest anybody or beat 'em up. But I can listen while you plot out a better strategy to deal with your problems than hiding in the woods. That won't change anybody's attitude or actions. How do you usually get home?"

"I used to hitch a ride with my grandfather or one of his deputies."

Roth's blood went cold. *Grandfather. His* deputies. "You're Piper's son?"

"Yeah. You know my mom?"

"Yes." The living proof of Piper's love for

another man rattled Roth—hard. But he'd expected Piper's child to be younger. Much younger. He needed to back away, to get his head on straight, to accept that Piper had moved on.

Damned fast by the looks of it.

Hell, she must have picked up her new guy while Roth was still in boot camp. It had taken him a hell of a lot longer to get over her. He'd been well into his second deployment before he'd realized that if he didn't get her out of his mind, he wouldn't make it home without a bullet in him. As the hunter and the hunt*ed,* a sniper couldn't afford to be distracted.

"You're the new chief?"

Roth struggled to suppress the emotions boiling in his gut. Maybe his feelings for Piper weren't as resolved as he'd believed them to be. "Yes. Roth Sterling."

"You aren't so bad."

"Who said I was?" Not that he needed to ask.

"My mom and grandpa and grandma. They've been acting all ADHD since you got here. They said I shouldn't bother you."

Interesting. What kind of man had Piper chosen to replace him? "What grade are you in?"

"Sixth."

The fine hairs on Roth's body rose. "That makes you what? Ten?"

"Eleven."

His? No. He couldn't be. Piper said she'd gone to the clinic.

Roth searched the kid's face. Piper's hair. Piper's mouth and nose.

But the boy had brown eyes. The same shade of brown that stared at Roth in the mirror every morning.

Denial screamed through him, exploding like a mortar round in his belly. No. No. *No,* damn it. Brown eyes were common.

"When's your birthday?"

"March twentieth. Why?"

He did the math. Too close to call without a calendar. But more likely than not. Had Piper lied? Piper, who'd always been honest as a July day is long.

"Just curious." Shock, anger and fear coiled and twined inside him like a pit full of snakes. He didn't want to be a father. He didn't know how. And he sure as hell didn't want to hurt some kid the way his father had hurt him.

He had to know the truth. But could he count on Piper to tell it? No. He needed proof. Inarguable proof. How could he get it? Strategies raced through his head, and then he remembered one of his Marine buddies bragging about his new job with a lab—one that could give Roth exactly what he needed.

"You know I have to take you to school and call your mother."

"You can't let me off this time? It's my first skip."

"Nope, but good try."

The boy sighed. "Would have been better if it worked."

"Come on. I have a cooler of sodas in the cruiser. Let's grab a cold one for the ride."

Good thing he'd packed a lunch and snacks for the day. He offered Piper's son a can and a straw and took the same for himself although his dry mouth had nothing to do with thirst. Fear—the kind he felt when he knew he had an enemy sniper stalking his every move—settled on his back like an overloaded rucksack.

"Grab a sandwich if you're hungry. They're ham and cheese. Mustard. No mayo."

"Cool. I hate mayo."

So did Roth. Coincidence? Or more?

"What's your name?"

"Josh."

Josh. *Josh* could be his son. But he hoped like hell he wasn't. He wouldn't pin that curse on any kid. "Climb in and tell me why you're avoiding the boys on the bus."

"I never said it was boys."

"You're too old for it to be girls."

Josh smiled, revealing Piper's dimples. Then his smile faded. "They're into stuff I'm not into."

"Like vandalism?" Roth asked as he started the engine.

Those familiar brown eyes widened. "Wh-what makes you ask that?"

He put the car in motion, aiming for casual even though casual was the last thing he felt. "The council gave me the heads-up. Back in my dumber days I used to be one of Quincey's troublemakers. My friends and I irritated a lot of people. I know the tricks, the ways to pull off crap and not get caught. If you know anybody who might be into mischief, warn them they're in my crosshairs."

Josh gulped. "Yessir."

"And don't be stupid enough to get caught up in their trouble. Trouble is part of what led to your grandfather running me out of town."

"Grandpa kicked you out of Quincey?" Josh asked in an awestricken tone between bites.

"Yep."

"Wow. That's kinda cool."

"No. It's not. I left a lot of things…unsettled. Running away never fixes anything. The issues are always waiting when you come back."

Like a son he knew nothing about? He wasn't a religious man, but he was damned ready to drop to his knees and pray for a bye on this one.

All too soon the school came into view. Roth had a million more questions for Josh. But they'd have to wait. Until he was sure. He parked by the entrance.

"Finish the sandwich then I'll walk you in. Don't skip class again. Your education is the only ticket out of town."

"Why would I want to leave Quincey?"

Surprised, he looked at the kid. When he'd been that age all he'd wanted was to get as far away as he could. "You like it here?"

"Heck, yeah. We have fishing and forts and camping and stuff. The kids who've moved here from the city don't even know how to bait a hook. How lame is that?"

"Pretty lame." But Piper's son didn't have a father who'd beat him at the slightest provocation. And sometimes without one.

Roth wanted to keep it that way.

"Did you want to leave Quincey?"

"More than anything."

"Why?"

He debated dodging the question. The kid would hear the truth sooner or later. "My dad was a mean drunk."

"My dad's dead."

Roth bit his tongue on the urge to correct Josh. Where it came from, he didn't know, because he didn't want to be a father and he didn't know for sure yet if he was. "Finish up."

Josh shoved the last quarter of his sandwich into his mouth, wadded up the plastic wrap and grabbed his can.

"Leave the trash. I'll take care of it."

"Okay. And Chief Sterling, thanks. For the ride. And the talk. And…y'know." Josh offered his hand.

An invisible noose tightened around Roth's throat. His arm felt like deadwood as he clasped the boy's hand. "You're welcome, Josh. Anytime you need to talk, look me up."

"Oh, and ah…could you like not mention the guys on the bus to my mom?"

Did Piper need to know? Yes. But did he want to betray the boy's trust? No. "As long as you can handle it without skipping or breaking the law, I'll stay out of it."

"Fair enough."

"You want to give me their names? It would save me a lot of trouble."

"No way. That would cause me a lot of trouble."

"Figured as much." He'd identify the culprits without implicating the kid.

Roth escorted Josh to the office, still feeling the imprint of that grasp long after they'd parted.

His son. Maybe.

Piper had some explaining to do. He drove straight to the vet's office. Madison looked up from the desk and stiffened as he entered. "Afternoon, Chief."

"Where's Piper?"

"She drove her father to the doctor's for his checkup." Her tone and expression were a lot less I'd-like-to-get-to-know-you-preferably-naked friendly than last time.

"When will she be back?"

Dr. Monroe shrugged. "Depends on whether or not they have dinner before driving home."

"Tell her I'm looking for her."

"I'll do that."

Roth returned to his cruiser and looked at the cans sitting side by side in his cup holders. He would make an afternoon trip to Raleigh to his friend Boonie at the testing lab.

He'd get the answers he wanted without Piper's help.

Chapter Six

"I met Chief Sterling today."

Josh's announcement jarred Ann Marie so badly she dropped a cookie on the kitchen floor. Her heart pounded, and her hands trembled as she picked up the broken bits. "You did?"

"Yeah. He's going to call because he busted me for skipping school."

"Oh, Josh." She knew she should ask him why he'd skipped. But she couldn't get the words past the panic rising up her throat. She hadn't foreseen Josh would do anything to draw Roth's attention and force the meeting before any of them were prepared.

"He gave me a ride to school and walked me into the office."

Lordy, Lordy. And now the two of them had been seen in public side by side. She could only hope no one would notice the similarities between them. They might be subtle, but they were there if a body took time to look.

Josh shoved a whole cookie into his mouth. "He told me Grandpa ran him out of town."

Her spine snapped straight. The fact that Roth Sterling had bad-mouthed her family superseded her reminder for Josh not to talk with his mouth full. "He did, did he? Did he tell you why your grandfather wanted him to leave Quincey?"

"Because he was a troublemaker."

Well, well. The truth. But only part of it. Then again, Lou hadn't known Piper was expecting when he'd railroaded Roth out of town. That bombshell had come a few weeks later after Ann Marie had found Piper hugging the toilet before breakfast. Lou might have committed a much more serious crime if he'd known his daughter's condition.

"What else did you and Mr. Sterling talk about?" She couldn't call him "Chief."

"Hunting and fishing and school and stuff.

He had a rifle when he was my age and *he* went hunting."

She grasped on the familiar grievance of Josh wanting a rifle. "*He* had to put food on his family's table."

"He was poor?"

How did you explain to an eleven-year-old that some people preferred liquor to food? You didn't. "Yes."

"Did you ever take food over to his house?"

The question took her aback. "I—I—"

"You're always feeding poor people. Like you did with that bazillion cookies you made a few days ago. You gave them all away! I barely got any."

"I took some to the church day care and, yes, I shared a few with some of the shut-ins."

"You're not giving these away, are you?" His eyes filled with panic, as if losing his cookies was the worst thing he could fathom. He had no idea.

"I know peanut butter is your favorite. We'll keep these."

"Good. So did you ever take food to the Sterlings?"

So much for her hope that he'd forgotten his question. "No."

"Why?"

"Roth's father…" She searched for the right words and the correct amount of information. She wasn't about to tell him Lou had forbidden her to ever set foot on the Sterlings' property. "He didn't appreciate visitors."

"Chief Sterling said his dad was a mean drunk. How mean?"

Roth had been full of truisms today. "Josh Hamilton, you know I don't tell tales."

"Oh, c'mon, Grandma. How mean? Like bite-the-head-off-live-chickens mean or just scaring-little-girls mean?"

"Dear heavens. Where do you come up with this stuff?"

"You didn't answer my question." He looked exactly like his mother with that one eyebrow hiked and his head tilted down.

"Seth Sterling killed your grandfather's brother."

Josh's cookie-filled mouth dropped open. "That was him? Quincy's only murderer was the chief's daddy? *Cooooool.*"

"No, it is not cool! And don't you dare let your grandfather hear you stay that."

"I don't mean it's cool that Roth's father killed Grandpa's brother. I mean it's neat that Chief Sterling's dad was a criminal and the chief was a troublemaker, but then he grew up and became a cop. It's like he's trying to make up for the wrongs he and his dad did."

Dumbfounded, Ann Marie gaped. Sometimes Josh said the most outrageous things.

But this idea might have merit. Was Roth repenting his misspent youth? And if he was, could she trust this new phase?

No. There was no way he could make amends for abandoning Piper when she had needed him most. Ann Marie's job as a mother was to protect her daughter and grandson, and that meant keeping them far, far away from the entire dysfunctional Sterling clan. Especially Seth.

"Take the broken cookie out to the squirrels for me, Josh, and see if the bird feeders need filling."

He snatched up the pieces and headed for the back door. His arm lifted.

"Don't you dare eat that, young man. It's been on the floor."

"Your floor is cleaner than most folks' dishes," he said with a full mouth, and she knew her squirrels weren't getting a treat. But she had bigger problems to worry about than her grandson eating a little dirt.

The minute the door closed she grabbed her cell phone and dialed Piper's number.

The phone dumped straight to voice mail. Of course Piper would have turned it off while in the doctor's office.

Ann Marie wasn't about to leave the horrifying news in a message. The only thing they could do now was wait to see if the new chief came knocking.

Roth and Boonie had been through hell and back on numerous deployments together. As the Navy Corpsman assigned to Roth's unit, Boonie had patched up too many Marines to count, and Roth had learned to read the prognosis on the man's face before he opened his mouth.

And the news wasn't good.

"He's yours, man. No doubt about it. Smart of you to save the straw."

Roth felt as if a concussion grenade had exploded nearby. His ears rang. His eyes hurt. He couldn't breathe.

Piper hadn't terminated her pregnancy.

He had a son.

A claustrophobic sense of being trapped surrounded him. His fight-or-flight instincts kicked in, making his heart race and his palms moisten. He wanted to run. Again.

His plan to get the hell out as soon as he

talked sense into his mother or arrested his father faltered.

Was it better to be a bad father or an absentee one?

He'd had the first. He'd prayed for the second, and his life had sure as hell improved after his father had been locked up.

"You okay, HOG?"

HOG. Hunter of gunmen. The title earned by a successful sniper.

Piper's words, her fears, suddenly became Roth's, too. What kind of father could a man who'd hunted other men be?

I'll never have the child of white trash like you. She'd been so eager to forget Roth she'd concocted a fiancé to wipe him from her past.

Roth met Boonie's concerned gaze. "She told me she'd had an abortion."

"She lied."

"But why? Why lie?"

"You're asking the wrong man how a woman's mind works. Has she asked for money?"

"No."

"Think she will?"

Piper had made one thing clear. She wanted nothing from him. "No."

"Eleven years of child support would be a big chunk of change. You sure?"

"Yes." He yanked himself out of his bubble. "Thanks for running the test, Boonie."

"These new two-hour deals are sweet. I just wish I'd been able to give you the results you wanted."

"You gave me the truth. That's what I needed." What he would do with it was a whole different issue. "I'll catch up with you later."

A heavy hand descended on Roth's shoulder. "Park your ass in the chair, HOG. I'm not letting you get behind the wheel until your head's on straight."

Roth debated arguing for all of two seconds, but Boonie was right. Roth's legs were weak and trembling as if he'd run a twenty-mile ruck in full, wet gear.

"You regretting life on the civvy side?" Boonie asked, his attempt at finding a saner, safer topic as transparent as the glass in a scope.

It had been Boonie who'd planted the idea of getting out. Otherwise Roth probably would have been a lifer. "No. You were right. I'd proved myself as a Marine, and I'd maxed out on the promotions for my specialty. It was time to move on to new challenges."

"Better learning and living than dying a hero."

"Yeah."

"What are you gonna do about the boy?"

Bam. Back to reality. "The right thing. As soon as I figure out what in the hell that is."

"Oohrah. The Marine way." The Corpsman might be Navy, but he'd been trained to think and act like a Marine.

"The right thing would be to give Piper money to support Josh and stay out of their lives."

"Can you do that?"

"I don't know. How can I forget I have a son and return to Charlotte like nothing's changed?"

"Copy that."

"But my line of work doesn't make for regular hours. SWAT teams can't clock out mid-crisis. We stay until the end. How can I work a kid into that life? I've seen coworkers try and fail. If Piper and I shared joint custody, Josh would end up waiting for me to pick him up, and some weekends I'd be a no-show. I don't want to be *that* dad—the one who lets his kid down."

He'd been disappointed by his father often enough to know how rotten it felt to be embarrassed by, ashamed of, disappointed in or flat out disgusted by a parent.

"Half-assed isn't your style. You're an all-in guy. Maybe you shouldn't return to the old job."

Roth rejected the idea immediately. "My life and career are in Charlotte. Quincey is only a brief detour."

"You're only talking a few years. Six or seven. Then your boy will go to college or do whatever eighteen-year-olds do. You can handle it. You've faced worse."

Roth sucked in a lungful of air, fighting for calm, fighting the real reason he didn't want to commit to fatherhood. It took conscious effort to pull himself back from the edge of fear. Yes, fear, damn it. And he wasn't proud of it.

Boonie waited.

Roth had trusted the guy with his life. Literally and figuratively. Could he trust Boonie with his darkest secret? Roth's lungs emptied a heavy breath.

"My father was a drunk, abusive, murdering sonofabitch with a temper he couldn't control. I'd like to believe I'm better than him. I've sure as hell worked hard at it. But I can't be sure. And if I'm wrong, Josh and Piper will suffer."

"I've never seen you drunk, and I've never

seen you lose your cool—not even when some jarhead deserved a fist in the face. You aren't anything like your father sounds."

Roth stared at Boonie and the certainty in the man's eyes.

"It's like the battalion commander always said, believing you'll fail is the best way to guarantee it. You have to decide, HOG. Are you in or are you out?"

Never doubting his ability to get the job done had kept Roth alive during his deployments. How could he be any less committed now? He stiffened his spine. There had to be a way to make this work. All he had to do was find it.

Roth knew.

Piper could tell from the moment she saw him leaning against the police cruiser with his arms and ankles crossed outside the vet clinic. And the telltale sign wasn't because he looked furious but because he looked calm. Deadly calm. His muscles weren't tense, and his respiratory rate appeared normal. That very lack of emotion terrified her.

She didn't know this man. The one he'd become. The one who could kill as a routine part of his job then continue with his day.

He didn't speak as she closed the distance between them. He watched her without so much as the twitch of an eyelash. His crisply pressed navy blue uniform only added to her anxiety.

She stopped two arm-lengths away. What if she hadn't dropped by after her father's appointment to finish some paperwork? Would Roth have forced this meeting at home? In front of Josh?

"You lied. Don't bother to deny it. I have DNA proof that Josh is my son."

The low, controlled tone of his voice sent adrenaline rushing through her veins. "Proof?"

"I picked him up for skipping school today. Gave him a soda. Took the straw to a DNA lab." Clipped phrases spelling out doom.

"I told you I went to the clinic." And then her fear transformed into anger because he hadn't been there for her at that crucial moment— the one where the rest of her life had hung on one decision.

Her heart had insisted she do one thing. Her mother and her father had each demanded other equally unacceptable alternatives. She'd been terrified of making the wrong choice because no matter which decision she made someone would be unhappy.

"What I neglected to tell you was that I chickened out and ran crying from the building. And when I climbed into my father's car and begged him to take me home he told me to go inside and do what needed to be done or I would have to leave Quincey because I wasn't going to humiliate him."

The memory egged her on. She stepped forward until she stood chest to chest, nose to nose with the man who'd let her down. "What I didn't tell you was that I chose to leave everything and everyone I loved behind to have my child."

"Our child."

"No. He ceased to be yours when you shoved money in my hand and told me to 'take care of it.' He became mine and only mine when you took the easy way out and ran away from your responsibilities. I carried my baby. I gave birth to him—alone—with no one but the hospital staff by my side. I have raised him."

He gripped her biceps and the heat of his touch penetrated her fury, making her heart race for an altogether different reason. She hated that despite everything she still felt the tug of attraction. She covered the reaction by shrugging off his hold, moving to her car. She threw her bag onto the seat.

"Don't worry, Roth. I—*we*—don't want or need anything from you. You can pretend you never found out the truth."

"Josh believes his father's dead."

"Would you rather he knows the truth? That you never wanted him to be born?"

She almost missed his barely noticeable flinch.

"As far as I'm concerned, Josh's father is dead. The man I loved, the one who was brave enough to defy my father and make me fall in love with him, the one I prayed would come after me and tell me that he'd made a terrible mistake and that he wanted to be with me, is dead. He died the day you abandoned us. And I want him to stay that way."

A nerve twitched in the bow of Roth's upper lip—the only evidence that this confrontation got to him in any way. Did he care so little about the devastation he'd left behind?

"I don't know how to be a father."

"Do you think I knew how to be a mother? I learned by trial and error. Mostly error. But at least I tried."

"You had your parents' example to follow. My role models were an alcoholic father who beat a defenseless kid and the woman he claimed he loved, and a mother who took the abuse as if she didn't deserve better."

"You had your grandfather, Roth."

"He died when I was thirteen. He hardly had time to be an influence." He raked his fingers through his hair. "You should have told me about Josh, Piper."

"And how exactly was I supposed to do that, Roth? Even if I thought you deserved to know—and I didn't and still don't—you didn't tell anyone where you were going. Not even your mother knew how to find you. Or if she did, she wouldn't tell me."

"You spoke to my mother?"

"Once. In a weak moment. Before I left I went to her house and begged her to tell me where you'd gone."

"I didn't tell her I'd enlisted. I didn't want her to worry. I told her I'd gotten a job out of town and that I'd send money."

"And I was shipped off in disgrace to live with an aunt I'd only met once. Lucky for me—" she couldn't keep the sarcasm from her voice "—Aunt Agnes really had broken her hip and she had to take me in whether she wanted to or not. She didn't have anyone else who could care for her or put up with her judgmental attitude."

"I'm sorry you had to endure that. I want to get to know Josh."

"No! You're not a good role model."

"What does that mean?"

"You were raised with violence and you've made a career out of it, reinforcing every lesson your daddy pounded into you. Josh is at an awkward age and I'm trying to teach him that aggression isn't the answer to his problems. I certainly don't want him anywhere near Seth when he gets out of prison."

Roth's expression turned lethal. "On that we agree."

"Stay away from my son. I don't want you getting his hopes up only to let him down like you did me."

"That won't happen."

"Oh, really? How long do you intend to stay this time, Roth? You're renting. Month to month. And you may have asked my mother to find you a house, but still, a rental house. That's noncommittal. Temporary. How long before you decide you've had enough of Quincey and Josh?" *And me.*

The muscles of his jaw bunched. "Piper—"

"Can you deny you plan to leave?"

His hesitation gave her the answer she needed. Before he could argue, the roar of a diesel tractor engine turning into the parking lot made replying impossible. She spotted one of her least favorite people.

"Oh, look, your buddy Chuck's here—the one you sacrificed our future for. The one who meant more to you than me and our child."

"Damn it, Piper, we're not done."

"Yes, we are. We've been *done* since you chose him over me twelve years ago."

Piper took advantage of Roth's distraction as the tractor chugged to a halt dangerously close to his cruiser to jump into her Jeep and make her escape.

"Say it ain't so, bud," Chuck said as he climbed from his tractor. "Tell me you didn't volunteer to come back to this cesspool after making the great escape."

Roth wanted to go after Piper. But she was too angry to listen to reason right now. He'd give her time to calm down before trying to make her see his side of the situation.

"Chuck. It's good to see you. And yes, I did. But so did you." He'd intended to look his old friend up, but the past five days had been too full to fit in a drive out to the farm.

"Yeah." Chuck shrugged as if uncomfortable. "You always swore you'd never come back, but I guess with your daddy locked up you got no reason to stay gone."

"He's getting paroled." Roth couldn't get over how much his former best friend had aged. Chuck's football muscles had turned to flab. He looked like Chuck Sr. had before Roth had left town.

"No shit?" The stench of whiskey preceded Chuck's extended hand and chest bump embrace.

"How much have you had to drink today?"

"Dressed like a cop. Playing cop. Funny, man." Chuck's bloodshot eyes scanned Roth's face. "You are kidding. Right?"

"No."

"You're peeved 'cuz I popped the top on a beer or two without you."

If there was one thing Roth knew how to identify, it was someone who'd had too much to drink. That wasn't a two-beer buzz making Chuck unsteady on his feet.

"I'm concerned because you're operating heavy machinery under the influence on Quincey's streets."

Chuck flung his arms wide and stumbled. "It's not like it's my car. I don't drive that anymore since I lost my license."

Lost his license. This got better and better, as Piper had probably expected it would. If this was typical behavior for Chuck then no wonder she was angry Roth had chosen Chuck over her. But he'd give Chuck the benefit of the doubt—for now. One incident did not make a pattern.

"Get in the cruiser."

"Are we going to grab a beer? There's this new joint down the road I'd love to show you."

"No, I'm taking you to the station."

"You're a riot, man." Chuck's eyes narrowed then his expression turned ugly. "Thought you were my pal. Give a buddy a break, *Chief.*"

Chuck tagged on the title with enough venom to nick Roth's anger. He reined it in. "I am giving you a break by not making you take a breathalyzer test, which I suspect you would fail, then I'd have to arrest you and impound your tractor. Let's go to the station and catch up."

Visiting would give Chuck time to sober up and Roth time to look into Chuck's record.

"I'd rather we catch up over a drink. You can buy the first round."

"Another time. Tonight I'm on duty. Let's go."

"Gonna cuff me before you put me in?" More surly attitude.

"Not unless you get stupid." Roth opened the passenger door. "Sit up front."

Chuck fell into the seat. Roth climbed in the other side. This wasn't how he had expected their reunion to go. "Buckle your seat belt."

"For a three-block drive?"

"It's state law."

"What? You follow rules now?"

"Yes. And I enforce them."

With a lot of muttering under his breath, Chuck complied. "What you been doing since you split Dullsville?"

"I wrote and told you I'd joined the Marines. You didn't reply. You're the only one of the guys who didn't write back." Roth steered toward the station.

"Prolly never got the letter. Me and Joan have moved around a lot."

"Joan?"

"The wife. The Marines? Seriously? What for?"

"I needed discipline, a sense of purpose and a steady paycheck." Roth nearly choked on his own tongue when he realized he'd recited the exact words Chief Hamilton had hurled at him outside the recruiting station. But, he acknowledged with hindsight, they were true.

"A bit drastic, but okay. Puts food in the belly. And the gov'ment ain't gonna run out of money and lay you off."

"What about you? What happened to college?"

Chuck plucked at the seam of his oil-and-mud-spattered jeans. "That didn't work out."

"Because you lost your scholarship?" Roth hoped Piper had lied, but was beginning to suspect she hadn't.

"Man, I was framed."

"For cheating?"

"Grapevine's already working, eh? Piper's never liked me anyhow. Best thing you ever did was dump that bitch. Did you know she had some other guy's brat?"

Anger and the need to deny Chuck's claim hit Roth hard and fast. He contained both reactions by clenching his fists on the wheel. He didn't have the right to defend Piper anymore, and he wasn't ready to share the news of his paternity yet—especially given he didn't know what he would do with it and wasn't sure if he could trust Chuck.

"Did you cheat?"

"Sterling, we both know you were the brainy one in our little quartet. Let's just say I needed some help to pass if I wanted to stay on the team."

Roth swallowed his disappointment as he parked outside the station. "Are Joe and Billy still in town?"

"Nah, they lit out for Raleigh a few years back. Got tired of farming, I guess, and didn't want to work for that conglomerate that's buying up all the land."

He'd counted on the guys keeping him from going insane while here. "Come inside."

He waited for Chuck to precede him and registered he'd unintentionally fallen into the habit of keeping anyone he'd arrested in plain sight even though he hadn't charged Chuck. Roth debated patting him down before taking him into the station, but this was Chuck. So he didn't.

The two officers he'd sent home this morning jerked upright when he entered. They sat behind their desks doing nothing as far as Roth could tell. He paused at Morris's desk. "Did Deputy White get all the weapons cleaned?"

"Don't know, ah, sir. He didn't say." The

man's face turned red and he wouldn't hold Roth's gaze.

Jones found a sudden interest in shuffling papers. Roth scanned the room for a reason. His gaze landed on the whiteboard he'd hung this morning to mark their comings and goings. It would act as a temporary scheduling board until he could set up a computerized version. Beside Roth's name a four-hour block had been marked off in red with "long lunch."

"Have a seat in my office, Chuck. I'll get you a soda." On the way to the break room he paused by the board, erased "long lunch" and inserted "split shift."

He turned to Morris and Jones, who both hunched their shoulders as if uncomfortable. "As I told Deputies White and Aycock this morning, until I get a feel for my team—your strengths and your weaknesses—I'll be working the first half of each day with the morning shift and the latter part with the second shift. Clearly I overestimated Deputy White's ability to relay that to the second shift as instructed.

"Idle time is wasted time. Every piece of equipment in this building needs to be clean and fully functional if and when we need it. My pistol was a misfire waiting to happen.

It didn't look like it had ever been cleaned. If you have time to sit, you have time to break down the equipment and clean it. If you don't know how, I'll teach you."

Morris's chin jacked up. "We don't get to do much shooting around here, so stuff doesn't get dirty."

"That's going to change. Morris, I'd like a total inventory of every firearm and round we have on the premises, and Jones, because you're the only one with any computer training, next week after the new scanner arrives I'd like for you to supervise the conversion of our records from paper to computer."

"We're going to computers for everything?" Morris asked with a touch of panic in his voice.

"The town council has budgeted for it. Laptops will be installed in the patrol cars. Going electronic will help us communicate with other departments. Right now any traffic stop is hazardous because you don't have access to basic information. There's also an increase in gang activity in the areas surrounding us. We need every heads-up available to be proactive. If you can operate a cell phone, you can handle a computer. You'll get training on all the software."

Roth had been shocked to learn they still did things the old-fashioned way in Quincey— with pen and paper. One of the reasons the town council had hired him was because he was willing to oversee the digital conversion and make the force technologically current. He figured it wouldn't take more than a couple of months.

He opened a drawer and located Chuck's file. It was over an inch thick. He retrieved a soft drink and a package of crackers, returned to his office and slid both toward Chuck. Roth tapped the file. "You've been busy."

"Nothing to do here."

Roth scanned the pages, report after report of the same kind of shenanigans they'd pulled in high school with multiple driving-while-intoxicated charges thrown in. One item caught his eyes. "Shoplifting?"

"Just wanted to see what the big deal was. Movie stars do it all the time."

They'd both grown older, but apparently only one of them had grown up. Roth rose and closed his office door. "Do you have any children, Chuck?"

"Yeah. Two. Why?"

"I spent my life ashamed of my father. Don't do that to your kids."

Chuck lurched to his feet and stood nose to nose with Roth. "You sonofabitch. Don't come back here actin' all high and mighty an' insult me like that."

Roth didn't flinch from the intimidation attempt. "Sit down and shut up or I will arrest you. You've had four Driving While Impaired arrests in ten years. That's a Class F Felony. Habitual Impaired Driving. I don't know how you've managed to avoid jail time, but I can have you locked up for a minimum of twelve months with almost no effort. And I could probably charge you with enough today to get even more time. Why has no one forced you to attend a substance abuse program?"

"I don't have a drinking problem."

"Your record says otherwise."

"Don't go all official on my ass, Sterling."

"I haven't. Yet. But if I catch you intoxicated in public again—I don't care if you're walking or riding a bicycle—I will charge you. And you will do time. I'm sure you remember how much crap I took for having a father in prison. Set a better example for your kids."

He yanked open the door. "I'll get you the information for a substance abuse program—you can enroll voluntarily. I'll expect proof of attendance."

"And if I don't?"

"You'll wish you had." He pushed the phone forward. "Finish up, then call your wife to come and get you. And Chuck, don't expect any favors from me. I gave up a hell of a lot for you twelve years ago and you pissed it away. I won't make the same mistake twice."

Chapter Seven

Roth sat in his cruiser outside the animal clinic at 6:50 a.m. waiting for either Piper or the doc to arrive.

He didn't know how to be a father and the idea of screwing that up and failing the boy scared him spitless. But he wouldn't back down from the challenge.

And the only way to get to know his son short of an expensive and time-consuming legal battle was to make Piper believe in him the way she once had.

To accomplish that he needed a strategy to infiltrate Piper's world. That meant blending into a town he couldn't wait to leave, forming friendships he didn't intend to keep beyond this "deployment," and becoming an integral part of her landscape. He'd even have to make peace with his worst enemy—Piper's father.

All skills he'd honed in the Corps.

The unexpected passenger in his backseat provided the perfect cover to begin implementing his plan.

A ten-year-old blue extended cab pickup with a camper shell on the back turned into the lot. The same truck had been here last time he'd stopped by. Madison sat behind the wheel.

Roth climbed out and opened the back door. A whimper and the flick of a tail greeted him. The dog struggled to rise but gave up. "It's okay, bud. The doc will fix you up."

Roth carefully scooped up his passenger and met the vet at the clinic's door. "Who handles strays?"

Dr. Monroe looked less than thrilled to see him. "The county animal control office if you can wait for them to get all the way out here. Why? What do you have?"

"I found this guy out on the highway. Looks like he was hit by or thrown from a car. He's pretty banged up. Recognize him?"

The hostility on Madison's face morphed into concern as she peeled away the jacket

Roth had wrapped the dog in and studied the raw patches on the mutt's head. "He's not one of my patients. The scrapes look recent. Let's get him inside for an exam."

She quickly unlocked the door and hustled down the hall, flicking on lights.

"We're pretty rural and not far from the highway, so unfortunately we get a lot of pet dumps out here. Bring him in here."

Here was a small treatment room with a hip-high stainless-steel table. It hadn't changed much since Roth's last visit well over a decade ago. He set his bundle on the cold metal. The vet went into action, talking soothing non-sense as she gently prodded.

"No collar. Underweight. Fleas. Besides the obvious neglect and abrasions, it looks like he has a hip injury, but I can't tell the extent of the damage without X-rays."

Roth waited for her to follow her words with action, but she remained by the table, simply stroking an uninjured portion of the dog's head.

"Aren't you going to take the X-rays?"

She leveled a look at him. "Why run up the expense if animal control will probably put him down?"

Roth recoiled. *Kill only what needs killing,*

the sniper code echoed in his head. "Why euthanize him? He has a good disposition. He has to be in pain, but he hasn't snapped or growled once while either of us handled him."

"True, but he's older and he's not by any stretch of the imagination an attractive dog. It's unlikely he'll be adopted. Unless you're taking him."

"My apartment doesn't allow pets. Can't you find a home for him?"

The front door clicked open. The dog cocked his head. Roth heard the quiet squeak of rubber-soled shoes approaching. Piper?

"I can try to find a home, but I can't make guarantees. People prefer puppies. And in case you haven't noticed, we're a two-woman office. We don't have a night crew to attend animals left here."

"What do you do with your overnighters?"

"Either Piper or I take them home. If they're critical or postsurgical, I camp on my couch."

Piper appeared in the doorway. He involuntarily drank in the sight of her. She looked good with her hair in one of those braids—the kind he'd always unraveled one lock at a time. Her pink scrubs accentuated the tint of her cheeks.

Blue eyes flicked briefly to his but ricocheted away quickly. "What do we have?"

"The chief picked up an injured dog on the highway."

A little of Piper's stiffness eased and a hint of a smile touched her lips. "Roth always rescued strays. He had a three-legged dog and a one-eyed cat when we met. He used to do odd jobs for Dr. Jones in exchange for their care."

"Really?" the vet asked in a tone that snapped Piper's spine taut. The women exchanged a look full of subtext that Roth couldn't decode. Snipers read body language well. It was often the only way to tell the difference between the good guys and the bad. But he was at a loss here. And he was pretty sure the message he was missing concerned him.

Piper moved closer to the dog, close enough that her flowery scent drifted to Roth. She petted and studied the mutt, tilting her head in an all too familiar way—one that reminded him of tasting the soft skin beneath her ear.

"Medium-size boxer mix in serious need of TLC. Shall I start a chart?"

"Might as well. Looks like he'll be our guest. The chief wants us to find this fella a family. I'll need pictures of his hip and a full spectrum of lab work."

Piper's attention transferred to Roth and his heart stalled. He'd been taught to control his body—every nuance from his respiratory to his heart rates. Why did years of discipline vanish around her?

"You have blood on your hands."

The movement of Piper's pink lips made him realize he'd been staring at her mouth. Damn, he wished he could forget all the magic those lips had once created. He forced his gaze away and processed her words.

Did she mean literally or figuratively? He looked down and spotted the brownish-red smears. She wasn't talking about his past career. This time. "It's nothing."

She pointed to the sink in the corner. "Wash up. You don't know where he's been or what he has. And you'll need to wash your coat to get rid any fleas or parasites. Check yourself for ticks when you get home. I'll get started cleaning this guy's wounds."

He dutifully scrubbed. As soon as he turned off the water he heard the front door latch click again.

Madison waved Piper away. "Walk the chief out and take care of whoever's out there. I've got this guy."

Roth followed Piper down the hall, his gaze automatically dropping to her butt. He missed the snug jeans she'd practically lived in twelve years ago. Her scrubs concealed her curves. The need to tug the band from her hair, to run his fingers through the silky strands and sink deep into her body ambushed him. Images of the two of them intertwined, of her above him, beneath him, wrapped round him, rained on him from all sides like incoming enemy fire. There was nowhere to duck for cover from the mental shrapnel.

He forced the pictures from his head. Regaining Piper's confidence did not include getting into her pants, tempting though that might be.

Lovin' her and leavin' her. He couldn't do that to her again. He couldn't do that to himself. Because he couldn't guarantee he'd be able to claw his way out of the black hole that cutting her from his life had sucked him into.

He *would* leave Quincey. Having Josh complicated matters and might force Roth to extend his stay short-term, but he would escape this town and the foul memories attached to it.

If he stayed he risked turning into what everyone predicted he would. His father's son.

* * *

Piper silently groaned when she saw who stood by the desk. Her least favorite person and her least favorite patient. Without an appointment. Just what she needed on a day that had begun badly.

"Good morning, Mr. McNulty."

McNulty looked from Piper to Roth. His thick white eyebrows winged upward and his faded blue eyes filled with speculation. "You two back together?"

Piper's nerves snarled. "No."

She jerked her gaze to Roth, who'd answered simultaneously. Then she focused on Mc*Nutty,* as most of Quincey referred to him. The retired science teacher was the town's worst busybody—worse even than her mother's assistant. "The chief brought in a stray dog."

"You might want to consider a reunion. That boy of yours needs a daddy, and you haven't shown any partiality to the fellas around here."

"What brings you in today?"

"Rascal hasn't eaten in two days." He hefted a cat carrier.

It was all Piper could do not to jump back. McNulty's ferret liked to bite—especially

Piper. But the vile critter gave her the perfect excuse to get rid of Roth, and for that she could even be thankful for the hateful varmint.

"Let me show Chief Sterling out then I'll check with Dr. Monroe and see if she can work you in. Have a seat."

McNulty sat, and she pulled open the door and turned to Roth. "Do you want us to call and report what we find?"

"Yes. Piper, we—"

"It'll probably be late this afternoon before we have all the results. Have a good day, Chief Sterling."

He opened his mouth. She shook her head slightly and tilted it toward the waiting room, hoping Roth would take the hint and say no more.

Roth studied her for a full fifteen seconds then he tucked his jacket under his arm and grabbed her hand. Startled by the sudden move, she gasped and tried to tug free, but he held tight and pulled a pen from his pocket. The warmth of his grip seeped through her palm, up her arm, jump-starting her heart into a rapid jungle beat.

"Here's my cell number. I'll cover the expenses, but try to keep them down."

The pen tickled erotically across her skin as he wrote, stirring up trouble below her navel. Her breath became shallow. Her nipples tightened. She prayed he didn't notice, but when she risked a peek at his face, that's exactly where he was looking. Shame scorched her skin. The moment Roth stopped writing she yanked her hand away. Their gazes locked. She couldn't find words.

Roth dipped his head and left. Piper gulped the moisture that had inexplicably flooded her mouth. Damn him for still ringing her chimes.

She turned, her eyes falling on the observer she'd totally forgotten—the one who hadn't missed a second of the exchange. Great. It would be all over town before most folks finished reading their paper that she still had the hots, as Madison had put it, for her old flame.

"I'll be right back." Piper fled to the exam room.

Madison glanced up from the patient. "Did you read the *Quincey Gazette* today?"

What did that have to do with anything? "No."

"You should. One of the councilmen wrote an interesting article about Roth. You say he rescues strays and yet you think he's a killer?"

"He can do both. McNutty's here."

Her boss rolled her eyes. "Put him in exam one. And Piper, there's a good chance you've misjudged our new chief. He might not be the irresponsible man he once was."

"If you think he's so great, you can have him." Feeling sick to her stomach she raced toward Rascal and his owner, eager for once to have to focus on dodging the ferret's teeth and avoiding his nosy owner's prying. Both would keep her brain fully occupied.

Roth, gossip and her boss's defection. Tuesday was showing signs of being a winner of a day. Not.

Roth's stomach growled. He'd been on patrol since four and he needed food. Better to focus on the hunger he could feed and forget the chemistry between himself and Piper.

He tossed the soiled jacket into the trunk and left the car in the clinic's lot. The walk to the diner would clear his head.

"Morning, Chief."

Roth did a double take at the man passing by—a stranger. The warm greeting was a first. "Good morning."

A few steps farther and the pharmacist waved through his window. Roth waved back.

What was going on? He entered the diner. Heads turned. People made eye contact and nodded when he scanned the place. Not everyone, but about a quarter of the patrons. The only thing notably missing was the open hostility he'd enjoyed the last three times he'd stopped in for a meal. Odd.

"Good morning, Chief," May called from behind the counter. "Sit wherever you like. The usual?"

He tried to conceal his surprise. The waitress had barely spoken to him previously and had only grudgingly taken his orders. He'd lumped her in the Lou Hamilton–supporter category. "Yes. Thanks, May."

Luck was on his side today. First the dog and now a seat at the counter beside Ronnie Craig—one of the few people in Quincey who Roth had actually loathed years ago. And while he'd prefer not to sit with his back to the room, today he'd make an exception because he and Ronnie had unfinished business.

Roth slid onto the red-and-chrome stool. His target, a sorry excuse for manhood, stiffened but didn't glance his way.

"You still making moonshine?" Roth asked.

"What's it to ya?" the man snarled.

"You used to supply my father even though you knew he had a drinking problem."

"Seth's problems weren't my business."

Anger coiled in Roth's gut. "If you're brewing and selling, I suggest you get your still out of my jurisdiction. I have the power to do more than bust up your equipment now."

Eyes full of hate turned his way. "So that was you. Suspected as much since I never had any problems after you left town. You had no right vandalizing my property."

"And you had no right to manufacture and sell illegal liquor or to provide an alcoholic with the fuel he needed to beat his wife. If I catch even a whiff that you're brewing for anything more than your private consumption again, I'll have the Alcohol Law Enforcement division all over you. ALE and I won't look the other way. Understood?"

Without a word, Craig yanked out his wallet and threw money on the counter then stomped out. Roth watched him all the way out the door.

May slid Roth's breakfast and a copy of Quincey's weekly newspaper in front of him. "Might want to come back 'round dinnertime. Cook's working on a new pie recipe. If it tastes as good as it smells, it's worth a try."

"Thanks. I'll consider it."

"Morning, Chief," someone said as they passed behind Roth. He replied automatically to that and each of the subsequent greetings that came over the next ten minutes while he ate his steak sandwich. What in the hell was going on? Why the change from frosty to almost warm?

He finished and reached for his wallet. "May, could I have my check?"

"'S'already paid. Lowry took care of it."

He frowned. "Who's Lowry?"

"He didn't live here back in your day. He served twenty years with the Army and retired here 'bout five years ago. He paid your tab on his way out. You might want to look him up, compare your medals and swap war stories. He don't have a lot of friends, being an outsider and all." She tapped the newspaper. "'S a real good story 'bout you in today's *Gazette*."

A news story could explain the change in attitude. He hadn't told anyone about his commendations, but they were a part of his résumé. He left a tip and rose. "Thanks for the info. I'll take a look."

But uneasiness settled over him. When something looked too good to be true, it usually was.

* * *

"The chief's here!" Josh shouted from the den and every muscle in Piper's body snapped taut. From the excitement in his voice she knew he wasn't talking about his grandpa.

She spooned the last meatball into the sauce and set the ladle aside. Footsteps thundered to the foyer. Piper heard Josh open the door as she washed her hands.

"Hi. What're you doing here?" Josh asked.

"Dr. Monroe told me your mom brought home the dog."

The deep rumble only confirmed her fear— her worst nightmare was *here*. In her home.

"Yeah, he's here. Want to see him?"

"I do."

Piper cringed as she joined them in the foyer. Roth's espresso-dark eyes met hers then slowly rolled over her, making her stomach do somersaults.

"Evening, Piper."

"Roth."

"Doc Monroe said the patient cleaned up well, but I wanted to see for myself."

"I'm calling him Sarg, short for Sergeant," Josh informed him, and Roth's eyes widening in surprise. "We read the article about you in today's paper during English class. Cool stuff. And since you found Sarg, I thought it would be neat to name him after you. He's in the den. C'mon." Her son dodged around her, leaving Roth to follow.

Of course her son was impressed by the article. According to the council member who'd written the gushy piece, Roth was practically a superhero who had served his country with honor and received several commendations for his actions. But the story had glossed over his role as a sniper—a cold-blooded killer.

Piper wanted to barricade Roth's path and ask why he hadn't called before dropping by. She wanted to send him away. She wanted to make her heart quit racing like a stupid schoolgirl's every time she caught sight of him. She couldn't do any of those things.

"Why are you here?"

"To see the dog." The sharpness of his gaze and the tension in his muscles belied the innocent comment.

"I don't believe that for a second."

"Chief, ya coming?" Josh called.

After a beat Piper reluctantly unclenched her fists and let the intruder pass.

"Dr. Monroe says Sarg only dislocated his hip, and the scrapes will heal. He should be fine in a few weeks. He already knows how to catch. Watch." Josh tossed a ball into the air. The dog caught it without getting up. Her son rewarded their visitor with a liver treat. "He knows 'shake,' too." Josh demonstrated.

"He must have been somebody's pet before he was dumped." Roth knelt and scratched the uninjured side of Sarg's head. The dog licked his hand, literally lapping up the attention.

"Mom says I can't keep him," Josh informed Roth, his voice full of resentment.

Here we go again. "Josh—"

"And she won't let me have a cell phone or a rifle so I can hunt, either."

Oh, boy. Her son at his I'm-so-deprived finest.

"Can you pay for them?" Roth asked before she could defend her decision—not that she owed Roth any explanation for her parenting choices.

Josh blinked. That clearly hadn't been the response he'd anticipated. "Well…no."

"Then she's right, Josh. Until you can afford to buy luxuries, you don't need them."

She hadn't seen that coming.

"But everybody else has dogs and phones and rifles."

"Josh, nobody gave me anything. I had to work and earn the money to buy what I needed. It made me appreciate what I had. My first rifle belonged to my grandfather. He left it to me when he died. I'd have rather had him a few more years."

Piper hated the tug on her heartstrings. Rumor had it Seth's behavior had gotten worse after Roth's grandfather had passed.

Josh's face screwed up in his thinking-hard expression as if he were trying to figure out how and why his attempt at manipulation had failed. "I'm only eleven. I can't get a job."

"I worked at your age. I cleaned up Dr. Jones's kennel every weekend and I helped my dad fix cars after school. The first earned me a little spending money. The second taught me a trade."

Wow. Piper closed her gaping mouth. *Not bad, Roth.*

"Your grandfather used to hunt. Doesn't he take you with him when he goes?"

"He was going to start last fall, but his stroke messed up his trigger finger. He can't shoot anymore. He says that's why he's not chief. He can't pass the target test."

"That so?" Roth glanced at Piper for confirmation, but she refused to confirm or deny. She wasn't helping the man who'd taken her father's job.

"Can't you adopt Sarg, Chief?"

"My apartment doesn't allow pets."

"I wish I could keep him. I'd walk him and bathe him and everything." Beseeching brown eyes swung her way.

Piper sighed. Some days reasoning with an eleven-year-old was like teaching a parrot to talk. You had to repeat everything a hundred times. "You have school, and I work. It's not fair to Sarg to keep him locked up all day, and we don't have a fenced yard."

Roth placed a hand on Josh's shoulder. "Tell you what. I'll keep Sarg during the day until he's adopted or his owners reclaim him. He can ride in the patrol car with me. And you keep him at night."

Dismayed, Piper shook her head. Roth was trying to worm his way into her son's affections. "That is not a good idea."

"Really?" Josh completely ignored her. "Could you? He'd be like a K-9 cop."

"I can pick him up every morning and give you a ride to school. Then after school I'll pick you up and drop you and Sarg off here."

"Wow, that'd be great!"

Damn him for pushing his way into her son's life. "Roth—"

"Something smells good," he said with a knowing look in his eyes.

"Mom's cooking spaghetti and meatballs. My favorite."

"Mine, too."

"She always makes a ton. You should eat with us. Grandma's playing Bunco with 'the girls.'" Josh made quotation marks with his fingers and crossed his eyes. "A hen party. Old hens. You should hear them when they play here. Cackle, cackle, cluck, clu—"

"Joshua Hamilton." She wasn't sure what she was scolding him over—the unexpected and unwelcome invitation to dinner, the dog-exchange deal or maligning his grandmother and her friends.

Josh made a face at Roth, and in that moment two identical pairs of brown eyes shared a silent communication—one that excluded her. And she didn't like it.

"I'd love to stay for dinner. If it's okay with your mom."

Nothing like putting her on the spot. If she refused, she'd seem rude and Josh would be upset. Consternation raced through her. She didn't like Roth invading her house or befriending her son. She wanted him gone. Permanently, this time. "I—"

"Great! I'll go set an extra place at the table." Josh raced from the room.

On one hand, she was pleased that Josh was voluntarily setting the table without her nagging. On the other hand... Piper glared at Roth. "I'll ask again. What are you up to? You manipulated that invitation. Using a child is low—even for you."

The smugness faded from his expression. "I'm trying to insure Josh doesn't skip any more school. Did you ask why he's skipping?"

"We discussed it."

"But did you ask *why* he's skipping?"

She replayed the conversation. "No. I forbade him from doing it again and took away his video games for a week."

"The school said skipping is a new behavior for him. People don't change patterns without reason. Talk to him."

Apprehension ticked her spine. "What are you not telling me?"

"He didn't give me specifics, but even if he had, I wouldn't betray his confidence unless I thought he was in danger."

She hated that after only five days in town he knew something about *her* son that she didn't. "I'm his mother. I have a right to know."

"For whatever reason, he felt comfortable talking to me. If you want him to have an adult to hash over tough decisions with, you'd be wise not to burn that bridge."

Why did Josh have to choose to *him?* Why not his grandpa? "I don't want you staying for dinner. It's not fair to gain his friendship and then let him down. We both know you will."

Roth's expression blanked. She didn't have a clue what he was thinking as he held her gaze until she wanted to squirm.

"I'm not the same man I was twelve years ago, Piper."

"Oh, so you're ready to settle down and raise a family now?" His recoil was slight, but she caught it. "I didn't think so."

Josh raced into the room. "All set. Let's eat. I'm starving."

Roth held her gaze, and she was certain he'd force his company on them despite her wishes. Then he looked at Josh. "I'm sorry, Josh. I forgot I needed to run patrol by the school again. We've had some vandals painting the gym. I'll join you for dinner another time."

Josh's face displayed an odd combination of disappointment and uneasiness, making

Piper wonder if he knew something about the vandalism.

"What time do I need to pick you up in the morning?"

"You don't." Piper had to limit their contact. Unfortunately, protecting her son meant she'd see more of Roth than she'd prefer, but that was the lesser of the two evils. "Josh has enough trouble getting himself ready in the morning without adding dog chores to make him late. I'll take Sarg to the clinic with me. You can get him there."

"Aw, man," Josh grumbled. "I'll get up. I promise."

"No. But the chief can pick you up after school and bring you and Sarg home—as long as your homework doesn't suffer and you remember that this is temporary. Sarg still needs a permanent home. Understood?"

Josh's entire body drooped. "Understood."

"Go wash and put the garlic bread in the oven. I'll see the chief out then I'll join you."

"See you tomorrow afternoon, Josh."

Josh flipped a wave and plodded off—the picture of dejection.

Piper yanked open the door with a little more force than necessary and motioned for Roth to leave, then followed him out, shutting the door behind them. "Do not play games with my son. I'll see you in the morning."

And then she stepped back inside and shut the door in his face, wishing she could block Roth Sterling from her mind just as easily.

Chapter Eight

After a nearly sleepless night of worrying about Josh and his interactions with Roth and whether or not her secret might get out, the last thing Piper needed to see was Roth's patrol car waiting for her when she arrived at the clinic. Knowing this would be a daily ritual until she found the dog's owner didn't improve her mood.

Roth unfolded from the driver's seat and her stupid heart commenced that little skippety-do-dah thing. Ignoring what could only be described as a Pavlovian response, she climbed from her Jeep then reached for the dog and set him on the ground.

The second Sarg spotted Roth his tail started swinging. Loping on three legs, he towed Piper toward the man she wanted to avoid.

"Heel, Sarg," she ordered, and the dog instantly dropped to her side.

"Morning, Piper."

She flushed as hot as a menopausal woman. "Good morning."

The words came out harsher than she intended because she was angry with herself for responding to his simple greeting.

Roth squatted to pet the dog. Sarg wagged practically his entire body, wounded hip and all.

Madison's comment nagged at her. Roth had always been great with animals. How could he be both a rescuer and a murderer?

Piper didn't know. But he could. He did. He *had*.

Shoving the emotions out of the way, she focused on facts. "Sarg is incredibly well mannered and housebroken. That makes me suspect he's someone's missing family member and not an abandoned dog. I'll email the other vets' offices in the area and see if anyone's reported a missing pet."

"Did you scan for a chip?"

"Yes. He doesn't have one. I want to make

sure Josh doesn't get attached to something that's only temporary."

"You've made that clear."

"I was referring to the dog."

"But we both know you meant me. Piper, I don't claim to have all the answers. I've known I had a son less than forty-eight hours, and I'm still working it out. But I won't turn my back on Josh. I'll be there for him both emotionally and financially."

"I don't want or need your money."

"He might feel differently when he wants a car or a college fund."

Maybe. Probably. But Roth hadn't been there for her before, and she doubted he'd hang around for Josh. Parenthood was a novelty to him now. What would happen when he realized how much work it involved?

Still…she owed him for last night and struggled to find the words courtesy demanded. "Thank you for supporting me last night. Josh was hoping to find an ally in you. That's why he tried to back me into a corner."

"You're welcome. But I meant it. Josh needs someone to talk to and something to fill his time. Especially now."

"There you go again. Hinting at something I need to know, but telling me nothing. He's my son, Roth. I have a right to know if you think he's into something he shouldn't be."

"I don't think he is yet. The mayor told me we have some vandals in town. Given the nature of the damage, he and I suspect kids. I know firsthand how tempting becoming one of the cool crowd can be. I'd rather Josh not become part of that."

Piper shook her head in denial. "He can't be part of it. My mother is there every day when he gets home from school. We account for his whereabouts at all times."

"Except during school hours. But that's not when the past vandalism has occurred. That's happening late at night. Any chance Josh is sneaking out?"

"No. His bedroom is on the second floor and he'd have to walk by my open bedroom door to get out."

"You sleep light enough to wake every time he gets up?"

"Yes. Do you think Josh knows who's doing it?"

"Possibly. But don't push him. Getting him to name the perpetrators could cause trouble for him. I'll find them without implicating Josh."

Sarg rolled onto his back, displaying his

belly in submission, as if he'd already decided Roth was his new master.

"Carpooling him every afternoon won't implicate him?"

"We have the dog as cover."

She hated that Sarg provided an excuse for Roth to spend time with her son. Josh was already developing a case of hero worship and this would only exacerbate that. Despite her frustration with the situation, when Roth bent over the mutt Piper had to fight an odd compulsion to reach a few inches and test the texture of his short, spiky hair.

Neglected hormones were a bitch.

He caught her looking. "We had canines on base each time I was deployed. I always envied their handlers. Dogs were a comfort, a touch of home and normalcy."

She flinched. "Roth, I don't want to think about your military career or what you're capable of doing. I especially don't want to think about that man spending time with my son."

He straightened and his unapologetic eyes met hers. "I'm not that man here, Piper. I don't need to be."

"If you mean as a civilian, your SWAT career says otherwise."

"Protecting and serving—whether military or civilian—is a different mind-set. When it's your fellow soldiers or innocent civilians being picked off like targets at a turkey shoot the goal is to make the casualties stop. That means eliminating the threat as expediently as possible with minimal collateral damage. I realize the strategy is not pretty. But it is necessary and effective."

His cool certainty that his actions were justified only reinforced her fears. But what could she do short of packing up Josh and running away? Not an option.

"Josh gets out of school at two forty-five. This carpool situation is a short-term deal. And do not, for any reason, tell him who you are."

"I wouldn't do that without talking to you first. What have you told him about his father?"

"That his father was a wonderful man and I loved him dearly. He doesn't need to know his father wasn't the man I thought he was."

Roth pressed his lips into a thin line. "For now I'll accept your decision. But I want him to know and understand my choices."

"And destroy his love for his grandfather?"

"It might not come to that."

She couldn't see it happening any other way. Her feelings for her father were certainly on shaky ground after the recent revelations. She hadn't forgiven him for his dishonesty. The ride to his last doctor's appointment had been a tense and silent one, but she didn't want Josh to see his grandpa as a liar who bent the law to suit his purpose.

"I have to get the office ready." She thrust the leash at Roth and their fingers bumped during the exchange. Sparks danced up her arm.

Her hormones had blinded her to the true Roth Sterling before. She wouldn't let it happen again. There was much more at stake now and she could not afford to weaken.

"Sarg!" Josh broke into a run across the lawn of the middle and high school toward Roth's patrol car, then he caught himself, slowed and tried to stroll like one of the cool guys.

Roth's gut muscles tightened even as he fought a smile at Josh's typical preteen behavior. Having a kid was one hell of a responsibility. Was he up to it?

Oohrah. If not, he'd go down fighting. But he didn't like marching into foreign territory without a plan. And right now he had zilch. He was out of his depth, ill equipped and smart enough to know it. Parenting Josh and getting out of Quincey were in direct opposition and he'd yet to find navigable middle ground.

The dog twitched at Roth's feet. "Stay. Sit," Roth commanded and the dog obeyed. Only his thumping tail gave away his excitement.

Josh dove to his knees with enough force to grind the grass stains in deep. Piper would love that. It would have earned Roth a whupping. But he couldn't see Piper reacting that way.

The boy rubbed and nuzzled the mutt, who seemed to enjoy it, reinforcing Piper's belief that this wasn't a dumped or abused dog but a lost one—one that some kid like Josh was probably bawling over. Finding the original owner meant disappointing the current custodian.

While Josh fussed over the canine, Roth scanned the students to see if anyone was paying too much attention to Josh's meeting with him.

No. But the bus kids exited a different door and Josh had skipped school to avoid the bus. Chances were the boys Roth wanted wouldn't be coming out this entrance.

"Load up, Josh. Let's get you home before your grandmother calls in a missing persons report." He opened the door and motioned for the dog. Sarg climbed in, only slightly hampered by his sore hip.

Josh hesitated. "Can I sit in the back with Sarg?"

"Sure."

Once they were buckled in Roth put the car in motion. He didn't have a lot of experience conversing with preteen boys—let alone one he'd fathered. He searched for a topic they had in common. The dog seemed safe.

"While I was patrolling today I took Sarg on a bit of a field trial. He knows a lot of commands and responds very well."

"He's smart."

"He's also very likely someone's lost dog."

"Ah, man. Now you sound like my mother. I know Sarg is only mine till we find his owner. But if Mom sees how responsible I am with him and his owner never claims him, then she might let me keep him."

"I wouldn't get my hopes up, Josh."

The sight of the kid's dejected face in the rearview mirror pulled at something inside Roth. He wanted to fix the problem and there was no fix. "Did you know the military has used dogs throughout history?"

"Really?" The comment had the desired effect.

"They started out as sentries, guards and messengers. Now they're one of our best weapons against IEDs."

"Bombs?"

"Yes. Dogs 'see' with their noses as well as their eyes and they can detect explosives much better than any of our sophisticated equipment."

"Cool."

"Some MWD—military working dogs— are equipped with Kevlar tactical vests that have infrared and night vision, as well as a camera and speaker so their handlers can see what the dog sees and give commands from a distance. Sometimes the MWDs wear special goggles called 'doggles.'"

He was pretty much reciting from a handbook, but the kid didn't seem to mind.

"Did you ever work with dogs?"

"No, but there were usually K-9 troops on base. They could play football with us one minute then be lean, mean fighting machines the next."

"I have to do a report and a presentation

on a career I might like to have. I wouldn't mind being a military dog trainer if they get to use all that nifty gear."

"Most military dogs, no matter which branch they serve in, are trained at Lackland Air Force Base in Texas. That's a long way from Quincey, and you'd have to join the Air Force."

"Oh. That's not good. Couldn't I train them here and send them off when they're ready?"

Josh was getting attached to a stray after only a day. Roth couldn't see the kid spending months with a dog and then easily parting with it. "No. The dogs have to go through a special course and have to pass all kinds of aptitude tests along the way to progress— kind of like you do in school."

"Bummer. Do you think Sarg is smart enough to be a K-9 warrior?"

"Maybe. But he's the wrong breed."

"Could you keep him and use him as a police dog?"

Roth laughed. Josh had a one-track mind. "You're pushing it, kid. But it's a good angle."

"I don't want him to go back to his owner. Whoever had him before didn't take good care of him. Sarg was covered in fleas and ticks, and he wasn't wearing a rabies vaccine tag."

"That just means he lost his collar, and that he's been missing long enough for his flea prevention medicine to wear off."

"But his feet weren't raw like those dogs that cross the country looking for their owners."

Smart, observant kid. "True."

"Why is Mom mad at you, Chief?"

The unexpected, out-of-the-blue question startled Roth. How much honesty could Josh handle? And what could Roth say without going against Piper's wishes? "Your mom used to be my girlfriend and I hurt her."

"You hit her or something?"

"No. I'd never hit a woman. And don't you, either." He couldn't shake the revulsion at that thought. "But I let her down. She needed something from me that I couldn't give her."

"Money?"

"There are more important things than money, Josh."

"Only people who have money say that."

"That's true." He turned into the driveway and hoped their arrival would curtail the conversation. "Have you and your mother discussed you finding a part-time job?"

"Not yet."

"Think about it. You can only work a few hours because of your age and school. But you might be able to earn a little spending money and come summer you could work more and bank some bucks."

He climbed out of the car and opened the back door. Piper's Jeep wasn't parked beside Ann Marie's sedan in the driveway. An odd feeling slid over him. Disappointment?

Wanting to see Piper wasn't good. They had no future other than pertaining to the boy they'd made.

"Tell your mom I'll see her in the morning." And no, damn it, that wasn't anticipation quickening his pulse. "See you, kiddo. Study hard."

"Josh wouldn't be so desperate for a father figure if you hadn't cut his out of his life."

Piper heard her mother's raised voice as soon as she entered the house. Alarm and dismay raced through her. Where was Josh? And *not again*. She was sick and tired of playing referee.

Her parents' battles had escalated since Roth's return, and the risk their angry words would be overheard had also increased. She dropped her bags on the foyer table and hurried toward the kitchen.

"Running off Sterling was the best thing I could have done. He was worthless and you know it."

"Not to your daughter. She loved him and you nearly destroyed her. And you lied to me. You said you had proof Roth had stolen Gus's car."

Piper should never have shared what she'd learned about her father's manipulation of facts with her mother, but she'd had to know if her mother was also guilty.

"I told you what you needed to hear."

"You don't get to decide what I need to hear, and you don't get to play God. Josh needs a father and Piper will never find one with the poindexters you bring home. She hasn't had a date in over a year. And I'll tell you something else, Lou Hamilton. Your damned pride cost me years with my grandson."

"Stop!" Piper shouted. Both parents' heads pivoted toward her. "Where is Josh?"

"He's walking that flea-bitten mutt," her father groused. "I don't like it, Piper. I don't like Josh and Sterling spending time together.

Josh is a bright kid. He'll figure things out and hate us for lying."

"And whose fault will that be?" Ann Marie sniped.

"Mom—"

Her mother gave her a false smile. "I'm sorry, honey. I didn't hear you come in."

"That's the point. What if I'd been Josh? You two need to meet on neutral territory. Better yet, don't meet at all. You especially don't need to fight about you-know-who in this house or anywhere else you could be overheard."

Her father puffed out his chest. "I did the right thing."

"I swear, Lou, your refusal to admit you made a mistake is one of the things I hate about you."

Feeling a tension headache coming on, Piper ripped the clip from her hair. "Enough already. You're rehashing the same arguments. The past is over. It can't be changed. We have to find a way to deal with our current predicament."

"I don't want Sterling or his no-account family in Quincey," her father groused.

Her mother shook a finger at him. "That's only because you're afraid people will find out what you did. How supportive will our friends and neighbors be when they find out you framed an innocent man and you threw out your daughter when she needed you the most?"

"That's it! Josh and I are eating out. I can't stand to be in the same house when you two argue like this. I wanted my son to grow up surrounded by his grandparents' love, but you can't even be on the same block without war breaking out.

"And do you want to know why it upsets me? Because I'm the one who started this when *I* fell in love with the wrong man. *I* got pregnant, and *I* decided to keep my baby. *I* caused this. Me. *My* choices ended your marriage. Maybe Roth isn't the one who needs to leave Quincey. Maybe it's me."

Heartsick, she pivoted on her heel and left.

"Now look what you've done." Ann Marie forced the words past the lump in her throat. She couldn't lose Piper or Josh. They were her reasons for getting out of bed every day.

"Me? You're the one screaming and hurling accusations."

"Not accusations. Facts. How can you live with yourself?"

Lou's broad shoulders snapped back. "I did what was best for Piper. I didn't want her to end up like Eloise Sterling, dirt-poor and physically abused. That kind of violence runs in families. Roth's daddy did it. Statistics say Roth will, too. I don't regret getting rid of him."

That was essentially what she'd surmised and told Piper, but hearing him confirm it was a plus.

"But trying to force Piper to have an abortion…" Lou slumped. "I admit that was wrong. It wasn't my decision. It was hers. You're right. I was afraid people would think that if I couldn't control my own daughter, I couldn't control this town. So I sent her away. To save my pride. But I missed her. Every damned day. And I was glad—I know I said I wasn't—when you insisted she come home. Now the idea of not having her and Josh in our lives…"

He mashed his lips together and looked away, clearly choking up, the big galoot. His one redeeming characteristic was his love for his grandson. "Not a day goes by that I don't thank God Piper disobeyed me. That boy… he's my life. Especially now."

That he didn't have the job that defined him.

Empathy welled in Ann Marie's chest. It was the first time Lou had ever admitted he had regrets.

She reached out to put a comforting hand on his shoulder but drew it back before making contact. She didn't trust herself. Her feelings for her husband were all over the map. She loved him. She hated him. She missed the man she'd married—the one who'd treated her like a queen and who'd always made time for them. But he hadn't been that man in a long time. Sometime before this mess with Piper had started he'd become cold and unreachable. She didn't know if he'd had an affair or if he simply stopped loving her.

"I'm not completely without guilt. I tried to pressure her into giving up the baby for adoption. If either of us had had our way, we wouldn't have Josh. We both made mistakes. The point is we want the same thing now—to protect Piper and Josh and to keep them here.

"Piper doesn't believe Roth will be around for the long-term, and I suspect she might be right. He hasn't scheduled a time for me to show him any of the rental houses. If he and Piper were to get back together, and they decided to leave Quincey…"

The gravity of the situation lay over the room like a heavy, silencing blanket.

"What are we gonna do, Ann Marie?"

"First, we need to find out Roth's intentions, then we'll have to work together to insure the outcome we want."

Ann Marie wished she had more confidence in her plan—or lack thereof. "We have no choice but to stick to our original story since I've told it all over town for eleven years. But I can't help feeling we're holding on to a ticking bomb. I only hope that if it blows, this time you'll stand beside your daughter and grandson and not behind your stupid pride."

"I won't make the same mistake twice. I can't bear losing those two. But the only way to guarantee the silence is to get the Sterlings to leave Quincey and stay gone."

"Agreed. But we're not breaking the law to make that happen this time, you hear?"

"The ends—"

"Do not justify the means, Lou Hamilton. *Me* telling lies and *you* twisting facts is what got us in this mess. No more of that."

His features twisted as if he were planning to argue more, but finally he nodded.

"I hear ya. All right. I agree. But we need a better plan."

"Then you come up with it, because I don't have one."

And this time she hoped she could trust him.

"I know what I'm doing my report on," Josh said around a mouthful of cheeseburger.

"That's great. When you finish chewing you can give me the details."

Though his lips remained sealed as he hastily chomped, his eyes gave her that "Oh, Mom" look. "I'm going to write about Air Force dog handlers."

"I thought your presentation was supposed to be about a career you wanted."

He leaned forward, excitement practically oozing from his pores. "I'd like to train dogs."

"Joshua Hamilton, if this is another attempt to convince me to let you keep Sarg, it won't work."

"It's not. The chief told me about the MWDs—that's military working dogs—on the way home from school today, and that's what I want to do."

The military? Where he would be shot at? No way. She tried for logic with Josh. "You can be a dog trainer without enlisting, and there's no guarantee that they'll allow you to work with dogs once you've signed those papers."

She and Roth would have a little talk. She didn't want him making his career sound glamorous. Not that she had anything against the military, but it was not for her son. She wanted Josh safe and that meant away from flying bullets. It had been bad enough that her father carried a gun all those years, making her mother a nervous wreck, and even though he'd often bragged about never having to draw it on anyone, his brother had been killed in the line of duty.

"But military dogs are awesome. They get to wear flak jackets with night vision and cameras and speakers and stuff. Regular dogs don't. Those dogs are heroes—just like the chief. They serve their country and save guys and stuff. Tomorrow I'm going to ask the chief if he'll be my guest on Career Day."

Dismay knocked the air from her lungs. "I thought I was your guest."

Josh rolled his eyes. "But, Mom, all you do is test dog poop."

"I do more than that." Not long ago Josh had loved spending time at the clinic, "helping" her with her duties. In fact, he'd begged to spend part of his school holidays with her.

"Yeah, maybe. But the chief has had three really cool jobs. You've only had the one."

Coldness enfolded her. She was already losing her son to the man who'd never wanted him—one who was only interested in Josh now out of a sense of duty. Josh would be crushed when Roth showed his true colors.

She had to stop it. But she didn't know how to keep them apart or to cure the case of idolization her son had contracted—not without Josh getting hurt.

"What about asking Mr. Lowry? He spent twenty years in the Army. I'm sure he's had a lot of interesting experiences. And now he has the hunting store."

"No way!"

She didn't understand the revulsion in his voice. "I thought you were interested in hunting rifles. If you interviewed Mr. Lowry, he might show you the stock he has in the store and teach you about the different guns."

"Mom," he said in that parents-are-so-dumb voice. "Until you'll let me go hunting I don't need to know about rifles. I want the chief to be my guest. He's the neatest guy in town. He'll be the best Career Day guest ever."

She wasn't getting anywhere with Josh. She had to go to the source of her problems. Roth. And each time she had to face him she had to admit one thing.

She still wanted him—physically.

Chapter Nine

Roth eased his foot off the gas as he drove toward the riverside of Quincey. It wouldn't do for the chief to be caught speeding. He still had issues with two of his deputies, who would like nothing better than to write him a citation.

Following a tip he'd picked up in the diner, he pulled into the Hunt and Bait shop, a long, low cinder-block building. The place hadn't been here in Roth's day. There were two pickups in the parking lot—neither of which he recognized. The sign on the door said they closed at seven. He had five minutes.

He stepped inside and scanned the shop,

immediately spotting the fifty-something guy behind the counter. Scar on the right side of his face. Medium build. GI haircut. A display of two rifles and four shotguns hung on the wall behind him. The remaining walls were decorated with a taxidermist's dream collection of fish, fowl and mammals.

The muffled sound of sporadic gunfire permeated the space. Out of habit Roth started a mental tally of shots fired and made a note to insure the gun range met safety specifications. Regulation was not his job, but if there was an accident, cleanup would be his problem. Better to be proactive.

"Evening, Chief." The man behind the counter reached across a glass display that held six handguns of assorted make and caliber along with miscellaneous clips and gun-cleaning paraphernalia. "Tate Lowry."

Roth shook his hand. "You bought my breakfast. Thanks."

"You're welcome."

"I'm looking for Lou Hamilton."

"He ain't gonna be happy to see you."

His history preceded him. "Don't I know it?"

"That's him on the gun range. Range use

is free for Quincey P.D., by the way, if you want to keep your skills sharp."

"Thanks. I'll take you up on that."

"It's only four lanes, but it's the closest indoor facility for forty miles and rarely busy. Come back when you don't have business to take care of, an' we'll swap stories."

"I heard you were a Master Sergeant. I'm sure you have a few."

"Yessir. You'll find Lou through there." Lowry pointed toward a red steel door marked Live Fire Beyond This Point. "Take as long as you need. I got nowhere to be tonight."

Roth opened the door and the erratic pops grew louder. He spotted Hamilton in one of the shooting booths. The paper target down range had only one hole in the top corner despite the dozen shots he'd heard discharged.

Roth stepped into the range control officer's position and observed the former chief's struggle with pressing the bullets into the semiautomatic pistol's clip. Then Hamilton caught sight of Roth and stiffened.

The stroke had taken a toll on more than Hamilton's manual dexterity. His left eye and shoulder, as well as the left side of his mouth, drooped slightly.

"Have you considered switching to a revolver? They're easier to load. Fewer rounds, but just as effective short-range."

"I don't need your advice, boy. Your kind's not welcome around here."

"Roths and Sterlings founded Quincey. *My kind* has been here longer than yours."

"And when your grandpappy Roth died they put the last good one in the ground. None of you Sterlings has been worth a damn in the past fifty years since the cotton mill closed."

Roth let the insult roll off his back. "You were left-handed before your stroke."

"What's it to ya?"

"Josh says you can't take him hunting because you're having trouble with your firing hand."

"What I can or cannot do is none of your damned business."

Roth had learned that the proudest men were the hardest to assist but also the ones who needed it the most. Rescuing a downed comrade who insisted on doing everything solo could get both of you killed. But the "never leave a man behind" creed meant making the effort despite the risk.

"The Corps taught me to shoot with each hand. I worked with friends to become proficient at shooting with their weak hands when injury sidelined them. I'm sure you had elementary school teachers trying to make you write right-handed. I could help you polish those rusty skills."

"The only way you can help me is if you stay away from my daughter and grandson and make sure that murdering bastard Seth stays the hell out of my town."

"Nobody wants my father to be behind bars more than I do. And the only reason I returned to Quincey was to make damned sure he didn't pick up where he left off. As for Piper and Josh, I've made mistakes. I'm not sure how to amend for them now, but I'm working it out."

"Work on it back in Charlotte where you're an 'asset to the team'—" Hamilton quoted the newspaper article "—and not just a pain in my ass."

Roth's irritation finally got the better of him. He had one more ghost to lay to rest and he wasn't letting Hamilton stop him. "How 'bout I talk and you listen for a minute. I tracked you down to thank you for shipping me off to the Marines. They were good for me. I'm sorry I wasn't here for Piper, but she told me she wouldn't have the baby. Either way she sure as hell deserved a better man than I was twelve years ago."

"That's the only thing you've said worth hearing. Quit while you're ahead."

"I still don't like the way you went about it. You knew damned well I didn't steal and wreck Gus's car. But bending the laws and ignoring stuff right under your nose was the way things were done around here. Like Ronnie Craig's still. Your brother would still be alive if you'd shut Craig down decades ago."

Hamilton paled. "Don't you dare bring my brother into this you sonofa—"

"And my mother wouldn't have gotten the crap beat out of her on a regular basis if you'd done your job."

"A drunk will find his liquor somewhere, and your mother brought that on herself by refusing to press charges every time Seth beat her. If she'd done what she oughta the first time Seth laid a hand on her, he would have been locked up sooner and my brother would still be alive. But she hid it and lied to cover for him."

All true. "You should have found another way to nail my father. You knew what he was doing."

"Don't try to pin your father's faults on

me. And let me tell you something, Sterling. If you hurt my baby girl or that boy of hers, you'll rue the day you returned to this town. And if your father gets anywhere near either of them—" Hamilton popped the clip into his weapon. Then he rested the pistol on the firing bench but didn't release it.

Roth stretched into full intimidation mode, looking down at the older man. "You're not communicating a threat to an officer of the law, are you, *Mr.* Hamilton?"

The *mister* jab worked. The former chief jerked ever so slightly and his face reddened.

"Just stating a fact. Chief." Hamilton practically spit the last word.

"Neither of us wants Piper or Josh hurt, and you can be certain I'll keep them as far away from my father as possible. But that's my problem. Yours is making sure your cronies who've been skirting the law get the message. I won't put up with their crap, and I won't take any from you. Understood?"

"You talk a good game, boy, but you don't have the *cajones* to follow through. You'll turn and run before you get the job done— just like you did twelve years ago."

The words stabbed Roth like a Ka-bar to the gut. "You're wrong. And I'll prove it."

He did intend to leave, but this time he wouldn't be running. This time he'd go on his terms and when he was damned good and ready. Not one second before.

Definitely not before he figured out how to do right by his son.

The fist hammering on Roth's door brought him to his feet in a hurry. 9:00 p.m. Who would be calling at this hour? And it wasn't a friendly hello given the force of the five blows.

He grabbed his Glock and tucked it into the back of his waistband before approaching the door. He'd removed his belt, holster and boots, leaving him at a disadvantage.

The peephole he'd installed yesterday revealed Piper. He exhaled and his muscles relaxed, but the pounding in his chest quickened instead of slowing as he flipped the locks and opened the door.

She looked good with her hair rippling over her shoulders and a sweater and jeans encasing every curve of her body. But her eyes burned like twin blue flames.

"What do you think you're doing?" she demanded.

What exactly was she angry about? His

talk with her father? He stalled, waiting for a clue. "I'm kicking back, watching baseball, winding down."

A white line circled her lips. She barged in, bumping into him and making him step back. "You are *not* taking my son from me."

Not her father. Josh. What had he said that riled her? She stood before him as a fierce warrior, a mother defending her young. He hadn't seen this woman before. In their dating days Piper had always been a gentle and soothing ray of sunshine in his bleak life. And he had to admit he found the intensity in her eyes, the flare of her nostrils, the I-will-annihilate-you stance damned sexy. Maybe even sexier than the gentle version.

This woman would fight for herself and her child. She wouldn't cower in the corner and apologize for some imagined slight, and she wouldn't put up with abuse from a man who'd claimed he loved her—a man who'd said all the right things when he was sober but didn't mean any of them.

If she'd been this strong twelve years ago, would he have left her?

Irrelevant. He had. Piper may have changed, but who he was hadn't. He would always be

Seth Sterling's son. Genetically and statistically he was not father-of-the-year material.

He shut the door. "I'm not trying to take Josh from you, Piper."

"You're trying to brainwash him into joining the military. That'll take him from me and it will put him in harm's way. If you don't stop, I won't allow you to see him."

A threat. And he didn't take threats lightly. He didn't know how he would work Josh into his life yet, but he wouldn't allow that opportunity to be taken from him before he figured it out.

"Do you really want to go there? He's my son, too. And from what I've heard, your father's buddies are not sitting on the county's judicial benches anymore. No court will keep me from Josh."

Her body, even her breathing, stilled then her throat worked. "He's only eleven, Roth. It's my job to keep him safe. I limit his exposure to the violence he sees in movies, video games and on TV. I don't need you to make that all seem not only right, but exciting and appealing."

Frustration rose within him. "You haven't heard a word I've said. My job was to make the violence stop with one shot as opposed to a barrage of bullets or bombs. A carefully selected target means fewer rounds fired and that translates into fewer casualties."

She closed her eyes and when she opened them he saw trepidation. "My head understands what you're saying. But my heart cannot process the idea of stalking a man for hours, days or months with the deliberate intent of taking his life. How do you turn it off? How do you stop being that cold-blooded killer when you enter the real world, Staff Sergeant Sterling?"

There were no words to alleviate her fears. There had been enough negative stories in the news to prove some veterans had the transition issue she feared. His actions would have to do the talking, and he wasn't sure he'd be around long enough for those to be effective. For the first time, leaving Quincey lost a little of its appeal.

"You're a good mom, Piper."

"You can't know that."

"Given your fear of me, you still came charging on to my turf to protect Josh."

"I'm not afraid of you, Roth. I don't know what to make of the man you've become. What I fear is the devastation you can cause in my son's life."

"I'm not here to cause trouble. I'm here to prevent it. My father's being released and I want to protect my mother. The same way you want to protect Josh. And from what I've seen of Josh, he knows right from wrong and he's respectful of people and property. Looks like you've done a good job.

"And you didn't have to, Piper. You could have taken the easy way out. Like I did. When I look back on my life, walking away from my responsibility to you is the only moment that shames me."

Her mouth opened slightly, and damned if a flash of something hot didn't kindle in his groin. "You were scared."

"And you weren't? But you found courage. I was—still am—afraid that I'm my father's son."

Her softening expression eroded his defenses. He focused on the present. "Where did this fear that I'm trying to steal Josh come from?"

She averted her gaze. "He wants you to be his guest for Career Day."

"And that's a problem why?"

"I was supposed to be his guest."

Understanding dawned. She felt displaced. "Do you want me to refuse when he asks?"

"That would hurt his feelings."

And she'd rather have hers hurt. "If he asks and I agree, I'll give the standard speech I give to anyone who indicates interest in a military career. Go to college first. If serving your country is still your first choice when you have other options on the table, then you'll go in as an officer."

"You'd do that?"

"I would never deliberately do anything to put Josh in harm's way."

When a tear pooled in the corner of her eye, something inside him torqued and he cupped her face, stroking his thumb along her smooth cheekbone. Her gasp reflected the shock blasting though him like a rocket propelled grenade.

Acknowledging the problem was half the battle. "It's still there."

"What?"

"The fire."

"No, it isn't." She said it with certainty, but he knew from the quick rise and fall of her breasts that she lied.

"Don't say that like a challenge or I might have to prove you wrong."

Her eyes rounded and she arched away. "Don't you dare, Roth Sterling."

"Oh, babe, you know better than to dare me." Even though every fragment of common sense he possessed screamed he shouldn't, he bent his head and covered her mouth with his.

Instant detonation. Fire blasted through him. Her lips were soft, moist and parted in surprise. He sipped, then traced his tongue along the warm, satiny seam. She tasted familiar yet different. But good. Damned good.

She shivered then her tongue met his, stoking the bonfire inside him until his pulse nearly deafened him. Her left hand fisted in his shirt at his waist. Her right spread palm-flat over his jackhammering heart then it glided ever so slowly upward, scorching a path from his neck to his nape. Her nails scraped lightly as she gripped him, and a shudder of raw need racked him.

He tilted her head back so that he could get more of her sweet mouth. Her thighs brushed his and his erection pulsed hard. She shifted closer—so close that when she wound her arms around him her breasts mashed against his chest.

He wanted her. Here. Now. In his bed. On his floor. Against the door. Anywhere. A groan rumbled up his chest. How in the hell had he ever been strong enough to walk away from the combustion she caused? He still wasn't the man she needed, but knowing that didn't kill the hunger.

Her hand jostled his Glock, shifting the hard barrel against his spine. She went rigid in his arms then tore herself away. The passionate flush of her cheeks faded to ashen. "You're carrying a gun? Even at home?"

"It's late. I didn't know who'd be at the door. And I do have a few enemies here."

Shaking her head and groping behind her, she retreated until she collided with the jamb.

"That shouldn't have happened, forget it happened, it won't happen again." She yanked open the door and raced down the sidewalk. Roth reached for the knob determined to follow, but he caught himself, fought himself, and after a few seconds he found the strength to push the panel closed and bang his forehead against it.

What could he say? Because she was right. He shouldn't have kissed her, shouldn't have opened that Pandora's box. Because now he wanted more.

But no matter what he wanted he couldn't start something with Piper and then abandon her again. His life was a Cluster Foxtrot at the moment. His departure was about the only thing he could guarantee.

He was not the man she needed. And he probably never would be.

Piper glanced up and caught Madison studying her. Again. "Have I developed a weird rash on my face or something?"

"Did you sleep with him?"

Piper didn't have to ask who. "No!"

Madison smiled and walked to the procedure room.

Piper pursued her boss. "What does that smirk mean?"

"It means that despite everything you still have it bad for Roth."

"You are insane." But her face burned with a combination of shame and guilt because it was true. Last night's foolish kiss had been hotter and more arousing than anything in her past. She should have pushed him away. Instead she'd reveled in the rush of desire pumping through her veins.

"I'm insanely close to the truth, you mean. Piper, you're so agitated today that even our patients are picking up on your mood and getting fidgety. Methinks you and the chief had a close encounter."

Was she so transparent? "Why would you say that?"

"Besides you being as jumpy as a flea looking for a new host? Mrs. Peabody said she saw your car parked outside Roth's apartment very late last night."

Piper wanted to smack her forehead. She'd seethed all evening after her dinner with Josh, and then as soon as she'd gotten him to bed she'd raced out the door to confront Roth. Not once had she considered that the eyes of Quincey would be watching.

"Nine o'clock is not late."

"It is late for a woman to go visiting a man by Mrs. Peabody's standards."

"I had to tell Roth to quit preaching military propaganda to Josh. I don't know what he told Josh, but my son has a sudden burning desire to join the Air Force and train dogs. In *Texas*. It's all he could talk about during dinner. And he wants Roth instead of me for Career Day."

"Ooh. Not good. I can understand why you're upset. But from Josh's standpoint you have to admit the chief is new and exciting. You're his mom. Moms, by definition, are not exciting."

"According to my son, my job is boring."

"Remind him of that next time he begs to come in."

"Don't worry. I will."

"You know, a little roll in the hay with the chief might relieve some of your stress and make your life a little more exciting."

A gurgle of disgust rolled up Piper's throat. Unfortunately, it sounded a little too much like a groan of desire. She hoped Madison didn't pick up on that.

"I'm not interested in repeating my mistakes. Last time Roth asked me out only because his friends dared him to and he wanted to irritate my father. Who knows why he's made a move this time? He's probably trying to get closer to Josh."

"He made a move?"

Argh. She needed to watch her words more carefully. "It was just a kiss."

Madison smiled knowingly. "Roth already sees Josh every day because of the dog. I doubt *just a kiss* was targeted to get more of what he already has. I think he wants you as much as you do him."

"Think what you want, but you're wrong. Roth won't stick around, and I will not get involved with him because I do not want to get used and dumped again. I'm more concerned about Josh. He's already developed a serious case of hero worship. He'll be disappointed."

"Stop using Josh as a shield. He's a kid. If his feelings get hurt, he'll recover. That's part of growing up. This is about you and Roth, Piper. You're older and wiser now. Maybe the timing is right. With that kind of chemistry you ought to give it a shot."

There was definitely chemistry, but that's all it was, and she didn't want the volatile concoction to blow up in her face.

Madison's gaze shifted to the window. "Speak of the delicious devil. There's your man now."

"He's not my man," Piper corrected automatically as she joined Madison at the window. But knowing it and saying it didn't stop her pulse from leaping wildly when she saw him on the street looking tall, dark and desirable in his uniform.

"He could be yours—at least until you've worked him out of your system." Madison tsked. "Is he writing a parking ticket? Your mother's assistant is not going to like that."

"He's not in my system. And Doris's car is blocking the fire hydrant."

"Admit it. You're craving a big bite of that muscular body. And she's parked there for as long as I've had this office. Your father never ticketed her."

Piper had learned long ago to keep up with Madison's dual conversations. "I am not a dieter who needs to binge on something bad for me. And he is bad for me. Doris's breaking the law repeatedly doesn't make it right. If we had a fire in the clinic, we'd have a problem. She needs to be ticketed." Why was she defending Roth?

He looked up. Their gazes met through the pane. Piper's breath and heart hitched in unison like a pair of dogs yanked on their leashes. How did he do that to her given the hell he'd put her through? He nodded. Her lips tingled with the memory of last night's kiss. She spun away and caught Madison's appraising gaze.

"Oh, yes, you definitely have it bad."

"I don't have it bad. I just don't want him here."

"Before my husband…died…our sex life was as amazing as I imagine yours and Roth's must have been. After Andrew…was gone… I tried sex a couple of times because I needed to feel alive. It wasn't a good experience either time. The spark was missing.

But I think—I hope—the body gets past the numbness after a while. I think yours has."

That was the most Madison had ever shared about her past. Piper focused on that rather than her boss's astute observation. "I'm sorry for your loss."

The words sounded empty, trite.

"Don't be sorry. Just take advantage of your opportunities. We won't live forever and we might as well enjoy every moment we have left. Have you even had a sexual relationship since Roth?"

Piper's face burned. "Yes."

"Who? When? How did I miss it?"

She didn't want to confess, but didn't know how to get out of it. "He was a real estate agent from Raleigh. My mother introduced us. And it was before you moved here."

"What happened?"

Piper wished she were anywhere but here. "You really don't want to know."

"Yes, I do. Then maybe I'll understand why you're so afraid of letting the chief make your toes curl."

"I dated Austin for a few months. He was good-looking and successful and great with Josh. I decided my parents might be right about him needing a father. So I decided to take it to the next level and—" The humiliation hit her hard, as if it had only been yesterday. "I called him Roth…in the middle of… you know."

"Oh."

"Yeah. Oh. I don't understand why I did it because I am so over Roth Sterling. But—"

"Maybe you're not over Roth. How did the guy take it?"

"Not well. He told me to give him a call if I ever got tired of living in the past. I didn't call. I couldn't. I was so embarrassed. And I haven't let another relationship go that far because I can't be sure I wouldn't repeat the catastrophe."

Madison nodded. "I get that. But I have a suggestion. If Roth used you before, why not use him this time? It's one way to be sure you're over him."

"Use him?" Piper shook her head so hard it was a wonder she didn't give herself a concussion, but she had to dislodge Madison's tempting suggestion before it started to make sense. The very idea of using Roth for sexual pleasure made her blood run hot. But the reality… No way.

"C'mon. You'll have your fun then he'll be gone."

"Madison, I can't. The last time he dumped me I was able to leave town and avoid the gossip. I didn't have to live with everyone knowing and staring and talking behind my back. But this time I wouldn't be able to run and hide. My life is here. Josh's life is here. I will not let Roth ruin that or run me away from my home again."

Chapter Ten

Ann Marie's outer office door slammed against the wall. Lou. So much for the fresh plaster and paint.

"Damn Roth Sterling to hell," Lou snarled as he stomped through her reception room. He paused on the threshold of Ann Marie's office and looked at Doris. "There's a parking ticket on your windshield."

Ann Marie heard her assistant squawk then scurry out, moving much faster than her usual snail's pace. Lowering her reading glasses, Ann Marie looked at her husband. Anger had mottled his face and made him breathe heavily. If he didn't calm down, he would work himself into a heart attack, and while she couldn't stand to live with him after everything he'd done, she wasn't ready to bury him.

"What has Roth done to get you so riled up this time? Not the parking ticket, I'm sure."

"He wants to teach me to shoot right-handed."

"You're saying he offered to help you regain your shooting skills?"

"Yes. And the bastard *thanked* me for forcing him to enlist. Can you believe that?"

Well, well, well. Ann Marie leaned back in her chair as her mind assimilated the facts. Roth had returned to look out for his mama. He'd picked up the stray dog that had stolen Josh's heart, and okay, maybe hers, too. And Roth had been wonderful with her grandson.

In four days Roth had started tongues wagging all over town because he was trying to stop people from doing the things they shouldn't be doing—things Lou had ignored because he and the offenders had known each other since their diaper days. And then there was the write-up in the paper.... It couldn't all be fiction. That little worm of a councilman didn't have that much imagination.

Now Roth had offered to help a man who'd done him wrong?

Ann Marie tapped her pen against the blotter. Had she let the past prejudice her against Roth? Who was he now? The admirable man he appeared to be or the hell-raiser who'd abandoned her daughter?

Everybody made mistakes and bad decisions. She ought to know. She focused on Lou's glowering face. "Are you going to accept?"

"Are you out of your ever-loving mind, woman?"

"Sit down, calm down and think about this. You want to be chief again. Piper is convinced Roth will leave town once he's had his fill of the busybodies. Don't be stupid, Lou."

"Stupid!"

Lou was a logical man. She had to put this in terms he could accept; otherwise his elephant-size pride would get in the way.

"Passing the qualifying test could put you in a position to get your job back when and if Roth leaves. And can you think of a better way to keep an eye on him and find out his intentions than spending time with him?"

"You want me to befriend the bastard who knocked up our daughter and told her to get rid of his own son?"

"You ordered her to get rid of Josh, too.

You tried to strong-arm her the same way you did Roth. Only Piper inherited too much of your stubbornness, thank goodness."

"That's a fact."

"Lou, we need to know if Roth's matured into a man we can trust around Josh. You're in the best position to find out. No court in this country will deny a decorated military veteran shared custody of his child. If Roth chooses to exercise his parental rights, he will have an influence on Josh whether we like it or not."

Lou stared at her, and slowly the stiffness eased from his body. His expression shifted to resignation, then he shook his head and gave her a slightly lopsided smile that melted her heart, and reminded her how close she'd come to losing the big stubborn, opinionated galoot.

"I knew I married you for good reason. You're a pretty smart cookie."

The compliment rattled her.

"All I'm saying is that if Roth thinks he can help you, let him try. What can it hurt?"

And in the process she'd find out what Roth Sterling was really made of and decide if she needed to get on Lou's bandwagon and run the bastard out of town.

* * *

"Do you like baseball, Chief?"

Roth checked on his passengers in the rearview mirror and met Josh's brown eyes. His father's eyes. But Josh's gaze held none of the malevolence of Seth's. Roth intended to keep it that way.

"Baseball is my favorite sport."

In deference to Piper's wishes he didn't add that he'd picked up his interest in the Corps. Watching games via satellite in the mess hall had often been his platoon's downtime activity during deployments. Baseball, like the handlers' dogs, had provided a taste of home and a sense of still being connected to the real world. "You?"

Josh's head bobbed, dislodging Sarg's licking tongue. The kid would miss that mutt. A fleeting thought of buying a house with a fenced yard and keeping Sarg flickered across Roth's mind, but he instantly dismissed it. Keeping the dog meant staying in Quincey. And there was no way in hell he'd do that one day longer than necessary. And Josh…well, Roth still hadn't figured out that puzzle piece.

"Will you come to my games, Chief?"

"When do you play?"

"I don't know yet. We have our first practice tonight."

"When you get your schedule let me know. I'll work in as many games as I can." Baseball. With his son. Who'd have thought that would ever happen?

"You could come tonight and meet everybody. It's at Blue Jay Park at six-thirty."

The idea of seeing Piper again, kissing her again— Not gonna happen. "I might be able to stop by after my patrol."

"Did you play on a team in school?"

"No. I had to work and the equipment was too expensive."

"Bummer. Did you ever throw in the yard with your dad?"

"No. But my grandfather and I used to play catch in a field near the house." He'd loved those days. With his grandfather around he'd felt a lot safer, as if someone were watching out for him and his mom. His father had still smacked them around, but not as hard and he'd never left marks then.

They rode in silence until Roth turned the car into Piper's driveway. He climbed from the cruiser and opened the back door for Josh and the dog.

"Chief, would you be my guest for Career

Day? It would be neat for you to tell everybody what you did in the Marines."

The invitation Piper had warned him about. He'd been waiting for it. "I thought you were taking your mom."

"Everybody already knows what she does and it's boring. All she does is give shots and clean up poop."

"You said you wanted to work with MWDs. During a deployment, that includes every facet of your partner's care—the kind of tasks your mom does. Veterinarians are few and far between over there. The handler does his own dirty work, including cleaning up after his canine partner."

"My friends would rather hear about you."

"Only because I'm the new guy in town."

"And because you've had exciting careers that nobody around here has had."

"What about Mr. Lowry?"

"He creeps some of the guys out 'cuz of his fake leg, and he doesn't like kids coming into his store."

Roth hadn't noticed a prosthetic, but then Lowry hadn't come out from behind the counter. "He stocks guns and knives and things kids could get hurt on. I wouldn't want kids running loose in there, either."

"Yeah, I guess. But if you come to Career Day you'd get to meet some of the single moms."

That jerked him up like a parachute harness. "Josh, are you trying to set me up?"

"There aren't that many single people in Quincey. You need all the help you can get."

Dating advice from an eleven-year-old? He struggled to keep a serious expression. "And you know this how?"

"Grandma and Grandpa think Mom should find me a dad. I hear 'em whispering about it."

The innocent remark hit like a gut punch, knocking the amusement right out of him. The idea of Piper kissing another guy the way she'd kissed him last night...

"Grandpa's always introducing men to mom, but she says he has bad taste."

"Your mom told you that?"

"I heard her telling Dr. Monroe that all Granddad's men are mama's boys."

Roth wiped his face to hide a smile. He'd have to remember to watch what he said around this little parrot. "Think about it, Josh. If you were bringing home men for your daughter would you bring troublemakers or hell-raisers?"

"Guess not. You could always ask Mom

out. Unless you have a girlfriend back in Charlotte."

He should have seen that coming. "I didn't leave anyone special back in Charlotte, but I don't see your mom and me dating."

"But she went to your place last night. The kids in school were talking about it."

Damn gossips. "She came to talk to me about Career Day. About you."

"Oh."

"Lay off the talk of the military. It scares her. Moms don't like the idea of their boys going into harm's way."

"I didn't think of that. Did your mom worry?"

"I didn't tell her where I was because I didn't want her to worry."

"So you, like, ran away from home when you were twenty? That's how old the paper said you were when you enlisted."

When Josh put it that way it didn't sound good. "Yeah, and by not telling my mom where I was she couldn't tell me when she moved away. It was a shock to find out she wasn't at home waiting for me when I got out."

"You mean you didn't visit?"

"No." Because he hadn't wanted to face Piper or his cowardice.

The door opened, revealing Ann Marie. She waved and walked toward the car. "I baked cookies for Josh's baseball team today. There were a few extra and I thought you might want some."

Roth barely concealed his surprise. Piper used to bring him her mother's cookies, and Ann Marie definitely knew her way around the kitchen. His mouth watered in anticipation as he accepted the plastic bag. But he couldn't suppress the spark of suspicion. Why was she being nice?

"Thank you."

"Josh, honey, run inside and get started on your homework. We'll have to leave for practice as soon as your mom gets home."

"See you later, Chief." Josh raced inside with the dog on his heels.

Ann Marie treated Roth to one of those looks that moms around the world mastered— the kind that made you want to confess even if you didn't know what you'd done. He kept his mouth shut.

"Lou told me you offered to help him with his shooting."

"That's right."

"Why would you help a man who framed

you, threatened your mother and ran you out of town?"

Nothing like getting to the point. He couldn't tell her the truth—that when he left town he wanted the chief to be ready to retake the reins. "I can't fault the chief for protecting his daughter. I hate to see a man lose the ability to do something he enjoys, and I want him to be able to take Josh hunting."

"You won't be around to do that?"

By fall he'd be in Charlotte. "I don't hunt anymore."

"Why not? You were easily the best shot around. It used to drive the older men crazy when you brought home bigger trophies than they did. Your grandfather taught you well."

"I was never in it for pleasure or the trophies. I hunted to feed my family. That's no longer an issue."

She searched his face. "I see."

But she didn't. Nor did Piper. Killing for the sake of killing had never been his goal. He'd hunted to survive as a child and later as a Marine. That was one reason he and the military had been such a good fit. He'd been living by their "kill only what needs killing" creed since he was old enough to carry a rifle.

Too bad Piper would never believe that.

And why did he care what Piper thought?

Because now they shared a link that would tie them forever whether he liked it or not.

Piper sighed in relief at the sound of the car door slamming and turned toward the parking lot. Her heart sank when she spotted Roth instead of the coach.

Roth strode in her direction, his long legs gobbling up the space. Her pulse lurched and her lips warmed. Damn that kiss. Was she cursed to relive it every time she saw him?

"What are you doing here?" she whispered the instant he reached her side. She tried to ignore how good he looked with evening shadow darkening his jaw. "You can't keep popping up. People will talk."

"People are already talking thanks to your visit last night."

"Probably not one of my better decisions."

"Relax. The park is in my jurisdiction. Patrolling it is my job." He scanned the boys milling around home plate. "What's going on? I thought practice started thirty minutes ago."

"The coach hasn't arrived yet. That's not like him."

Someone's cell phone rang. One of the fathers excused himself to answer it. Moments later he stepped grim-faced onto the nearby bleachers and clapped to get everyone's attention. "Listen up. Bad news. Coach Buddy was in a car accident in Wilson this morning. He's broken his arm and leg. And he'll be out of commission for a while."

Chaos erupted as everyone talked at once. Roth whistled—one loud, shrill blow, silencing the crowd. "Is the coach all right otherwise?"

That he'd care about someone he didn't even know surprised Piper.

"Yes," the father said. "His wife says he's out of surgery. But he'll be flat on his back for at least four weeks. We need a volunteer to fill in until he returns."

Heads downcast, the parents shuffled their feet. No one raised a hand. Piper's frustration mounted. She couldn't volunteer. Some nights emergencies at the clinic made her late for games and her mother or father had to drive Josh. Plus the clinic was open every other Saturday so she missed those morning games altogether.

Too bad her father wasn't here. She might have been able to strong-arm him into stepping up to the plate, so to speak, even though his only interest in baseball was watching Josh play.

"C'mon, people. The Rockets will not have a team if someone doesn't step forward. Y'all know I can't," the man pleaded.

Beside her Roth straightened. "It's temporary? Only until the regular coach can get here?"

"That's right."

More silence. Roth scanned the crowd as if willing someone to volunteer. Josh's gaze sought hers then Roth's and his shoulders and mouth drooped. He'd been talking about this season for months, and he would be so disappointed if it was cancelled.

"I'll do it," Roth said, startling Piper and making her want to shriek in dismay. "I should be able to schedule myself around games and practices, but I'll need an assistant to back me up in case a call comes in or I can't break away."

Voices clamored again, this time with parents willing to be second-in-command.

"All right!" Josh yelled over them all and pumped his arm in the air. "Chief, Chief, Chief..." Josh chanted, and the other boys joined in.

Piper shot Roth a glare. His darkened

cheeks surprised her. Was he not used to the attention?

"Grab your gloves and some balls and hit the field to warm up."

The boys raced off, their whoops filling the air.

"Why are you doing this?" Piper demanded. "Why are you forcing yourself into our lives?"

"Because Josh loves baseball, and working with these kids might help me discover who the vandals are."

So it wasn't just another attempt to worm his way into her son's affections—even if that would be the end result.

Movement in her peripheral vision caught Piper's attention. She peeled her gaze from Roth's as a woman sidled up to him. Piper stifled a groan. Tammy Sue and her spoiled, bossy son had been a pain in Piper's backside ever since the Weaver duo had settled in Quincey two years ago.

"Hi there, Chief. It's real nice of you to volunteer. I'm Tammy." The piranha offered her perfectly manicured hand and lingered, in Piper's opinion, far too long over the handshake before Roth pulled free. "That's my boy, the tall one. Robbie. He's been the team's best pitcher for the last two years."

"Since I don't know the boys, I'll have to evaluate each player's strengths and weaknesses before making that determination."

Tammy blinked at the deflection of her blatant attempt to lobby for her son and cut a sly glance at Piper. "I see your mama baked cookies for the team again. Nice of her to do that for you since cooking's not your strong suit."

Piper stiffened. "I can cook."

"Not as good as me, I'll bet. I am amazing…in the kitchen. Chief, you'll have to come over and sample my Southern hospitality sometime. Robbie and I would be happy to have you."

And not just for dinner, Piper decided. Talk about obvious.

"Thanks. Ladies, if you'll excuse me I need to meet my team." His gaze hit Piper's before he strode off. She could have sworn she saw a "be nice" warning in the dark depths.

"I hear you two have a history," Tammy said.

"We have a past. It's over."

"Good. Because I intend to be his future, and I don't share my men." With a toss of her long, dark hair Tammy sashayed off, her skinny butt swinging in a way that would make a call girl proud.

The impulse to stick her tongue out hit Piper hard and fast, but she refrained because the childish gesture wasn't the best way to set an example.

She exhaled and deliberately walked in the opposite direction—to the third base side of the diamond. She didn't want Roth. That meant he was available to any other woman. Any woman except Tammy Sue Weaver, that is.

Piper's chest burned. It wasn't jealousy, she assured herself. It was the homemade pizza she'd had for dinner. And her attitude wasn't sour grapes. She was simply looking out for Roth's best interest. No man, not even the one who'd left her and who was now trying to steal her son's affections, deserved to have to put up with Tammy Sue's backstabbing bitchiness.

And if the worst-case scenario should happen and Roth stayed, Josh certainly didn't deserve Tammy Sue for a stepmother.

Roth waved goodbye to the boys and strode off the field after an hour's practice. Coaching was a short-term commitment. A month.

Six weeks at the most. He could handle that
without disrupting his plans.

He needed to check the log on the new laptop in his cruiser. Even though he had officially
clocked out before coming to practice, he'd like
to know if there had been any calls while he'd
been occupied. The radio clipped to his shirt
had been silent, but he wasn't convinced the
equipment was as good as it should be.

"Chief," a male voice called out.

Roth turned. A pack of six men walked toward him. Instantly on alert, he rolled to the
balls of his feet and searched their faces. He
didn't see malice, but he quickly cataloged
their descriptions nonetheless. He'd been
catching a lot of flack for the tickets he'd been
writing and the laws he'd been enforcing.

The same man who'd reported the coach's
condition earlier stepped forward, hand extended. "Mike Bass. Thanks for volunteering.
Most of us commute, so getting to games and
practices on time can be a challenge."

"Especially if there's a wreck on the highway," another man added.

"We're glad to have you here," Mike said.
"We all moved to Quincey because we wanted
to raise our kids in a small-town, but I guess

none of us took into account how things were done here."

"What he means is we're glad the town council hired someone from outside the good-ole-boy network."

"I'm from here. What makes you think I'll be any different?"

The men laughed. "You're already shaking things up," Mike said, and the other men chorused agreement.

"Have you had problems?"

"I wouldn't call it problems, per se," a third man said. "But laws are not unilaterally enforced."

"Meaning?"

"Locals get away with stuff newcomers don't."

Roth had suspected as much.

"And our concerns about the recent vandalism have been brushed off with 'boys will be boys' responses."

"I'd like to hear your concerns."

"C'mon over to the house for wings and beer one night after practice."

"As long as I'm not on duty."

Piper and Josh walked past and Roth's radar immediately zoomed in on the woman who'd short-circuited his brain.

"You can bring Piper if you want. She gets along with the wives."

"Piper and I aren't dating."

The men said nothing, but every one of them wore an expression of disbelief. Apparently even Quincey's new blood had adopted the gossip habit.

The boys joined their fathers in the lot carousing and jostling each other. Within minutes they'd piled into their cars and driven off, leaving Roth alone. The fathers were all roughly his age. They had wives and families. Roth had neither except for Josh. And for the first time, solitude held no appeal.

He checked his watch. It was too late to follow Josh and Piper home to question Josh about the boys on the team. Just as well. He needed to form his own opinions.

So home alone it would be. And tomorrow he'd lay one more ghost to rest before he went on duty.

Chapter Eleven

Roth parked his truck beneath the sprawling oak he used to climb and stared at the old house where he and his grandfather had spent so much time.

Gus had been a no-bullshit, no-excuses kind of guy, and Roth doubted forgiveness was in the old man's vocabulary. But Roth had to try. And he was long overdue in the asking.

Gus stepped out of one of his two garages. He was still tall and lean, but his shoulders were a little more stooped and deeper lines grooved his face. How old was he now? Eighty?

He crossed the yard. His wise eyes sized up

Roth, then he extended his hand. "Wondered how long it would take you to come see me."

Roth returned the handshake. Gus still had a decent grip. "I wasn't sure you wouldn't greet me with your twelve-gauge."

"No reason to. I know you didn't wreck that car."

Roth stared. "How do you know?"

"That Vette meant as much to you as it did to me. Hell, you probably had more hours' work in her than I did, and you probably cried as hard as I did when you saw her wrapped around that tree."

"Came close."

"Hamilton was convinced it was you behind the wheel and nothing I said changed his mind. And you wouldn't tell him any different. You were loyal. Like your grandpappy. Wilson was the best friend I ever had right up till his last breath. An' I ain't saying that 'cuz he left me his Corvette."

That car, along with the hunting rifle, had been Roth's last tie to his grandfather.

"I respect your loyalty, son, but I guess you've heard how that turned out. Chuck's still...well, he's Chuck. More muscle than brains and not too dependable."

"What makes you think Chuck was responsible?"

"He's the only one you would have lied for and the only one of your friends cowardly enough to let you take the blame. I don't know how he convinced you to let him drive—"

"He didn't. He took the car while I was writing up your bill."

"Figured it had to be something like that. Then three days after the wreck you lit out for parts unknown. Not a word to anybody. I figured you were running from something else. Maybe you got tired of living in your daddy's shadow."

"A little of both."

"I hope you came to terms with whatever it was. If not, it'll follow you like a fine bloodhound no matter how far you go, and you'll be running the rest of your life. Can't fix your problems if you don't look 'em in the eye."

The words sounded so much like something his grandfather would have said Roth's throat tightened. "I'm working on it."

"I'll get it," Piper called as she descended the stairs after her post-work shower Friday evening. She opened the front door. To Roth.

Her heart dropped to her fuzzy slippers.

He looked so good in pressed navy pants and a white shirt with the top two buttons unfastened. And she... Ugh. She wanted to run upstairs and lock herself in her room. She'd washed off the remnants of her makeup and pulled on her rattiest, most comfortable clothes for family movie night. She'd barely taken time to brush her hair.

Use him. Piper instantly rejected Madison's suggestion. It didn't matter that simply being near him made Piper's body dance like a wind chime in a summer storm. She had to think about Josh.

"Why are you here?"

"Ann Marie invited me to dinner."

She was going to kill her mother. Slowly. But not in front of the chief. No witnesses.

Her mother's heels tapped into the foyer. "Don't leave the man on the doorstep, sweetie. Roth, come in. I'm glad you could make it, and I hope you like chicken and dumplings."

"Yes, ma'am."

"Josh, the chief is here." Her mother's announcement prevented Piper from convincing their guest to reconsider his dinner plans.

Stampeding feet were echoed by the scrape of galloping doggy nails on the hardwood floor. "Hey, Chief. Long time no see."

Roth smiled, making Piper's stomach loop-the-loop. He checked his watch. "At least three hours. Did you get your homework done?"

Josh made a face and rolled his eyes. "Yes, sir. Even my math."

That explained why Josh had been working so diligently when Piper had arrived home. It was a conspiracy.

"Way to go." Roth held up a palm and Josh slapped in the high-five ritual. Piper felt excluded. And she didn't like it. The tighter these two became the more crushed Josh would be when Roth showed his true colors.

"Josh, why don't you take the chief to the den," she suggested.

Roth gave her a look that said he knew she was trying to get rid of him then followed Josh.

Piper turned to her mother once Roth and Josh were out of hearing range.

"What do you think you're doing?"

"Josh needs a good male influence."

"He has Daddy."

"Someone younger. And Roth is his fa—"

"Shh."

"Piper, they need to get to know each other."

"They're doing that every day after school

and during baseball. Having him here is too risky."

"We will be careful. But I'll tell you the same thing I told your father. There's no better way to keep an eye on the man and find out exactly what his plans are than to keep in him plain sight."

"You and Daddy discussed this? Without me?" The last thing she wanted was her father scheming behind her back.

Her mom fussed with her hair in the mirror, clearly evading Piper's gaze.

"Mother?"

"You are hardly unbiased. We didn't discuss *this situation* exactly, but the general sentiment of keeping friends close and enemies closer."

Definitely a conspiracy. "I do not like inviting Roth into our home and deeper into Josh's life. And you know why."

"I'm not as convinced as you are that Roth will leave Quincey."

"He will. I can't believe you ambushed me."

"If I had told you my intentions where would you be? Not here, I'll guarantee that. You and Madison would have found some excuse to drive to Raleigh or Greenville for the evening."

"You know it."

"I have a plan. Don't mess it up." Her mother marched to the kitchen.

A plan. Dread wound through Piper like a kudzu vine. She debated going the opposite direction—out the door. Her home, her last sanctuary from Roth, had been invaded. And she had no recourse except to suffer through the evening or admit to Roth that she didn't trust herself in his company.

Use him.

"Oh, shut up," Piper muttered under her breath, and headed into battle—the kitchen—to confront her mother. "What kind of plan?"

"You are the one who said the past is over. I'm going to find out everything I can about who Roth is now."

"And how will you do that?"

"Sweetie, I'm not telling you because you are a horrible actress and an even worse liar. You can't help. Just watch and learn."

Piper's uneasiness over the evening multiplied tenfold.

"This is nice," Roth said as he looked around the den.

Ann Marie smiled because he'd obviously overlooked Josh's pile of boy paraphernalia that no amount of nagging or picking up behind him could eliminate.

"Piper decorated this room. She's much more practical than I am when it comes to taking rambunctious, growing boys into account. I'm sure she could help you with your place if you need it."

"Mother!" Piper protested as she joined them. "Roth's place is fine the way it is."

"Oh, that's right. You've already seen his apartment. But then so have several other single women. I hear you've been getting a few home-baked deliveries since you arrived."

"A few." A tight smile stretched Roth's lips, and there was a hint of irritation in his eyes. Good. She liked that he didn't enjoy women showing up on his doorstep unannounced.

But the tinge of jealousy on Piper's face was quite the most telling result of the exchange. It turned into a warning glare, which Ann Marie ignored. Somebody had to find out Roth's intentions.

"Please sit, Roth, make yourself comfortable." She waited until he did. Josh piled on the sofa beside him. Lordy, those two resembled each other. That could spell trouble.

"Have you had a chance to drive by any of the homes on the list I gave you?"

"All of them. None fit my needs."

"And what exactly are you looking for?"

"I'll know it when I see it."

"The rental choices are certainly limited. If you were buying there are better homes available, and you wouldn't be stuck with builder-beige walls and carpets. You could choose any color scheme. Piper has a great sense of color."

"Mother!"

"But Mom, he doesn't have a girlfriend to help him, so you could do it," Josh added. "You know how much fun we had painting my room."

Bless Josh for helping the cause. She'd bake her grandson a batch of brownies next week. "If you decided to purchase a home, you'd also need to decide if you wanted a starter or something that you could be comfortable in for years."

Roth's expression gave away absolutely nothing. "I haven't sold my place in Charlotte yet, so buying is out for now."

"House or condominium?"

"Condo."

"Is it on the market?"

He hesitated ever so slightly. "It needs work before I can list it."

Interesting. His hesitation, not the need for work. Every listing needed work.

"I'm sure you already know there are tax and investment benefits that come with ownership that you don't get when renting. You'll need to reinvest any capital gains as soon as possible once you sell your condo. How soon do you think that'll be?"

"It depends on when I can do the work. My focus now is on familiarizing myself with this job and upgrading the department."

Upgrading the department—something Lou had resisted for years. The man was technophobic.

"I have a colleague in Charlotte if you'd like an agent referral. Perhaps he can take a look and tell you what you need or recommend someone to do the repairs for you so you won't have to make that drive."

"I'll let you know when I'm ready for that."

Piper glared again. "I apologize for my mother. Once she starts talking business she doesn't want to stop. Is dinner ready yet?"

"I don't have a problem with someone being passionate about his or her work," Roth replied.

Ann Marie gave him points for the right

answer. "Why don't y'all head to the dining room? I'll dish up."

She'd learned two very important things from tonight's little get-together. Roth had one foot in Quincey and one still in Charlotte. Perhaps Piper's certainty that he wouldn't stay wasn't completely unfounded.

And second, and by far the most important thing she'd learned, Piper wasn't over him. Josh wouldn't be the only one heartbroken if Roth left.

Ann Marie wanted her daughter and grandson to be happy. That meant she had to find a way to make Roth stay.

Roth sat back, his stomach full from too much good food and his face hurting from an excess of grinning. He hadn't known what to expect when Ann Marie had issued the invitation, but now, despite her initial inquisition, he was glad he'd ignored his doubts and accepted.

Dinner in the Hamilton house had been nothing like the silent, guarded ones of Roth's childhood. He'd shared similar evenings with married Marines or other SWAT members and their families, but he'd never pictured himself as belonging. He'd always been the outsider. An observer.

But tonight had been different. Josh was his family. And more meals like this one were possible. If he—or his father—didn't screw it up. And he'd be lying to himself if he didn't admit he wanted more.

More nights of watching Piper's eyes light up with silent mirth when Josh told his baseball and fishing stories, more of hearing her laughter escape when she couldn't contain it, more of watching her hair slide across her shoulders when she buried her face in her hands over something Josh had said. More of the electric charge that hit him each time their eyes met across the table.

He caught Piper's gaze on him again. She'd begun the evening uptight and unwelcoming, her face an expressionless mask, but she'd slowly unwound. And watching her unwind had had the opposite effect on him.

She'd never been more beautiful than she was now, staring at him with her eyes warm and filled with approval. She hadn't looked at him like that in a long time. And he'd missed it. He hadn't realized how much. Something inside him flickered to life. Something besides the ever-present desire. Something a lot like yearning.

Ann Marie rose, breaking Piper's mesmerizing spell and garnering Roth's attention.

"Dinner was delicious, Ann Marie."

"Wait until you try my Death by Chocolate Mousse. Josh, help me with the dessert."

The pair left the dining room.

Piper groaned and slumped in her chair. "She's going to kill me with her rich Southern cooking."

Roth smiled at the good-natured complaint. "Not a bad way to go."

"She went all out for you tonight. Don't get used to it."

"I'll keep that in mind. Josh has a wicked sense of humor."

"He's certainly the class clown sometimes. He didn't get that from me."

"Nor me."

She tilted her head and assessed him through narrowed eyes. "I wouldn't be so sure of that—especially after seeing the two of you in action. I don't remember that teasing side of you. You were always so serious."

"I had a lot on my plate trying to take care of my mother and make ends meet with the garage." And he'd been so damned deep in love with Piper that humor hadn't been part of his behavior pattern. He'd been desperately trying to figure out a way to be the man she needed.

"You're very close to your parents despite your exile to Florida."

"Their breakup is my fault, and I guess I always felt a little guilty about that. And then there's Josh. He needs a man in his life. Us living here means my father comes over often."

"How is their divorce your fault?"

"They're not divorced. They're still married. That should tell you something. Separated twelve *years?* I mean, really?"

She glanced over her shoulder at the closed door. "My decision to continue my pregnancy divided them. Dad wanted...what you wanted. And Mom couldn't forgive him for that or for sending me away. So they split and didn't tell me about it until I came home and discovered their living arrangements. I've been trying to get them back together ever since. Although now that you've told me the truth about Dad's part in your leaving I'm not sure why my mother would want him back."

"Maybe they've stayed apart because they're better off that way."

She shook her head, causing the light to glimmer like strands of gold in her hair. "If you'd asked me ten days ago, I would have said they're soul mates. They're too stubborn to forgive and forget and move on. Now... I'm not so sure."

"Soul mates? You believe in that fairy tale?"

"You would, too, if you ever saw them together. When they're in the same room they give off enough energy to light Quincey. When they're apart it's as if their inner glow dims somehow. They feed off each other. Even their arguments seem to energize them. And when Dad had his stroke, Mom was a mess—totally unlike her I-can-handle-anything self. If that's not love, what is? Bonds like that should not be broken."

How had she held on to that romantic streak? "I'm not sure it's possible to forgive someone for a mistake so grievous it changes the course of your life."

Like his mother's decision to stay with a man who hurt her and their child.

Like his father's decision to murder that deputy.

Like his decision to run from Piper and his

responsibility to her and Josh. He wouldn't blame Piper if she never forgave him.

Wait a minute. Who said he wanted her forgiveness?

But he did. He wanted her to understand that at the time he'd thought he was doing the best thing for her.

The door swung open and Josh and Ann Marie returned carrying tall sundae glasses filled with the mousse and topped with whipped cream and a cherry.

"The cherries were my idea," Josh announced.

Roth winked. "Good idea."

He was about halfway through the rich, creamy dessert when he noticed Josh was focused more on him than the dessert. "What's up, bud?"

Josh squirmed in his chair. "The kids in school said your dad used to hit you. Did he?"

The unexpected question caught Roth off guard.

Piper gasped. "Josh—"

"It's okay. My father did hit me, Josh, and he hit my mother. He was a mean drunk who couldn't control his temper."

"I always wished I had a dad, but I guess it's better not to have one than to have one like that. Is that what made you become a cop? Because you want to lock up guys like him?"

Insightful kid. "Yes. I don't like people who victimize others."

"Nah. Bullies aren't cool."

That sounded more like personal experience than a generalization. "Do you have bullies at your school?"

Josh looked down, stirring his dessert instead of eating it. "Every school has bullies. Don't you watch the news?"

"It is the hot topic right now." But no doubt about it, Josh was dodging the question. Tonight was not the night to press for details. He'd try again on one of their rides home when the boy would be less likely to worry about his mother and grandmother overhearing. Roth didn't want the kid to face retaliation from his so-called friends.

"Josh, come help Grandma load the dishwasher."

"But—"

"Now, young man, if you want to have time to watch the movie before bedtime."

Roth rose. "Ann Marie, dinner was delicious, but I'm not staying for the movie. I'm going to make another sweep around town.

It's Friday night and our vandals might be out."

"I understand. Thank you for coming." Once again, the two retreated behind the swinging door.

Piper tucked her hair behind her ear. And for some damned reason the memory of nibbling her lobe charged forward. "I'm so sorry, Roth. I didn't know the kids had been talking about your father."

"Don't be. Josh asked a fair question. It's no surprise that people would gossip. It's what I expected all along and one of the primary reasons I moved away."

The other reason had been Piper. Looking her in the eye now and knowing he'd let her down was not easy. Especially since he still wanted her—more with every passing moment spent in her company.

If he didn't get out soon he'd repeat his mistakes—beginning with nibbling that lobe.

Chapter Twelve

"Walk me out?" Roth asked.

The request sounded innocent enough, but given the awakening effect his laugh had had on Piper's hormones this evening, she wanted to refuse. Instead, she did what she'd been raised to do—the polite thing. "Sure."

She led him to the door and told herself to stop here. But he paused on the welcome mat, waiting for her. He must have something he needed to tell her that Josh couldn't overhear.

Thankful for once for the lack of street-lights, Piper followed him to his truck. Only a few porch lamps gleamed from the well-spaced houses on the street. He stopped between his truck and the trio of magnolias her mother had planted, trees that obscured half the nearby homes' view of them. What the neighbors couldn't see, they wouldn't gossip about.

Roth looked at the navy blue sky liberally littered with stars. "I remember nights like this. Lying on a blanket on the riverbank and listening to the water and the nocturnal animals in the brush."

His words painted a vivid picture of hours spent wrapped in his arms, hours when she'd been so in love she couldn't believe the world could be more perfect. Or so cruel.

"Life was a lot simpler then. We knew what we wanted and never imagined that we might not get it."

He looked at her. "Do you ever wish you'd listened when everyone told you to stay away from me?"

"If I'd listened, then I wouldn't have Josh, and I wouldn't have had that magical summer."

"It was magical. Remembering it got me through a lot of tough nights." His smile seemed distant, as if he were looking back instead of at her.

"Don't say things like that."

"Why not? It's true."

She did not need to know that.

"Is your mother matchmaking?"

Piper stiffened, hating that he'd picked up on that vibe, as well. "She'd better not be."

"She did a great job of convincing me what a wonderful woman you've become." Suddenly he was standing too close and she hadn't even seen him shift. "But I already knew that."

Her breath caught. He traced her jaw with the tip of his fingers and desire shimmied through her. "Roth, don't—"

"You have become an incredibly strong woman. If you'd been this strong back then, I don't know if I could have left you even though it was for the best."

She refused to revisit the what-might-have-beens no matter how hard that one tugged her. She'd wasted too many years wallowing in them. "I was strong then, too."

"No, babe. You were the baby bird peering over the edge of the nest for the first time. You had the whole world ahead of you. I would have held you back."

"I didn't want the world. I wanted you." She wished the words back. But darn it, that *babe* had gotten to her.

"And I wanted you. God help me, Piper, I still do."

His words hung on the air between them then he bent his head. She ordered herself to back away. But her stubborn feet didn't listen. And even though she knew she shouldn't, Piper rose to meet him. Their lips touched, clung, separated. Her heart missed a beat when their gazes met and held. The hunger churning inside her reflected in his dark eyes. It was just desire. But it sure felt good. Without saying a word she closed the gap.

He grasped her waist and yanked her closer—the suddenness of his actions throwing her off balance. Their mouths crashed together. She fell into him. The heat of him molded against her from breasts to thighs. They fit together as if they weren't out of practice from a twelve-year hiatus. And he felt good. So good she didn't want to be smart and end the embrace. Instead she savored each stroke of his tongue, each brush of his hands, and the thickening ridge against her belly.

He massaged her back, cupped her bottom, then tangled his fingers in her hair and kissed her so deeply it seemed he was trying to consume her. One desperate kiss melded into the next and the next. She clung, grasped, stroked and dug her nails into his muscles. When he shoved his thigh between hers and brushed over her sensitive center she shuddered.

He slid his hand beneath her baggy shirt then upward, scorching a path across her belly to stop beneath her breast. Her head spun, as if someone had spiked her sweet tea. All she could think about was skin. She wanted to feel his against hers. Damn the bra separating them.

Then a shaft of light splashed over them, burning through her closed eyelids. She eased onto her heels, breathing hard, and glanced at the house. Josh's window glowed, and his curtains were open. The fire inside her instantly went out.

She tried to back away but Roth's grip tightened.

"No, Roth. We shouldn't be— This isn't smart."

"You want me as much as I do you. I saw it in your eyes every time you looked at me tonight. I feel it in your body now."

She couldn't deny the truth. Every time he'd laughed she'd experienced the tug deep inside. She searched for sanity and pulled herself from his willpower-melting hands. "That doesn't make it okay. I don't want to be used and discarded again."

Use him.

"We're damned good together, Piper." He reached for her, but she dodged him. Somebody had to think about the future.

"Stop. That's Josh's room." Roth glanced at the house. "And long after you're gone he and I will be here, and we'll have to live with everyone gossiping about what happened between you and me. Then and now. I can't do that to him. And I can't risk people seeing the three of us together and connecting the dots. It's best if we ignore this chemistry."

"Do you honestly believe that's possible?"

No. *Yes.* "I'll make it possible."

That didn't mean it would be easy. But her son's needs came first. And Josh's happiness was far more important than a fleeting affair or her neglected hormones.

"Please go home, Roth. And in the future it would be wise if you'd politely refuse my mother's invitations."

The clinic door opened a few minutes after noon Saturday as Piper set the autoclave to sterilize the instruments.

Piper stepped into the hall. Roth stood at the other end holding a box in his arms. Her stomach swooped.

Not again. She wasn't ready for this. She'd never be ready. Josh keeping Sarg all weekend meant she was supposed to be able to avoid these daily encounters.

"I need the doc."

"Madison's gone for the day."

"Then I need your help." He looked so good in his boots and thigh-hugging jeans that her mouth dried up as he closed the distance between them. His expression revealed nothing. Not even that he remembered last night's kiss. But when he reached her side the fury burning in his eyes took her aback.

"What's wrong?"

"Someone hung a garbage bag full of kittens from the tree in Tate Lowry's yard."

Remaining calm and objective despite her disgust at the cruelty wasn't easy. You could learn a lot about people by the way they treated their pets, and not all of it was good.

"Are they alive?"

"Barely."

"Bring them in here." She hurried into the procedure room. He set the box on the exam table. Piper peeled back a towel to reveal four tiny kittens. They stirred, mewing and moving weakly. She placed her palm on one then each subsequent kitten then checked their gums. Her spirits sank a bit.

"They can't be more than two weeks old. Their eyes are barely open."

"There's no telling how long they've been separated from their mother. They probably need to be fed."

"They're cold and dehydrated. I'll have to warm them before I can give them formula. Kittens' digestive tracts become sluggish when they're chilled. They wouldn't be able to handle food, but they need fluids."

She rolled a heat lamp to the table and turned it on then fetched a heating pad for good measure. She could feel Roth watching her every move. Her skin tingled with awareness.

"Lift them and let me put this beneath them."

He carefully scooped all four babies in his big hands. But then Roth had always been gentle with her. She snuffed the thought.

Once the pad was in place she was grateful to have an excuse to turn away. She focused on steadying her hands as she filled four syringes and willed her pounding pulse to slow. She was too old to act like a schoolgirl with a crush every time she bumped into him.

"What is that?" he asked.

"Therapeutic hydration liquid. It's the same stuff you give human babies when they're dehydrated." She carried the syringes to the table.

"Where was Josh last night?"

Roth's authoritarian tone brought her head up. "At home. Why?"

"He mentioned some of the boys not liking Lowry. Lowry suspects kids did this. He says he's had similar problems before—no live animals, but he's found roadkill on the porches of his house and store and in his mailbox."

She recoiled in horror then his meaning sank in. "How dare you insinuate Josh is involved. You're crazy if you think he would be a part of something like that."

"If he was at home all night as you said, then he wasn't—"

"He *was* at home. You saw him there."

"Piper, I left at seven. Given that the kittens are still alive I'd say this happened later—much later—probably early this morning. Kids sneak out all the time. I did it. You did it."

Another burst of heat erupted inside her. She'd snuck out to meet Roth and to make love and lie in his arms beneath the stars—a memory he'd rekindled last night.

"I get up at five. Josh sleeps with his door open. He was in his bed then. If he left earlier, he would have had to walk past my room to get out. As I've said before, I'm a light sleeper. I'd hear him."

"If he isn't directly involved, he might know who is. I need to question him."

Her protective instincts kicked in full force. "I thought you said not to question him."

"Waiting for Josh to volunteer the information is no longer an option. The pranks have escalated into animal cruelty. I want it stopped. Now. Escalation is a pattern, not a solitary event."

"I insist on being present when you talk to him."

"As his parent you have that right."

She gulped down her fear. "Does he need a lawyer?"

His face softened in understanding. "I'm not planning to drag him to the station, Piper. Where is he today?"

"He's fishing with my father."

"When will he get back?"

"After lunch. Why didn't Mr. Lowry report the previous incidents?"

"He claims he did, but he was told 'boys will be boys,' and nothing was done about it. The fathers at baseball practice Thursday night implied the same thing about the recent vandalism."

"My father has never mentioned any incidents of this kind. I can't believe he or his deputies would ignore the reports."

"We both know your father's not above bending the law to suit his purposes. That's half my battle as chief—enforcing laws and rules that he chose to ignore. And if he's turning a blind eye to this, then I have to ask why?"

Why indeed? Did her father know something she didn't? Something involving Josh? She didn't believe for one second that Josh would harm innocent kittens. He'd helped her nurse too many orphaned animal babies and each one they'd lost had been hard on him. But it was better that he learn how to handle loss through animals than have the first loss be a grandparent he adored.

She needed to talk to her father and her son. Fear over what she might learn made it difficult to breathe. The pitifully weak mew of a kitten dragged her back to the present crisis.

"You can go. I'll take care of the kittens, and I'll call you later when Josh gets home."

"I'll help."

She wanted—needed—him gone. He rattled her thinking by simply being under the same roof, and she had to get her racing thoughts organized. Did Josh know anything about the incidents at Tate Lowry's? How much trouble would he be in if he did and hadn't come forward with information? Would he rat out his friends if they were the culprits? What would happen if he did? Or if he didn't?

"There's no need for you to stay. I'm sure you have work to do or something."

"I'm off duty. Tell me what to do."

"If you're not on the schedule, then why did you respond to Lowry's call?"

"He called me personally because he wanted something done this time."

This time. "How long has this been going on?"

"About a year."

During her father's tenure. She'd hoped it had begun after his stroke. This didn't look good.

With Roth's jaw set like a steel trap, she doubted she'd be able to convince him to leave, and the kittens' condition was dire enough that she didn't want to waste time.

"Hold a kitten in your hand. Make sure all four paws are on your palm so the liquid doesn't go into its lungs, then slowly feed it the solution. Like this."

She selected a white kitten and demonstrated. He scooped up a tiny tiger-striped ball of fuzz and mimicked her actions. His carefulness melted the ice around her heart a teensy bit.

"It's been a while, but I remember."

She'd bet he did. Plenty of people had warned her away from him when she and Roth had begun dating, but she'd seen something they hadn't bothered to notice. Roth had always made time for pets or people others didn't want. She'd discovered that early on when she'd caught the big, strong rebel searching a weed-choked field for orphaned baby bunnies.

"You're smiling. Why?"

She didn't want to say. But with him looking at her in that commanding way her resistance crumbled. "I was remembering that litter of rabbits."

He shrugged. "I shot their mother. How could I not take care of them?"

"Most people would have let nature run its course."

"Younger victims sometimes need help."

He'd never admitted it, but she'd known he felt guilty for killing the mother even though his family had needed the meat. Once he'd found the nest he'd been so careful with the kits, feeding and massaging each one until they were old enough to release.

She shook her head to banish the memory. She needed to remember who he was now, not who she'd once believed him to be. Because she'd been wrong to put her faith in a man who could walk away from her much easier than he'd left those bunnies.

"You won't be bringing a new stray into the office every week, will you?" She aimed for lightness but didn't quite pull it off.

"What would you have me do with them?"

A killer or a savior. Who was this man? Her heart and the evidence in front of her said one, but her head and his career choices said the other. He was a threat to her son's happiness and therefore hers, and that was all that mattered.

She returned the first kitten to the box and picked up the next. "Exactly what you've done. Bring them in. At least we should be able to find homes for the kittens—if they make it."

He lifted the remaining patient. "What are their chances?"

"Not great."

"Have any clients whose cat might have had a litter recently?"

"None that immediately comes to mind. But cats are pretty self-sufficient. They usually give birth without assistance and often hide their babies. And when times are tight animal care often gets cut from the budget. These could even be feral cats."

"Have you heard anything from Sarg's owners?"

"No. And Josh is getting more attached. My mother's not much better. She spoils that dog. I caught her cooking breakfast for him this morning to celebrate him spending the entire weekend at the house. Before I left the office yesterday I emailed pictures of Sarg to every veterinary clinic within thirty miles. I doubt I'll hear anything over the weekend, but maybe next week…"

Roth's eyes roved over her as they finished feeding the last pair, making her hyperconscious of every move, every breath. His and hers. And just like that the taste of him, the feel of him, the heat of him strummed through her body. She hated that he had this power over her.

"You should be a vet. It's not too late to go back to school."

"Even if I was willing to relocate and take Josh away from his grandparents—and I'm not—there's no money for college, and I'm not interested in sadddling myself with student loans. I'm focusing on setting money aside for Josh's future."

"If you'd let me help—"

"No. I am happy with my life."

"Without a man? Without a father for Josh?"

She frowned. "What has my mother said now?"

His slow smile weakened her knees. "It wasn't Ann Marie. It was your—*our*—son. He's a sponge."

Piper covered her uneasiness by turning away to wash her hands. She hadn't considered the possibility that Josh would share things with Roth that she'd rather he not know.

Roth joined her sink-side, his body heat enveloping her as he reached across to lather and rinse simultaneously instead of waiting his turn. The urge to lean into him was almost irresistible. She steeled her knees against it.

"He told me everything from your parents wanting you to find him a father to the chief bringing home mama's boys."

If it were possible to die from embarrassment, somebody would be calling the coroner now. She ripped a paper towel from the dispenser and put the width of the small room between them. "Like I said, I'm happy with my life. I don't need you or your money."

"Why haven't you found Mr. Right?"

"Why haven't you?"

"My career isn't marriage-friendly."

"It is now. Quincey is the perfect place to raise a family."

"You dodged my question."

"Maybe I'm happy alone."

He hiked an eyebrow. "Living with your mother?"

Low blow. "Her help with Josh is invaluable. She's there every afternoon when he gets home from school, and she watches him during school vacations and on Saturdays when I have to work."

"Did I sour you on men, Piper?"

Pride stiffened her spine. She wasn't about to share her relationship failures with him. There hadn't been many, but enough to reinforce her decision to depend solely on herself. "You give yourself too much credit."

"Why invent the fiancé?"

"To protect Josh from small-minded gossips. If the truth gets out, he'll be hurt. Right now he believes he had a father who was as excited about his impending birth as I was. I'd rather he not know his father considered him a mistake.

"The kittens have been fed. You can leave. I'll stay until they're warm enough to take home. I can care for them there."

"What about lunch?"

Not for one second would she admit that in her rush to get Josh out the door with her father she'd skipped breakfast and hunger pains had been gnawing at her stomach for hours. "We have food in our break room."

"Lock up behind me." He turned and strode down the hall, his steps nearly silent. But then he'd spent his military career sneaking up on people. She supposed he had to be quiet.

The door clicked shut and the energy drained from her, leaving behind a knot of worry. She had to talk to Josh before Roth did and find out exactly how much her son knew about the vandals.

And she definitely, *definitely* had to get control of her reaction to Roth. Because her strategy to avoid him wasn't working.

"Make those orders to go, please, May."

"You got it, Chief. Anything else?"

"Do you know anyone whose cat has recently had kittens?"

"Haven't heard mention of it. Why? You looking for one?"

"No. I found a litter, and I'm trying to locate the mother. Piper's trying to keep 'em alive now."

"I'll ask around. If one of these lunches is for Piper, then you'll want to add an order of Willie's lemon fruit trifle. Piper's partial to it."

Interesting how everybody knowing your business could work in his favor.

"Thanks. I'll take two."

Once May sidled off Roth scanned the crowded diner. At least half the customers were out-of-towners. Back in his day the only nonlocals had been folks who got lost and stopped for directions. Strangers had been the only ones who hadn't smelled the stench of his father's sordid past clinging to him.

In Charlotte no one had ever heard of Seth Sterling. Roth was judged by his actions not the rotten branches of his family tree. The same could be said for the military after they'd grilled the ever-lovin' hell out of him with all their psychological evaluations. And he liked it that way. He refused to let others' low expectations hold him back.

He had to admit he found some satisfaction in returning to Quincey as the top dog when he'd left at a low point. Still, he was smart enough to know he'd have never been offered the position if not for the new town council who hadn't known his father.

But coming in as Chief meant he'd already hit the rank threshold—same as he had as a sniper. He wanted more. Higher rank commanded more respect and each promotion took him further away from being labeled that drunk, white trash, murdering bum's son. So even if it weren't for his history here, he wouldn't stay long.

He noticed fewer smiles from the locals today—probably a result of the citations he'd been writing. But he wouldn't ignore obvious infractions. He might not be able to turn Quincey around during his short tenure, but he'd damned well make sure people quit looking the other way when safety concerns arose—the way they had with his mother.

The door opened. Chuck stepped inside. He spotted Roth, stopped, then scowling, pivoted and left. The little girl by his side—probably eight or nine—protested, but Chuck grabbed her hand and dragged her away.

Roth hadn't heard from Chuck about attending a substance abuse program, but it had only been five days. He'd give him a few more before following up unless he caught him intoxicated in public again.

May set a plastic bag on the counter. "Thought you and Chuck used to be friends. He ain't looking friendly today."

Roth laid his money on the counter. "Time and the choices we make change everything. Thanks for the lunch, May."

He hiked to the clinic. Watching Piper this morning had driven a knife of guilt deep into his gut. She'd been competent, sure and efficient. She loved working with animals.

Leaving Quincey had allowed him to find his path and live his dream, but in the process he'd killed hers, and there was no way he could resurrect it.

What if he'd stayed?

He dismissed the thought. He'd made the right decision. But he should have left her contact information. If he had, she could have told him about Josh, and he could have sent her some of the money he'd sent his mother. Then Piper might have been able to go to college as she'd planned. Hindsight was a harsh master.

Her Jeep still occupied the spot beside his truck. He raised his hand to knock, but decided to try the door instead. It opened. "Piper?"

Her rubber-soled shoes squeaked toward the waiting room.

"You didn't lock the door."

"There's no need. We don't keep money or drugs on hand. Everybody in Quincey knows that."

"We have strangers in town on the weekends who don't know that. Medical offices of any kind are prime targets."

She parked her hands on her hips, accentuating her narrow waist in the baggy scrubs—the waist he'd held last night. "Did you come to lecture me?"

"Preventing crime is my job." That meant watching out for Piper was his job. It wasn't personal.

Yeah, right. He wanted her. And last night he would have taken her to his place and had her every which way he could imagine if she'd let him. Self-discipline and restraint be damned.

He swallowed to ease the lust crushing his larynx. "I brought lunch."

"You didn't have to do that."

Her lack of enthusiasm nicked him like barbed wire. "I kept you after office hours. It's the least I can do."

She accepted the package with obvious reluctance. "It feels like a lot of food."

"Enough for two."

Dismay flashed in her eyes then her lips parted. His thoughts instantly detoured down the forbidden path. Last night's kiss had been more than he'd anticipated. A temptation and, in the light of day, a road strewn with IEDs.

"May sent some of Willie's fruit trifle."

"You can take yours and go. I'll be leaving soon anyway. The kittens are almost warm enough to feed."

"I'll follow you home and talk to Josh."

"Today?" The color leached from her cheeks. "Why? Are you afraid I'll coach him on what to say to you?"

"It would only be natural."

"All I'd say to him is to tell you the truth." But she focused on his badge as she said it. Not a good sign. But a mother should protect her child. He couldn't fault her for that.

"Piper, I don't want Josh to be involved any more than you do, and ruling him out as a suspect is the best place to start."

Normally, right was right and wrong was wrong. He'd never had a problem distinguishing between the two before, but when it came to Piper's son—*his* son—the usual rules didn't apply.

"Let's eat before the food gets cold."

A sigh signaled her surrender. He followed her down the hall, fighting the urge to check out her butt—and losing. Big-time.

If he were smart, this pull, his fascination with her would go nowhere. So why couldn't he turn it off? And why did every encounter with her remind him of holding her in his arms? Of being accepted, wanted and loved unconditionally.

Why did he ache to relive their past when he knew damned well that was not an option? She and Josh were better off without him.

All he had to do was get through lunch, question Josh, and then he would focus on his objective of making Quincey a safe place for his mother—and his son. To maintain that focus he would have to keep his distance from the very desirable Piper Hamilton.

Chapter Thirteen

Piper spotted her father's mud-spattered truck in the driveway and her frazzled nerves splintered a few more strands.

She glanced in the rearview mirror at the pickup shadowing her. Having Roth and her father in the house at the same time and in Josh's presence was too risky. One careless, angry outburst could reveal secrets that would destroy her son's world and could make him hate her.

She sprang from the car and raced to Roth's door even before his wheels stopped turning. She tried not to think about what had happened in this spot last night. But her body remembered, warmed, tingled.

"My father's still here. It would be better if you came back later."

"I'd rather talk to both of them now—before something else happens."

"But—"

"Piper, I'm coming in. It's up to you whether we keep this friendly or make it official business."

When he put it that way… With a sinking heart she stepped away from his truck. "I know you and my father have no fondness for each other, but for Josh's sake, please keep it civil and watch what you say."

Dread weighted every step and her clammy hand slipped on the doorknob. Roth followed her in, carrying the box of kittens he'd retrieved from her backseat. She heard voices coming from the kitchen, took a bracing breath and marched toward them.

Josh looked up, the excitement on his face the antithesis of Piper's negative mood. "Hi, Chief."

Piper's father smiled indulgently, then he realized Josh wasn't talking to him and his spine went rigid. He slowly turned, his face clamping into an unwelcoming mask.

For the first time Piper stood in the same room with all of her family and Roth. Twelve years ago he hadn't been welcome in the Hamilton household. Today wasn't much different—not with her father here scowling hard enough to curdle milk. A chainsaw couldn't have cut through the tension in the room. Sarg trotted over to say hello.

"Whatcha got in the box?" Josh asked, oblivious to the strained atmosphere.

"Kittens. I rescued them from the tree in Mr. Lowry's yard." Roth's gaze didn't waver from Josh as he said it.

"Cool. Can I see 'em?"

She didn't hear hesitancy or fear in her son's voice. That had to be a good sign, didn't it?

Roth knelt, put the box on the floor and peeled back the towel.

"Wow. They're tiny." Then worry crossed Josh's face as those brown eyes so like his father's found hers. "Will they make it, Mom?"

"You know how it goes with babies this small, Josh. We don't win every battle, but we do try our best." The dog sniffed. "Sit Sarg."

Josh rewarded the dog for following directions with a hug. "Can I keep one if they survive?"

"No," she and her mother chorused in tandem.

"Wait a minute. They're not big enough to climb a tree. Did their mother have them up there? Cats don't usually nest in trees."

Roth's gaze didn't waver. "Someone hung them in a garbage bag from one of the branches."

Josh's eyes rounded. She saw both shock and dismay in his expression. And then fear. Her heart skipped over the latter.

"You know anything about that, Josh?" Roth asked, still kneeling at eye level with her son.

"What in the hell kind of question is that?" her father barked.

Roth rose. "Lowry says he's had multiple incidents at his house and business. He believes kids are behind them."

Piper didn't know where to look—at her father, whose face and neck were turning crimson, or her son, who'd gulped and turned chalky.

Ohmigod. Both of them know something. But what?

Her father's jaw set defensively. "Just kids being kids."

"Leaving roadkill on someone's stoop is mischief, but these kittens were taken from their mother and left to suffer a slow death.

This is animal cruelty, Mr. Hamilton. So I'll ask again. Josh, have you heard anyone talking about picking on Mr. Lowry or know of a cat that recently had kittens."

"Course he hasn't," her father snapped. "And he knows that if he heard of such a plan and he didn't come forward, that could make him an accomplice."

Piper heard the warning in her father's voice. Josh paled even more.

Panic stole her breath. She fought for calm. "An accomplice? He's only eleven."

"Old enough to know right from wrong. Aren't you, Josh? That's why you'll help me now."

Roth's calm and steady voice did nothing to soothe Piper, but it worked on Josh—until he glanced at his grandfather. Josh shook his head vehemently. "I don't know anything about hurting kittens."

"But you know about kids picking on Mr. Lowry."

Josh kept shaking his head. "Nothing more than I already told you. Guys talk. Mr. Lowry creeps some of 'em out."

"I'll need their names. Then I can talk to them and rule them out."

Another quick glance at her father and Josh's lips started trembling. Piper could practically see the conflict in his eyes. He wanted to help, but he was afraid. Sarg barked and planted himself in front of Josh, clearly sensing the tension.

"Sarg needs to go outside. May I be excused, Grandma?"

"Yes, sweetie," her mother answered.

"Heel, Sarg." Josh raced for the back door with the dog at his side.

The minute the latch clicked behind them her father lurched forward until he stood chest to chest with Roth. Roth's extra six inches in height didn't appear to intimidate her father. "How dare you come in here and accuse that boy of malicious mischief."

"I'm not accusing Josh. I don't believe he did it. His reaction was too genuine. But I believe he knows—or suspects—who might be responsible. Lowry says he's reported numerous incidents to the Quincey P.D. in the past and no one has done anything to determine the culprits. Why?"

Her father's silence caused a cold knot of fear to form in Piper's stomach. The men glared at each other. She wanted to believe her father knew nothing, but after learning how he'd manipulated the facts twelve years ago, his integrity was the one thing she couldn't be sure of anymore.

"Leave things be, boy. You don't know the trouble you're stirring."

"I'm not trying to start trouble. I'm trying to stop it."

"That's rich, coming from you."

"Did you suspect Josh's involvement?"

"Listen here, you—"

Her mother, the perennial peacemaker, wedged herself between the men. "Gentlemen. Let's not say things we might regret or that might be overheard. The point is we have a problem. One that needs solving. We can't have someone going around murdering innocent kittens, Lou, and I certainly don't want Josh hanging around with boys who might do such things. Josh needs to help Roth, and he doesn't need you scaring him half to death."

Then her mother's gaze swung Piper's way. "Piper, I see a cord hanging from that box. Don't you need to plug in the heating pad?"

"Yes." But she wasn't leaving the men to duke it out—verbally or physically with nothing more than her petite mother between them. She plugged the cord into the closest outlet and set the box on a baker's rack out of Sarg's reach.

Ann Marie planted a hand on each man's chest and slowly extended her arms, forcing each to back up. "Roth, I pulled a pork roast out of the slow cooker. It's a new recipe Piper prepared this morning. Why don't you join us? And maybe we can ease the answers from Josh as we eat."

"We've already had lunch." Piper hastened to prevent him from accepting. She wanted the men separated—preferably by miles rather than feet. "Roth only needed to talk to Josh. But Josh doesn't know anything. So... we're done for now."

Roth's dark eyes drilled hers. "He knows something. He's not ready to talk yet. Thanks for the invitation, but I'll have to take a rain check."

Not if Piper had anything to say about it.

"Well, at least sit down and have a glass of iced tea. I want you to tell me how you plan to help Lou with his shooting."

Piper's head whipped around to her mother. "What?"

"Roth has offered to help your daddy learn

to shoot right-handed, and Lou is taking him up on that generous offer. Aren't you, Lou?"

Again the men's gazes dueled like gunslingers in the old Western movies her father loved. The testosterone in the air was thick enough to choke on.

"If he thinks he can help me, I'll let him try." But the tone of her father's voice was one hundred percent challenge and zero percent cooperative spirit. Him at his bullheaded best.

Her father and Roth spending time together with loaded weapons sounded like a recipe for disaster. And given the fact that she wasn't sure she could trust either of them, she had no choice but to object.

"I don't think this is a good idea. Dad has occupational therapists who work with him on his fine motor skills."

Roth's attention swung to her. "Piper, this is between your father and me."

His inflexible expression said, *Don't argue,* and something about his insistence seemed ominous. Why was he doing this? Helping his enemy wasn't something a rational man would do. "Why did no one mention this crazy idea last night?"

Her mother's hands fluttered as if she

weren't completely comfortable with the situation either. "It didn't seem important."

Not important?

"I don't want Josh anywhere near you when you're shooting."

Her father bristled. "Ain't nobody going to hurt that boy."

"Damn straight. But Piper's right. We don't need distractions. Once you're back on your game you can teach Josh about gun safety and take him hunting."

The men exchanged nods, and to Piper, seeing two men who hated each other in agreement seemed totally foreign. Then it hit her. If Roth intended to be around, why wouldn't he want to teach Josh? But she kept that question to herself.

She had more pressing issues to deal with. Having these two spending time together put her squarely in the middle, forcing her to try to protect not only her son, but each of the men who'd betrayed her.

Stonewalled.

Roth gritted his molars in frustration. Both Hamilton and Josh were withholding information. But Lou's interference had guaranteed Roth wasn't getting any answers out of Josh today.

"Walk me out, Piper."

Relief flooded her face and twisted the knife in his ribs. She couldn't wait to be rid of him.

He followed her to his truck. The wind caught her hair, blowing the strands and her scent in his direction and taking him to the days when being tangled in her hair was his favorite place to be.

Not where his head needed to go especially after last night's embrace had inflamed him to the point of not thinking straight. But at least he had sunlight working for him today instead of moonlight, stars and memories to obscure his vision.

"After that—" he nodded toward the house "—you have to admit they know something."

She hugged her middle and kept her distance. "It seems that way."

"You father is using fear tactics to intimidate the witne—Josh. I hope you know I would never do that."

"You were very good with him."

"I have to question Josh again. Away from Lou. And I don't want either of you coaching him on his responses."

"I understand. What is this about you and my father shooting together? You can't stand each other."

"Every Marine's a rifleman." She flinched, but he couldn't let that stop him. "That means if you want to stay a Marine, you learn to adapt after an injury or you get discharged. My platoon had our share of injuries and comebacks. And we all learned to shoot with our weak hand—just in case."

"But why do you want to help my father after what he did to you?"

The whole truth wasn't an option. "Your father's attitude affects my acceptance or lack thereof. If we settle the hard feelings between us, then maybe he'll quit trying to incite discord among his cronies."

"Good luck with that. He's bitter and resentful and afraid. You took his job and he's not sure he'll ever be back to normal again. He's been chief of police more than half of his life. He doesn't know how to be anything else."

Roth didn't want to feel sympathy for Hamilton, but he couldn't help it. He'd seen the same disconnect happen to coworkers—Marines and cops—when a disability took the job that defined them.

"He's served enough time to retire, but no one likes to be forced out. I'll do what I can to help him. His body and his willingness to try will determine the success or failure of the effort. I won't quit before he does."

She searched his face. "I don't understand you. Twelve years ago I thought I did. Then you left me and returned with a career history that—I can't lie—I have trouble accepting. Now this. Which are you, Roth? A killer or a kind man?"

"I'm whatever circumstances require me to be. But I swear to you, Piper, I'm not here to harm you or your family."

She stared at him, her blue eyes softening with acceptance. Everything inside him stilled. She'd looked at him the same way twelve years ago and once or twice last night. Heady, intoxicating stuff, those eyes of hers.

He raised his hand to cup her face before he realized what he was doing. Before he could pull back the soft warmth of her skin snared him and held him captive.

Her lips parted on a gasp and her dark lashes fluttered.

He instantly recalled the satin of her skin gliding against his as if he'd held her, tasted her, made love to her only yesterday. Her expanding pupils and rising color told him she'd taken the same mental journey.

Seeing her with the kittens then with Josh—she'd been protective, nurturing and determined to work miracles. All the things he'd loved about her before he'd made the mistake of leaving her.

No. Not a mistake.

Except for missing out on his son's growth and not doing his share financially, leaving Quincey had been for the best. For all of them. Piper and her son were better off away from a man who'd been raised by Seth Sterling—a man whose idea of love was not breaking any bones when he hit you. Other than his grandfather and briefly Piper, Roth didn't know any other kind of love.

Through sheer willpower he lowered his hand.

Piper had always been able to take away the ugliness of his life with her sweet smiles, her gentle touch, her sexy laugh and her belief that he was a better man than his father. Being with her had made him feel whole, complete, *normal*.

And he was far from normal. The life he'd lived, the things he'd seen and done guaranteed that. Not that he regretted a single shot he'd taken. In the same circumstances he'd still pull the trigger in each instance. Which only reinforced his point. Piper deserved a man who would nurture her the way she did her family and the animals that crossed her path.

He took a step backward before he forgot what was good for him. And her. Before he forgot his fragile promise to keep his distance and do the right thing by her.

"I'd like to talk to Josh again tomorrow."

"You can't spend part of every day with him without people talking."

Unfortunately, she made sense. "Monday then. But in the meantime, if he tells you anything about who he thinks might be responsible—"

"I'll let you know. And Roth, thanks for believing in him."

The gratitude in her eyes pulled him forward, but he caught himself midstep. He had a plan. He just had to find the fortitude to stick to it.

No matter the temptation.

"Quincey Animal Clinic. This is Piper. How may I help you?"

"Did Josh ride the bus home today?"

Roth. Piper's stomach swooped at the rumble of his deep voice in her ear. It was hard enough seeing him for the dog exchange each morning. She didn't need him calling, too.

"I thought you were picking up Josh?"

"I waited. He never came out to the car. I asked in the office, but there's not much the staff can legally tell me unless I make it official police business. I'd prefer not to do that."

Concern crept over her. "That wouldn't be good. I'll call my mother. She must have picked him up and forgotten to mention her plans."

It wasn't like her highly organized mom to let details slip, but they'd all had a lot on their minds.

"Call me if you find him first," he ordered, and disconnected, raising Piper's hackles. Josh really wasn't Roth's concern.

Piper dialed her mother. The phone dumped to voice mail. She sent a text message.

Did you pick up Josh?

While she waited for a reply she assured herself she had nothing to worry about. There was a perfectly logical explanation for Josh not being where he was supposed to be. This was a safe little town with negligible crime.

But what about the vandals? Who were they and what would they do if they thought Josh reported them?

Finally, her phone signaled an incoming message with a meow.

No. Showing a house.

Piper's pulse quickened. Josh had to be with her father. When the two of them started talking fishing they forgot everything else. She tried her father's house and his machine answered. She left a brief message. Her father didn't text and rarely remembered to turn on the cell phone he hated, yet she tried that number, as well. Again, no answer.

She crossed the waiting room to look out the door, but there was no sign of Josh on the sidewalks in either direction. Where could he be? Perhaps he'd stayed for tutoring. He'd been having problems with math, and they'd talked about him getting extra help. She grasped on to the idea and raced to call the school.

"Hi, Tina. It's Piper. Could you check to see if Josh stayed for math tutoring today?"

"He's not here, Piper. I was getting ready to call you. Josh missed all of his afternoon classes, and we don't have anyone down as having signed him out."

Apprehension squeezed Piper's throat. "Thanks, Tina. I'll see if my father picked him up."

But she was pretty certain her father would not take Josh out of school without cause. Was he trying to protect Josh from Roth's inquisition?

She disconnected. Josh had been a model student until this year. He liked school. If he had skipped again, then why? And when he was crazy about Sarg and the chief, why would he miss an opportunity to spend time with them…unless he was avoiding Roth and more questions? Did she dare call Roth or should she look for Josh herself?

If Roth was the reason Josh had left school early today, then she'd be better off looking for him by herself.

She hustled to her boss's office. "Madison, Josh skipped school this afternoon and he's missing. Do you mind if I leave early to look for him?"

"Go. Nobody else is scheduled this afternoon and I'll take the kittens home tonight."

"Thanks." Piper grabbed her purse and jacket and raced out the door. She spotted

Roth walking across the parking lot toward her and skidded to a halt. Her heart inched up her throat. He wore jeans and a long-sleeved chambray shirt. But even without the uniform he wore an air of authority that indicated he was here on official business.

Ohmigod. Had something happen to Josh?

"Is he with your mother?"

Not bad news then. Her lungs emptied. "No. Maybe my father—"

"Lou's at the gun range. Josh is not with him."

"Now I wish I'd given in and bought Josh a cell phone."

"Why would you reward him for going off the grid?"

Good point. But Roth hadn't been responsible for Josh for eleven years. He didn't understand her fear or her desperate need to hear her son's voice and know he was okay. "So that he could call me if he needed me. Josh might have gone home."

"I drove by the house. There's no sign of anyone there, and he didn't answer the door. Get in my truck. We'll look for him."

She balked, her protective instincts kicking into high gear. "I'll look. Josh is not your problem."

"He is now."

She had to figure out what was going on with her son before Roth, and possibly the law, became involved. Not that she thought Josh was in trouble, but…well, she couldn't be sure. "It's best if we split up."

He looked ready to argue then nodded. "You head east. I'll head west toward his hideout."

"Josh has a hideout?" What else did Roth know about him that she didn't? Her concern that she might be losing her son spiked.

"You didn't know he had a campsite at Deer Hunter's Creek?"

"No. I knew he liked to hike through the woods, but Quincey's safe, so I've allowed that."

"Call me if you find him."

"Roth, did you consider that he might be avoiding you?"

"Yes. And that raises the question, why?"

"What if those kids, the vandals—"

"Their acts have been nonviolent and non-confrontational to this point."

To this point. Piper turned and stumbled to her Jeep feeling sick to her stomach with worry. She drove home by rote and wandered through the house. There were no signs that

Josh had been there since leaving for school this morning.

She stood in his bedroom and tried not to panic over her missing little boy. Was he hurt somewhere? Did he need her? Or was he just playing hooky? She prayed for the latter even though that meant she'd have to punish him.

She returned to her car and headed in the direction Roth had ordered. Apparently her son had shared things with Roth that he hadn't shared with her. Unfortunately, that meant she had to count on Roth to help her find Josh.

But protecting her son from outside threats was her job, and right now, Roth was the biggest threat of all.

Frustrated at finding no sign of Josh near the bridge, Roth followed a hunch and drove to his apartment. Had Josh decided to confess what he knew and needed to do so out of sight?

Concern had replaced irritation. Roth didn't want to consider foul play. The cat incident had been an escalation from the destruction of property. Confrontational violence would be an illogical leap. For Josh's sake he hoped that would not be the case.

Sarg picked up Roth's agitation and whimpered in the backseat.

"We'll find him, boy."

Roth parked and strode toward his place. His steps slowed when he spotted Doyle standing in the courtyard of the apartment complex with a disgusted expression on his face. Sarg stopped beside Roth and sniffed the air. His fur-covered body stiffened with alertness, but his tail wagged—a sure sign Josh was nearby.

Muscles Roth didn't realize had kinked relaxed. He surveyed the scene. The terra-cotta flowerpots had been tipped over, scattering dirt and plants across the concrete surrounding the pool. Patio furniture sat on the pool bottom.

Somebody had thrown one hell of a tantrum. Josh? If so, why?

The apartment manager looked up. "Should I call this in since you're off duty? Or do you want to handle it?"

"I'm here. I have it. Any other damage?"

"Haven't found anything else yet."

"Know who did it?"

"Didn't see anyone and none of the other tenants are home."

No witnesses.

"Take a look around. Make a list of what you find then I'll write up the report. Let me put Sarg inside."

"You know I said no dogs."

"This is temporary—an hour at the most. I'll take him to the Hamiltons' when we're done. Piper's taking care of him until his owners are located."

Roth noted a footprint on his door as he unlocked his new dead bolt. A sneaker print by the looks of it. One similar in shape and size to the impressions at Josh's camp. Sarg alerted, his nose to the scuff, his tail swinging faster. The dog was becoming as attached as the boy.

Roth pushed open his door and scanned for signs of entry but found none. Everything was as he'd left it. He unsnapped the dog's leash. Sarg bolted for the terrace door beyond the dining room table and *bingo*. Josh. The kid sat on the deck with his knees drawn to his chin and his head down, arms hugging his legs. He hadn't spotted Roth yet.

At the click of the lock his blond head popped up and the eyes so like Roth's lifted. The red rims spelled trouble. But what kind and how much? What had led Josh to skip school and destroy the courtyard? Roth scanned for injuries and found none.

"Sit, Sarg. Stay." Roth opened the sliding door. Josh shot to his feet, his face a tangle of emotions from anger to fear, his body language defensive. He barely glanced at the mutt—a sure sign of distress.

Roth tilted his head toward the disaster. "That your handiwork out there?"

"What if it is?"

"Get in here."

Full of attitude, Josh tromped inside. Sarg stayed put, but his feet practically danced in place in his eagerness to greet Josh.

"What provoked your tantrum?"

"You kissed my mom."

Guilty. He'd never dated women with children, making this unknown and potentially hazardous territory.

"That wasn't her first kiss and it won't be her last. You can't vandalize property every time some guy takes a liking to her."

"Yeah, well, I thought it was cool and that maybe you and my mom might get together. But when I told the guys at school about it they said it's about time and that—" The kid's chin hiked up. "They said you're my dad."

Oh, hell. Roth had been in town only

twelve days and already the spit had hit the fan. He'd promised Piper he wouldn't reveal her secret. But what choice did he have? He wouldn't lie to the boy.

"Are you?"

"Yes, Josh, I am."

"You lied. And Mom lied. Everybody lied."

He had to hose down Josh's building hysteria. "Your mom had good reason."

"There's never a good reason to lie."

"Ninety-nine percent of the time I'd agree with you. But Piper wanted you to have a father you could be proud of and I wasn't it."

Josh blinked, his eyes filling with confusion. A little of his aggression deflated. "Whadaya mean? You were a Marine and a SWAT guy, and now you're the chief of police."

Stalling while he gathered his thoughts and plotted the best approach, Roth fixed Sarg a bowl of water and motioned the dog into the kitchen, then he poured two glasses of iced tea. He had to come clean, but he'd minimize collateral damage as best he could.

He passed Josh a drink. "Saturday night you asked me about my father. I told you he used to beat my mother and me, often for no reason that we could ascertain and that he had a temper—one he couldn't control. Especially when he was drunk.

"When I was fifteen he shot and killed your Grandfather Lou's brother when your uncle responded to a domestic violence call."

"Grandma told me that."

"But she didn't tell you that the day they handcuffed my father and carried him away was one of the happiest days of my life to that point because it meant the beatings would stop. I could take 'em. I probably even earned some of them. But my mother never did anything to deserve the abuse. Her only sin was getting pregnant by the man she loved. My grandfather forced them to get married. That's what you did back then.

"I loved your mom, Josh. But when she told me she was pregnant…" Swamped with regret, he looked at the son he hadn't wanted to have. "I was terrified—"

"*You* were scared?"

"Yeah, this Marine was terrified that history would repeat itself, and that your mom and I would be forced to get married, and that I'd turn against her like my father had my mother. So I took the coward's way out.

I told your mother I didn't want to be a dad, and I gave her money to end the pregnancy."

Josh's eyes rounded. "You didn't want me to be born?"

The pain in the kid's voice lashed Roth. "It wasn't about you, Josh. It was about me. I was afraid I'd hurt your mother. And you. Nobody deserves that. Your mom was the brave one. She threw my money in my face and told me she didn't want or need me in her life if I felt that way."

He deliberately left out the part about her swearing she'd never have white trash's baby. If the boy was lucky, the stench of Seth Sterling would never touch him.

"I thought I was doing the right thing for your mom and me. Turns out I was only doing the selfish thing for me."

"But you said Grandpa forced you to leave town."

If he were a vengeful person, this would be his opportunity. But he wasn't interested in taking someone else down to improve his own self-image.

Roth wasn't fond of Lou, especially after the frigid treatment on the range today, but Josh loved his grandfather, and Roth refused to undermine that relationship. He selected his words carefully.

"I barely graduated high school. Studying wasn't my thing. And I didn't have any money. I scraped by working in the garage my father used to run before he went to prison. My mom and I lived off the vegetables from her garden and the game I shot. I would never have earned enough to take care of your mom and you the way you deserved.

"Your grandfather knew I was headed down a bad road and hanging out with the wrong crowd. He didn't know about you when he encouraged me to enlist and let the Marines make a man of me. I signed up believing that your mom wouldn't have you. I don't regret joining the Corps. But I do regret turning my back on your mother and you and not following up to make sure she was okay."

"But my mom said my dad lived in Florida and he rode a motorcycle."

"She was trying to protect you from knowing what a loser I was."

"But...you're not a loser now. You're the chief."

"Through sheer hard work. I have my father's temper, and I've spent most of my life fighting to overcome it. From the looks of the mess outside, you've inherited the Sterling temper, too. You're going to have to learn to control it, Josh. If you don't, it will control you and destroy your life. Do you understand me, son?"

"Yessir."

"Damaging other people's property never fixes your problems. It only creates more trouble."

"But you weren't here. And I was so mad." Josh hung his head. "I was stupid."

Roth put his hand on Josh's shoulder wishing he could take away the kid's pain. But he couldn't. Facts were facts. And Josh had a tough road ahead.

"You weren't stupid. You were angry and felt betrayed—two valid emotions. How you dealt with those emotions is the problem.

"We all make mistakes. Abandoning you and your mom was my biggest one. What counts is whether or not you learn from your bad decisions and grow into a better and stronger person because of them."

"You came to Quincey. For me? For us?"

He hated to crush the boy's hope. "I'm sorry but no. I came back to look after my mother. My father's getting out of prison soon, and I'm afraid he'll hurt her again. I didn't know about you until I found you at the creek and you told me you were Piper's son. But you can't blame your mom for that. She was doing what was best for you."

"By lying."

"By protecting you the only way she knew how."

Josh stubbed his toe on the hardwood floor. "I don't know. Maybe."

"There's no maybe about it. She's put you first since the day she learned about you. You need to remember that she had options, options that were a lot easier than being a single mother. But she chose to have you."

Worried eyes sought Roth's. "Do you think she's sorry she did?"

Roth had wondered the same thing about his mother too many times to count. If he hadn't come along, she wouldn't have been tied to a beast. For some damned reason a knot clogged his throat. It took a couple of gulps to clear it.

"I know your mom's not sorry. She told me she could never regret having you. If you don't believe me, ask her.

"But first we need to take care of that mess." Roth jabbed a thumb toward the patio.

"Doyle has every right to charge you with vandalism. That could get you a juvenile record that would close a lot of doors for you down the road, especially military careers. I'm lucky your grandfather never pressed charges against me when I pulled stunts like this, or I'd have never been a Marine and I wouldn't be a cop now."

"You did stuff like this?"

"This and the kind of petty vandalism your friends are doing. Not the animal cruelty. And I'm not proud of my actions now. I'm betting you aren't either."

"No. So why'd you do it?"

Good question. "Like you, I had a lot of anger because nobody had helped my mom and me. When I look back I realize I was hell-bent on living down to everyone's expectations."

"Nobody tried to help?"

Gus had tried. But Roth had tuned out his grandfather's friend. "One man did. And I was so afraid of disappointing him that I did exactly that. It wasn't until I reached the Marine Corps and one of my drill sergeants screamed in my face, 'If you see yourself as a failure, you will become one,' that I realized I had to change my attitude."

"And you did?"

"I did. It didn't hurt that I was motivated by a strong desire to survive my enlistment." He pushed to his feet. "So what do you say we go out there and do what we can to minimize the collateral damage here?"

"How?"

"First, you're going to apologize to Doyle. You'll admit you messed up and offer to fix it. If you're lucky, he'll let you work off your debt instead of having me write the report."

Josh paled. "A police report?"

"Yes. However this shakes out, I'll stand by you, Josh. But you have to promise me no more skipping. No more tantrums. Control that temper. Or I'll cut you from the team."

"Yessir." Josh's bottom lip quivered. "You probably wish I wasn't your son now."

The knot returned to Roth's throat—only thicker than before. How many times had his father told him he wished Roth had never been born? Roth would never do that to a kid.

He'd never wanted to be a father, never pictured himself in this role. But he wouldn't want to be anything or anywhere else right now. He couldn't let Josh believe he was a mistake that had ruined lives.

Before he realized what he was doing he

crushed Josh against his chest and clapped the boy on the back. After the brief hug he put the boy from him.

"I'd never wish that. Say hello to Sarg then get started making amends."

Josh moved to the dog's side then lifted his face, his expression hesitant. "You're going to tell my mom?"

"I have to. From here on out we need nothing but honesty between us. But I won't call her until after you've talked to Doyle. Go on. I have your back."

Josh paused with his hand on the knob. "You loved my mom when you made me. Do you love her now?"

Roth's tongue stuck to the roof of his mouth. He searched for an appropriate answer and came up empty. He still felt something for Piper. Something strong and undeniable. Something he couldn't control. But love?

No. He'd never let himself love anyone again.

"We're getting to know each other again. Don't get your hopes up. I'm still my father's son."

"And I'm yours."

That was the problem. Some people weren't meant to be parents. Roth was convinced he was one of them. But this time he couldn't—wouldn't—run away.

See yourself as a failure and you will become one.

Not this time.

"Yes. You are. Son."

Chapter Fourteen

He's at my apartment. We'll talk when you get here.

Roth's terse words rang in Piper's head as she hustled up the sidewalk. Her insides were a tornado of fear, relief and unanswered questions. Roth hadn't offered any details before he'd disconnected, cutting her off midsentence.

Was Josh okay? Why had he skipped school? Why had he gone to Roth's?

She spotted Josh with a broom and a dustpan tackling the dark dirt strewn all over the pool area and her steps slowed as relief made her dizzy. He wasn't hurt.

He glanced up, briefly meeting her gaze, then he bowed his head and resumed scooping and sweeping, his cheeks darkening so much she could see the flush from thirty feet away.

Confused, she opened her mouth to question him, to scold him for scaring her, to tell him she was glad he was all right, but a firm grip on her upper arm silenced her. Roth's hand. She knew it, by her body's shaken soda reaction, even before she turned and found him towering over her.

"Wait at my place until he's done."

"But what—"

"I'll explain. Inside." His hand skimmed down her arm and his fingers laced through hers. Surprised by the intimate gesture, she tugged futilely. His grasp probably looked casual to an observer. To Josh. But she couldn't escape.

He towed her toward his apartment, his palm scorching hers and resurrecting memories of walking hand in hand with him everywhere they'd gone that long-ago summer.

She dug in her heels outside his door and scanned the patio area trying to figure out what was wrong with this picture besides Josh with a broom. The furniture was missing. She caught a glimpse of the white legs sticking up from the bottom of the pool. What had happened?

"I want to talk to my son."

"Later."

"But—"

"Piper, trust me on this one."

Trust him. A tall order.

Roth propelled her inside and closed the door, sealing her into his lair. His scent surrounded her, distracted her. Then his dark gaze met hers and the seriousness there filled her with trepidation.

"Josh knows."

"Knows what?" she asked even though she suspected her worst nightmare had come to pass.

"That I'm his father."

It took a moment to catch her breath. "Why did you tell him? You promised—"

"The kids at school told him. Apparently, the grapevine is as efficient and vicious as always."

Panic joined the emotional cocktail whirling inside her. "And he came to you?"

"For clarification. Yes. And when I wasn't at home his temper got the better of him. He wrecked the pool area."

Her heart sank, weighted by a barrage of

new worries. Her father was a cop. She knew how this worked. "Is Doyle pressing charges?"

"No. I encouraged him and Josh to work out a deal. Josh will clean up today's mess, and he'll do a little extra work around here on weekends for the next month. If he meets those criteria, then Doyle won't take legal action."

She pressed her icy fingers to her forehead. "Tantrums are not Josh's style."

"They're the Sterling style, which proves he's not just your son, Piper. He's mine, too."

She didn't welcome the new ownership in his tone. "But coming to you instead of me..." Her knees buckled. She landed the sofa. "He must hate me."

"I doubt it. I explained."

Alarm crawled across her skin, raising the fine hairs. "What *exactly* did you tell him?"

"That twelve years ago I wasn't smart enough to know a good thing when I had it, and that you made up the story about his dad to keep him from knowing what a selfish bastard his real father was."

Shocked, she stared at Roth. "What about my father's role in your departure?"

"I told him Lou offered me an opportunity to make something of myself and I took it."

"Why would you accept all the blame?"

"Because I'm the one who ran from my responsibilities."

Who was this man? Was he for real? She didn't want him to take responsibility. She wanted him to continue being the inconsiderate jerk who had shattered her heart and left her in dire straits. It made it easier to keep her distance and easier to be certain Josh did not need him in his life.

Roth sat beside her, causing the sofa cushion to tilt her in his direction. The proximity made her jittery and tingly. She could not handle raging hormones right now.

"Josh's actions remind me a lot of myself at his age. I was full of rage. Rage at my father for being a sadistic prick. Rage at my mother for putting up with him and not moving us to safety. Rage at myself for not being able to protect her. I see that volatile emotion in Josh, and I want to help him conquer it or to at least channel it into something less destructive."

He sounded sincere. And that scared her. "To do that you'd have to become a long-term, if not permanent, part of his life."

Roth glanced toward the window where she could see Josh righting another planter then his attention returned to her, his face stamped with resolution. "I know. And I will. Count on it."

This was the response she'd yearned for when she'd told him of her pregnancy. Hope flickered to life.

No. No. No. Roth had let her down before and she did not want Josh to experience that pain, disillusionment and disappointment.

What if Roth had changed? What if he could be there for Josh? And for her?

But what about his sniper years? The violence—violence he'd admitted was in his blood.

She didn't know what to believe, and trusting what she saw now and ignoring her fears of what he might be wouldn't be easy.

The door burst open and Josh entered with shame and remorse written all over his face. "I'm sorry, Mom. I screwed up."

She rose and pulled him close. "Yes. You did. But, Josh, I love you even when you make mistakes, and I will be here for you to help you work them out."

He hugged her then quickly stepped away as if embarrassed by the action—another sign she was losing her cuddly little boy to his pre-teen independence. "That's what the chief—*Dad* said."

Dad. Her heart lurched. As Roth had said, Josh wasn't only hers anymore. And she wasn't sure she was ready to share her son. But did she have a choice? Not without a fight that would put Josh in the middle—the way her parents' arguments had her.

She gathered her shattered composure and brushed Josh's hair off his forehead. "I'm sorry that you had to learn about Roth from the boys at school."

"It's okay. Dad explained that you made up the other story to protect me. And Dad helped me work out a deal with Mr. Doyle so he wouldn't press charges and I won't have a juvenile record."

Roth had done that? Her eyes sought his and he gave an almost imperceptible nod. "Thank you."

Roth rose. "No problem. But it's time to get Sarg out of here before Doyle loses his co-operative mood. And, Josh, remember what I said."

"Yessir. No more skipping or tantrums or you'll cut me from the baseball team."

Another surprise. Roth was handling the situation like a real parent.

It was time she quit fighting the inevitable

and let Roth into their lives. But that didn't mean she wouldn't watch him like a hawk.

Dad.

The word ricocheted around the interior of Roth's skull as he stared at his laptop screen. He couldn't concentrate on the deputies' schedules, looking for similarities between the vandalism reports he'd dug up or any of the other tasks he'd attempted since Piper and Josh had left three hours, twenty-one minutes ago. Not that he'd been watching the clock.

It wasn't like him to be restless or unfocused. Admitting defeat, he pushed away from his desk and headed to the kitchen to scrounge up dinner. At times like this he almost wished he drank. But the answers he needed wouldn't be found floating in a bottle of eighty-proof liquor.

Dad.

Each time Josh had uttered the word it had hit Roth like a Taser, robbing him of strength and breath and words.

Dad.

The heavy responsibilities attached to that single syllable daunted him like no other assignment he'd ever had. He was about to embark on the most important mission of his life. One he could not fail. He would rise to the challenge. Somehow. He'd traversed uncharted territory before. He could do it again.

Expect success if you want to achieve success.

Oohrah.

A knock provided a welcome distraction. He about-faced and checked the peephole. Piper. Why had she come back?

"Only one way to find out," he muttered and opened the door.

A blue canvas rectangle dangled from her fingertips and she gave a tentative, rueful smile. "I come bearing gifts and an apology."

"For?"

"For trying to limit your contact with Josh. You obviously know how to handle him. Making him work for the man he'd wronged is the perfect punishment. But how did you know? It's taken me years of parenting to figure out what to do and I'm still wrong sometimes. A lot of the time actually."

"The men in my squad often faced stressful situations that brought out their worst behavior. A Staff Sergeant's primary duty is discipline. That means learning to diffuse the emotions and channel them into something more productive, or make sure the penalty fits the infraction."

For the first time she didn't grimace when he mentioned his military career. Progress, he supposed.

"I guess I never saw you as doing anything but…stalking your prey."

"That was only a small part of my job, and for most of my time-in-service that wasn't my assignment."

"I brought dinner as a thank-you for today." She glanced past him. "Unless another woman has beat me to it."

He stepped out of the way, his lips twitching over the sharp edge of her voice. Was she jealous? Did he want her to be? His smile faded when he realized the answer was affirmative.

"Not tonight. Come in."

She did, but her uneasiness couldn't be missed. "It's just fried chicken, pecan green beans and garlic-cheddar biscuits."

"You remembered my favorites. Are you joining me?"

"I ate with Josh."

"Stay while I eat?" Not wise. But he needed the distraction of her company.

"I…" Her gaze bounced around the room.

"Okay. Mom has things under control at the house."

Her hesitancy reminded him of the old Piper, a girl who'd been alternately tentative and eager, shy and bold. A fascinating contradiction.

He led the way to the kitchen. Piper set the carryall on the counter and unzipped it. Delicious aromas filled his sinuses, making his stomach growl. He wasted no time fixing his plate then poured two glasses of iced tea and headed for the table.

"I often thought about the dinners you used to bring me, when I was having mess hall meals and MREs." He sank his teeth through the crispy skin of a chicken breast and juice ran down his chin. He mopped the trickle, chewed, swallowed.

If he was to succeed with his current assignment, he needed to be briefed. "Tell me about Josh."

"He has your mechanical ability. There's nothing he won't take apart or try to fix." The half amused, half exasperated way she said it, combined with a sassy look from beneath her lashes, was too sexy for words. One hunger faded, another reared its head. He intended to ignore the dangerous one.

"He's very good with his hands."

Gulp. She used to say the same thing about Roth, and he recalled where he'd had his hands when she'd said those words in the past. Swigging his tea, he tried to concentrate on the present rather than those steamy nights, but he couldn't prevent the heat from gathering in his groin.

He cleared his throat. "My mechanical skills served me well. They earned me promotions and a better pay grade more than once."

"It earns Josh a lot of time-outs. He hasn't mastered the art of putting things back together or keeping track of all the parts yet."

The irresistible curve of her lips hit him in the solar plexus. He closed his eyes and chewed, struggling to think of anything besides how good that smile had always made him feel.

Memories pushed themselves forward, of picnics when his only appetite had been for her. Back then he'd forced himself to eat whatever food she'd brought knowing the meal would end with both of them naked and other hungers being satisfied. Very satisfied.

Not where his mind needed to go.

Bite. Chew. Swallow. He ate by rote and didn't come up for air until his plate was empty. "Your mother's cooking is better than I recalled."

Her cheeks pinked. "That's not my mom's recipe. It's mine. Josh and I cooked tonight. We like to spice things up a bit."

"'S good."

Their gazes met and held and the memory of those summer nights lurked in her eyes. He couldn't look away. Then her lips parted. She flattened her palms on the table and straight-armed to standing. "I should go."

He commanded his legs to lift him, and again their eyes met. Sexual tension hung like dense smoke in the air, clogging his lungs.

The standoff lasted for several heart-pounding moments then Piper exploded into action, grabbing his empty plate and her glass and hustling to the kitchen. She deposited both in the sink then opened his cabinets until she found a clean plate onto which she piled the leftovers.

She moved so quickly her actions were a frantic blur, leaving no question that she knew where his mind had gone—and hers wasn't far behind. Hell, the image was so vivid he could practically feel the cool sheets against his overheated skin.

He touched her shoulder with the sole intention of asking her to calm down before she drove. She spun so quickly a strand of hair flew through the air and clung to her bottom lip.

He hooked the satiny lock and tucked it behind her ear before he could curb the reckless action. He had himself completely under control until his fingertip glided across her silky skin. She gasped and her eyes widened. The desire in the blue depths hit him hard like a pugil stick to the gut.

He ordered himself to stop even as he leaned over her, lowering his mouth to hers. But he didn't. Couldn't. With every fiber of his being he fought to slow things down and not scare her off with the strength of his need.

He sipped from her soft lips instead of devouring them, stroked her tongue with his instead of plunging deep, and caressed her with open hands rather than fisting his fingers in her hair, her clothes. But gentle and slow wasn't enough.

Calling on his shaking reserves he tried to pull back. Admitting Josh would be a permanent part of his life had been bomb blast enough. Roth didn't need to complicate things by making love to Piper.

But try as he might, he couldn't stop mapping her warm curves with his palms or re-acquainting himself with her sweet mouth.

Familiar. But different. Same desire, but exponentially more potent, as if denying it for years had incubated and strengthened her hold on him.

She pressed her hands to his chest. He knew he should let her go. Yet he bent over her, contracting his arms around her waist until her body contours molded his.

"Roth—" Her nose nudged his. "We—" Sip. "Really—" She nipped his bottom lip. "Shouldn't—" Her tongue erased the sting. "Do—" Her mouth brushed butterfly-light across his. "This—"

Knowing she was fighting and failing to resist the desire as hard as he was only magnified her effect on him. He knew that unless someone shot him dead where he stood he wouldn't let her leave before he sated his craving for her.

Use him.

Madison's ludicrous idea suddenly made perfect sense. Roth's kiss, his touch felt so deliciously sensual. So right. How could it be wrong?

It had been aeons since Piper had felt like

a desirable woman, since she'd occupied a space steeped in pleasure this intense. But Roth had taken her there.

The smart thing to do would be to leave and not get physical. His past made her uncomfortable and she was sure he'd abandon her again. But the present hunger overrode those concerns.

When he swept her off her feet and carried her to his bedroom she didn't object. She clung tighter, immersing herself in him and blocking out every thought, every doubt, every fear. She was a mature thirty-year-old. She could handle an affair.

He set her down beside his bed. The only light streamed through from the den, but it was enough to see his chest's rapid rise and fall, the sexual tension in his narrowed eyes, the flare of his nostrils.

Then he reached for her again. Each caress, each kiss, each of their harsh breaths became more frantic. She drank it all in, licking up the heady hunger. He stripped her shirt over her head and pushed down her jeans. Cool air bathed her skin.

She kicked her pants aside while reaching for his buttons. Her fingers fumbled at first, complicating the simple task, then his shirt pooled on top of hers and she saw his chest for the first time since he'd left Quincey. *Left her.* She pushed the twinge of misgivings aside. That was then. This was now. And now she wasn't expecting forever.

Muscles rippled where he'd once been whipcord lean. He had enough extra bumps and bulges to make her head swim with a need to glide her fingers over each one. But she didn't know where to start. Instead, she focused on uncovering the rest of him.

His jeans, specifically the thick ridge beneath them, caught her attention. She traced the hard line with her fingertips, earning a growl. Behind the top button his skin was hot and taut against her knuckles. The button and zipper gave way to more supple skin streaked with a thin line of dark hair.

She slipped a finger behind the waistband of his briefs and his abdominal muscles contracted. Hot hands cupped her shoulders, urging her to sit on the mattress, then he stepped out of reach and finished disrobing.

He straightened, displaying his perfect body and full arousal. She licked her lips in anticipation and curled her fingers into the bedspread. He closed the distance between them, palmed open her thighs and positioned himself close enough for her to touch his pectorals, to caress, to lick his nipples as she traced the indentions marking each of his stomach muscles.

He shuddered and laced his fingers through hers and carrying them above her as he eased her back onto the cool fabric. His mouth covered hers, seizing, taking, demanding a response from her.

Heat built deep in her core, making her yearn for relief. She wiggled beneath him but couldn't budge his solid weight, so she wound her legs around his hips. She wanted to urge him to hurry and yet she wanted him to linger over each delicious kiss and caress. She wanted. She wanted. She *wanted*. Him. Now.

His penis rested against her mound. She lifted and lowered her hips, caressing him through her panties the only way she could when he held her hands captive. The tantalizing stroke of his smooth shaft sent flares of arousal arcing through her.

He tore his mouth away and put a few inches between them, then trailed a string of featherlight kisses down her neck and across her collarbone to the edge of her bra, where his tongue took over. He marked a damp trail, then lifted his head and blew on it, making her nipples tighten and push against the lace.

He captured one peak gently between his teeth then tugged and suckled until her insides tangled. The fabric frustrated her. She wanted his mouth on her skin. She struggled to free her hands and remove her lingerie, but he held fast and continued the torment as if they had all night. The way he used to.

Those memories buzzed along her nerve endings. Then he moved to the neglected side and started the torment all over again.

"Roth, I need to touch you, too."

He held her gaze then finally released her hands. Before she could reach for him he flicked open the front hook of her bra and cupped her in his slightly rough palms. He rolled her nipples exactly the way she liked, and she lost herself in the sensations, the tightening twist of desire, the needy clench of her womb.

And then his mouth replaced his hands. Hot and wet, his tongue glided over her. The scrape of his teeth made her breath hitch. She squeezed her legs around him, pushing her center against his hard flesh.

He reared back and with one quick move stripped off her panties. He paused, his eyes raking over her, lingering on her belly. With one fingertip he traced a line that gleamed silver. A stretch mark.

Her desire waned. She tried to push his hand aside, but he wouldn't budge. "Don't."

"Are these from carrying Josh?" He touched another.

Was that awe in his voice? Not revulsion? "Yes. He was a big baby and ten days late."

Roth exhaled, his warm breath sweeping her abdomen. "I should have been there. For you. For him."

He couldn't have said anything more perfect. She cupped his face. "You're here now."

He dusted the blemish with his lips, then moved on to the next and the next, bestowing kisses across her panty line then lower. Her body stilled in anticipation, her muscles tensing for breathless seconds. Waiting. Waiting.

He massaged her thighs, easing them open and stroking the hypersensitive flesh from her knees upward. Then his mouth found her center. She jolted at the intensity, as with each flick of his tongue he sent white-hot flashes of pleasure through her.

He knew exactly how and where to touch her. Of course, he'd been the one to teach her what she liked, to show her how to make her body and his sing. Lying in a bed with him for the first time, she wasn't distracted by birdsong or animals in the woods, and she didn't have to worry about being seen by passersby or discovered by her father.

The lack of distraction allowed her to surrender to the magic he created. At least, she told herself that was why her response to him now was so much more powerful than before.

Release neared, coming fast—too fast. She bit her lip to stifle a whimper but it escaped as orgasm burst through her in uncontainable, uncontrollable spasms of ecstasy.

Roth transferred his caresses to her hipbone then he nibbled the inside of her thigh, giving her a moment to compose herself. She'd barely recovered when he renewed his passionate assault on her senses.

Sweat beaded on her skin like dew, and shooting stars streaked through her veins. She dug her fingers into his shoulders, relishing every second of his attention until it was more than she could bear. Another climax gathered, but she wanted more this time. She needed Roth deep inside her.

She ran her hand across the top of his head. His spiky short hair tickled her palm, arousing her even more. She cupped his chin and lifted him away from his intimate caress. "I need you. Inside me."

His eyes burned into hers as he ascended her body, pausing only to grab a condom from the nightstand drawer. Then he was in her arms, his chest gliding erotically against her breasts. She reached for him, but he caught her hands, planted a tongue-swirling kiss in each palm before releasing her, then his arousal nudged her. She lifted her hips and he drove inside.

He fit perfectly, filling her, stretching her. He found a rhythm, one she instantly recognized and matched. It was as if they'd never been apart. Each movement magnified the heat and tension coiling in her.

He buried his face against her neck. "You feel so damned good, babe."

Babe. The single syllable vibrated over each of her nerve endings. She caressed his back, his buttocks, learning his mature shape. The friction of her palms across his skin stimulated her right back to the edge.

"Roth," she gasped as his heavy thrusts pushed her across the threshold. Her body bucked as wave after wave of pleasure slammed through it.

He bowed his spine, his neck tendons

straining and his tempo quickening. A moan poured from her and his groan joined hers. Moments later the room went silent except for the sound of the breaths and the pounding of her heart.

She looked at the man she'd once loved more than anyone and without the haze of desire to cloud her thinking, misgivings cooled her skin. She couldn't do it—have an affair and not want more, surrender her body and not her soul. She should end this before it was too late.

Who was she kidding? It was already too late. She was falling for him all over again. For the man who rescued dogs and kittens, who took time for her father and her son.

For the man whose past scared her spitless.

Chapter Fifteen

Roth jolted awake but didn't move. A Marine never gave away his position.

It took a few seconds to figure out where he was—Quincey—and why he'd slept like the dead. Piper. Her scent combined with the aroma of their lovemaking filled his nostrils.

A whisper of sound to his left made him turn his head. Light from the den revealed her slipping off the bed.

"Where are you going?"

"Home. I can't have my car parked in front of your apartment any longer." Avoiding eye contact, she bent to scoop up her clothing.

He turned on the lamp. She snapped upright, clutching her shirt to her magnificent breasts. Damn. Was that a hickey on the left one? He hadn't meant to be rough. But she got to him and he'd lost control. Not good since he prided himself on controlling even his most basic urges.

The fact he couldn't around her should be enough to make him run. But, no. He wanted to be a part of Josh's life. Just not here.

"It's a little late to get shy on me, babe."

"Roth, I didn't come here for this. I meant to—" She ducked her head and her hair concealed her face. "We never—" She squared her shoulders and met his gaze. "I came over to discuss how we'll handle everyone learning you're Josh's father. But I got…sidetracked. If the boys at school are taunting Josh, they're only repeating what they've heard at home. The gossips will be vicious."

Her words deep-sixed his mood. He rose from the mattress. She stood inches away and, after a slow head-to-toe look, averted her gaze from his nakedness.

The urge to drag her into his arms sand-bagged him. "Tell them the truth. I can take the heat. I've faced worse."

Worry clouded her eyes and stilled her frantic attempt to untangle her panties. "I don't want to think about your job or you in danger."

He snatched the twisted fabric from her hands, turned the garment right side out and held it for her. She braced her hand on his shoulder and lifted one leg then the other. Her touch made a certain part of his anatomy salute at the memory of those legs wrapped around him.

"I was a Marine, Piper. Danger's part of the job description. First in. Last to leave."

She closed her eyes and swallowed, blindly yanking the stretchy fabric from his fingers and into place.

"But that's past. I'm here now. Where I need to be. For Josh. For you. I have your back." For as long as it took to complete this mission. The mission of being a father.

"It's not just you, Roth. It's my parents. It's me. We've all lied."

"Stick to my version of the truth—what I told Josh."

"I don't know if that will be enough."

"We'll make it be enough."

"Tomorrow. We'll talk and we'll figure this out. Tonight... I have to go."

He wanted her to stay. The realization shocked him. Worse, he wanted to pull her back into bed and sleep with her in his arms. Oh, yeah, he wanted more incredible sex first, but afterward he wanted to sleep with her hair draped across his shoulder and her sweet body curved into his side, with her fragrance filling his lungs.

He couldn't remember the last time he'd slept as deeply as he had in—he glanced at the clock. Had it been only an hour? But given the way she was edging toward the door he'd bet he wouldn't persuade her to stay for either sex or sleep.

In fact, she showed signs of regretting what had happened. The idea stung like a wasp. He was the one who should be having regrets. He'd promised not to love her and leave her again. Yet he'd set himself up to do exactly that.

The situation was like discovering he was in the middle of a minefield. Dangerous to go back. Dangerous to move forward. Resigned to picking his way step by step through this relationship, he dragged on his jeans.

"I'm pulling a twelve-hour shift tomorrow. I might be able to meet you for lunch, but there's no guarantee I won't get called away."

"You're not going to make baseball practice?"

"I'll be there. I'll call about lunch."

She nodded and turned her back to shrug on her bra. He watched every move in the dresser mirror. She had great breasts. Fuller than before. Before Josh. And her hips might be a little rounder. The curves looked good on her. His fingers itched to caress her butt.

Her eyes lifted and met his reflection. She made as if to cover herself, then lowered her arms, fisting her hands by her sides. She looked so sexy in her plain white panties and bra.

"I'm not sure tonight was...wise, Roth."

"It was inevitable. The chemistry we share is practically nuclear."

She finished dressing in silence, then stood, shifting on her feet, her anxiety as easy to read as the face of his watch. "Where does this leave us?"

Damned if he knew. He was used to having a tight rein on his life, but it held too many variables now. His father's pending release. His mother's safety. Josh. Piper. The townsfolk.

For the first time since before he'd left Quincey he had no idea where his life was going or what the future held.

"Let's take it one day at a time and find out."

He could tell his answer had disappointed

her. But he couldn't offer more. Not now. Maybe never. Because no matter what else changed, one thing remained constant. He was his father's son.

And even though she'd fallen for him twelve years ago despite his family, she'd never come face-to-face with the evil spawn who'd fathered him. Meeting Seth would likely kill any tender feelings.

She finger-combed her hair. "We'll have to be discreet. For Josh's sake I'd really rather not have everyone talking about us."

"Done."

"I have to go." She gathered her things and walked out. Without a backward glance. Without a goodbye kiss.

Letting her go was one of the hardest things he'd ever done—even harder than walking away from her the first time. But it was the right thing to do.

Piper tried to hide her apprehension from Josh as they drove toward the park for practice. He'd be on the field. But she'd be stuck in the stands with the parents she'd been lying to for almost a decade. She'd rather not have angst over that.

"How was school today?"

"Okay. The guys quit bugging me when I told them the chief, the coach, was my dad."

She would have given anything to spare him those awkward moments. "Have they been bugging you?"

He shrugged. "A little. Thanks for having me, Mom."

Where had that come from? "You're welcome?"

"Dad said you had easier choices than being a single mom. And you chose to have me. So thanks."

Dad would take some getting used to.

She reached over to touch Josh's cheek then remembered how much he hated that now and tugged the bill of his ball cap instead. "I wouldn't have it any other way. You're the best thing that's ever happened to me, Josh."

He smiled. "Cool. Do you think you and the chief will get married and have more kids?"

Shocked by the question, she swerved a bit on the road. "Josh, please don't say things like that. Roth and I are not even dating." Or were they? They'd had sex. Stellar, I've-seen-stars sex. But were they a couple? "I don't know if we'll end up together."

"But you went to his place last night."

Thank you, Quincey blabbermouths. "To take dinner as a thank-you for helping you with Mr. Doyle."

"I wish you would marry Dad. He's neat."

"You're getting way ahead of yourself, big guy."

"At least now I know why everybody started acting so weird when he moved here."

"We weren't sure how he'd handle the news about you."

"Yeah, I know. But knowing he's my dad is way more awesome than not knowing." A wide grin split his face.

"I'm glad." She turned through the park gates, her insides twisting even tighter when she spotted a dozen cars, including Roth's patrol car, in the lot. Still in uniform, he leaned against his front fender, straightening when he saw them. She pulled into a space. He crossed to her side and opened the door.

Her pulse went wild. She hadn't seen him since the hasty dog-swap that Madison had interrupted this morning. He hadn't been able to make lunch due to an accident call.

She climbed out. He didn't retreat, which left them close enough that she could smell him and feel the heat radiating from his body, close enough that she could see each bristle of evening beard and each eyelash.

Erotic memories tumbled over her, quickening her breath. The hand gripping her door frame was the same one that had touched her so skillfully last night, and that beard stubble had felt so good on her—

Stop! Kids present.

"Why aren't you on the field with the boys?"

"I waited to walk out with you."

Her heart flip-flopped at the considerate, supportive gesture. When she'd first discovered she was carrying Josh all she'd wanted was a man who'd stand by her. Now she had him.

But for how long?

"Hi, Dad."

"Hi, sport. Did you get your make-up work from the teachers?"

"Yessir. And I started on it this afternoon right after I finished my homework."

"Good. If you've completed it by Thursday, I'll let you take a turn at pitching."

"Awesome!"

Score yet another one for Roth.

"Mom, can I head out to the field?"

She wanted to ask him to wait for her, but

as Madison had said, Piper couldn't use Josh as a shield.

"You may." Unlike her he'd faced his peers already today and showed none of her trepidation as he sprinted off.

The temperature rating in Roth's eyes rose, making her mouth dry. He wanted her, a circumstance she'd have to be blind to miss. But was it more than sex? Maybe she should slow their relationship and find out.

"Want to come over tonight after you get Josh to bed?"

Her hormones screeched, *Yes!* So much for putting on the brakes. If she went to his place, she knew exactly what they'd be doing. And she wanted to go. Badly. Then reality slammed her back to earth. "I can't. Mom has her girls' night."

"I could come to your house."

"Tempting, but no. We both know what would happen if you did. And I'm not ready to have an intimate encounter with Josh only one wall away."

His mouth tipped in a lopsided, make-her-toes-curl smile. "You're afraid you can't resist me?"

Exactly. "I'd rather not take the chance."

"Another night then. I'd like to take you to dinner—somewhere outside of town."

"On a date?"

"Yeah."

"I'd like that."

He nodded and they walked side by side toward the chain-link fence surrounding the diamond.

"You didn't tell me Chuck was involved in the accident you were called to today."

"I don't gossip."

Not even with her? "Is he okay?"

"Drunks usually are." He paused by the opening. "Want to sit in the dugout?"

Yes. "No. I have to face them sooner or later."

A spark of approval lit his dark eyes. "Go get 'em. I'll see you in an hour."

He strode toward the boys tossing balls and warming up, leaving her to face her punishment for lying. She turned toward the bleachers and found Tammy Sue waiting to pounce. Oh, joy. At least she'd get the worst one out of the way.

"I should have known that if our sexy new chief gravitated toward you, there had to be a reason. He's Josh's father."

The parents in the stand went silent, making no effort to hide their eavesdropping.

"Yes. Roth is Josh's father."

"And he left you alone and pregnant to run off and join the military."

She refused to let Roth be her fall guy. He had a job here for as long as he stayed and people whose respect he needed to command. But she had to stick to the truth. No more lies.

"I told Roth I wouldn't have his baby. After he left town I changed my mind and I never let him know."

"And you made up a story about a fiancé—"

"To protect my son from vicious gossips who think nothing of hurting an innocent child. I'm sure you'd do the same to protect Robbie. If not, you're not much of a mother."

Then she reached into her pocket for the iPod Madison had insisted she bring when Piper refused to let her baseball-hating friend come for moral support. Piper stuffed the earpieces in and turned up the music. She brushed by Tammy Sue and climbed to the top row of the stands away from the other parents.

Quincey, the place she'd once considered a haven, had turned on her.

* * *

"You're stirring up a hell of a lot of trouble around here, boy," Lou growled without looking up from the bullets he was painstakingly loading into the revolver.

"Am I?" Roth asked as he reached the firing booth. At least the retired chief was speaking to him this time. In their previous two meetings Lou had uttered no more than a dozen words to Roth—most of those grudging affirmatives or negatives. But he had listened and switched to the revolver.

Lou slammed the cylinder into place. "Writing citations. Butting your head into personal business. Chasing those boys when they're not doing anything you and your crew didn't do."

"We didn't try to kill innocent pets or start fires in trash cans that could spread to adjacent buildings."

That earned him a grunt that could have been either confirmation or denial.

"Mr. Hamilton, if you don't like the way I'm handling things, tell me what you'd do differently, keeping in mind that I treat all citizens equally and will not play favorites. I'm taking care of infractions you've let slide.

We don't need vandals, arsonists, illegal liquor sales or intoxicated drivers in this town."

"Chuck needs help."

"I tried to help him. The accident yesterday proves he won't get help voluntarily."

"Heard you had the sheriff cart him off."

Roth's irritation with the whole situation boiled. "Are you faulting me for following proper procedure? Chuck's wreck was across the county line and not in my jurisdiction. Luckily, his was the only vehicle involved, and he didn't have his kids in the car. It could have been worse."

"I still have connections in Greene County. The District Attorney called. He claims you tried to strong-arm him into putting Chuck into a mandatory ninety-day residential treatment program."

"I explained to the D.A. that Chuck was a repeat offender with small children at home, and for their protection he needed an intervention. Getting him away from what enables his habit is the only chance he has of beating his addiction."

"Think it'll work?"

"Only if Chuck wants it to."

"You wrote Doris a parking ticket. *Doris*, for God's sake. What's that woman ever done to you? She ain't nothing but a harmless busy-body."

"Would you rather your wife's building or the clinic where your daughter works burn to the ground because the volunteer firefighters can't get to the hydrant?"

Lou held his gaze then finally nodded. "I see your point. But you could have warned Doris."

"I did. Twice. She ignored both warning tickets. Wonder why?"

Lou's face turned red. "I might not have pressed the issue. With Doris. Or Chuck." Lou cleared his throat. "For what it's worth, I commend you for taking action with that boy."

An admission. And gratitude? He was on a roll here.

"Someone needed to."

Instead of answering, Lou fired at the target. Two of the five shots hit the paper, but none made the circle. Still, it was progress from their previous sessions.

"You've been practicing without me."

"Don't have anything else to do since you took my job." Lou emptied the casings and reloaded. Once again it was an arduous process that Lou would have been able to do blindfolded before his stroke.

Sympathy pinched Roth. "This time try squaring your stance to the target. Turning sideways makes you vulnerable with the lack of protection your vest provides under your arm."

He pulled his flashlight from his belt and offered it to Lou. "Hold this in your left hand. Aim both the beam and the revolver at the target. The flashlight's weight will help you build up strength in your left hand. Once it's steady we'll switch to two-handed shooting."

Lou tested the position with both arms extended down range. His left arm wobbled, but he made an effort to correct it. He shuffled, adjusted, then slightly bent his knees.

"You're messing with Piper again."

Roth went on alert. Loaded weapon. Angry father. Not a good combination. Lou wasn't pointing the barrel at Roth now, but he could easily pivot. At this close range Roth would be hard to miss.

"We share a son and because of that we have a future. I'm not sure what that future entails yet. But I don't plan to hurt her again. Or Josh. I don't run from my responsibilities anymore."

"See that you don't." Lou fired all five rounds in rapid succession, leaving four holes in the paper, two of those in the outer bands of the target.

"You're getting there. Another couple of weeks and you'll be ready to switch to the HK and practice for requalifying."

"Pretty smart, ain'tcha?" Lou laid down the weapon and returned Roth's Maglite. "You were right. I didn't pursue the vandalism complaints because I suspected Josh and his crew might be involved."

Another admission.

"And now you know he's not?"

"Thanks to your little trick with the kittens, yes."

Roth pulled out his pistol, transferred it to his weak hand, aimed downrange and squeezed off thirteen successive shots. Each one drilled the center ring on the target.

"Show-off," Lou groused, but the words lacked rancor.

"It's nothing but training and repetition. You'll be doing the same in a matter of time."

"I was never that good a shot."

"Then you have a goal."

Roth ejected the clip and reloaded. "Since you claim to have time on your hands, I could use an extra set of eyes on the vandalism case. I can't put you on payroll. But the fact it's unofficial works to our advantage if no one knows you're on the lookout. And I mean *no one*. Not your cronies. Not even Ann Marie. Especially not Piper or Josh."

"Why the hell not?"

"We're working on the assumption that the perps are kids Josh knows, but we could be wrong. It's better not to tip anyone off. Nobody knows the back roads and alleys like you do. You'll spot anything that's out of place."

Lou hesitated then nodded. "You got it. But why are you helping me?"

"Because you didn't lock me up for being a stupid kid."

Lou studied him. "Couldn't. Your mama was depending on you."

Surprised, Roth stared. He had believed no one in Quincey had lifted a finger to help his mother, but apparently he'd been wrong.

Lou offered his hand. The men shook then Lou's grip tightened almost painfully.

"One more thing you need to know, Sterling. Ronnie Craig is selling his shine. We've turned a blind eye 'cuz it's the only income he has with that bum leg of his. But with your daddy due back next month it might be good if you cut off his local supplier. If Seth's still drinking."

"Nobody wants my father to be clean and sober more than I do. But I don't believe in miracles. I'll notify ALE."

"Don't think that because I tipped you off I won't be watching how you treat my gal and her boy."

"I wouldn't expect anything less."

Roth had made an important ally—as long as he didn't screw up with Piper and Josh.

Lou sailed into Ann Marie's kitchen Wednesday evening, interrupting her dinner preparations.

"Are you ever going to learn to knock or ring the doorbell like a guest should?"

"In my wife's house? Not a chance."

She noted the absence of his usual grumpy expression. She opened her mouth to ask what had brightened his mood, but he stalled her question by grabbing her around the waist, then planting a kiss on her mouth.

Her heart tripped almost as fast as her feet. Despite how wonderful it felt to be in his arms again she yanked free. "What are you doing, Lou Hamilton?"

He pulled a piece of paper from his pocket and spread it across the island. It took a moment to register that she was looking at a target. One with holes in it. A lot of holes.

He beamed. "Look what I did this afternoon."

The meaning sank in. He'd hit the target. "Oh, Lou. This is wonderful."

"Damn right it is. I scored more than I missed."

"Roth helped you with this?"

"He's spent a few hours with me at the range. His time. Not work time. I didn't mention it 'cuz I didn't want you to know if it didn't pan out. Sterling might not be such a bad guy after all."

She'd come to the same conclusion, and this only reinforced her opinion that Roth Sterling might be what her daughter and grandson needed.

The confident man in front of her reminded her of the old Lou—the one she'd fallen in love with.

Before she could stop herself she stepped forward and touched her lips to his. The instantaneous swoop of her stomach startled her. She quickly retreated. "Congratulations."

He looked a little confused then scowled. "Don't think you're gonna give me a teasing little peck like that then run."

He pulled her into his arms and kissed her. Really kissed her. The way he hadn't in fifteen years. Ann Marie absorbed the feel of his burly body against hers, the taste of his mouth and the scent of his cologne. She heated up in places that hadn't been warm in a very long time.

The click of the door opening followed by the sound of doggie nails on the hardwood floor jerked her to the present. Flustered, she freed herself from Lou's arms seconds before Josh and Sarg barged into the kitchen.

Her face burned like a teenager's who'd been caught necking. "Wash up, Josh. No dinner for you until you've rid yourself of dog germs."

Josh looked from her to his grandfather, his face a mask of confusion. "Is Grandpa staying for dinner?"

"No."

"Yes," Lou answered simultaneously.

Josh gave one of his long-suffering sighs. "Here we go again. Why are you both acting so weird?"

Ann Marie stuffed her shaking hands in her apron pockets. "We're not. Go. Wash. Now. Your mother will be here any minute."

She didn't want Josh carrying tales to his

mother. If he did, Piper would put her through an inquisition. And how could she explain what happened to her daughter when she didn't understand it herself?

Chapter Sixteen

Piper pulled into her driveway dreading the news she'd have to share with Josh tonight. At least her father was here. Maybe he'd find a way to help soften the blow.

A truck turned in behind her blocking her in. Roth's truck. A burst of adrenaline raced through her bloodstream making her skin tingle.

Roth stepped out wearing a black polo shirt and jeans that accentuated those muscles she'd mapped two nights ago. He swaggered toward her.

"Evening, babe."

Babe. The endearment glided over her like a caress. "What are you doing here?"

"Ann Marie invited me to dinner."

Apparently that talk she'd had with her mother about not springing guests on her had failed to sink in. But things had changed and Piper actually wanted Roth's company. But not while her father was here. If her daddy caught wind of her and Roth's intimate activities, she wasn't sure what he'd do.

Roth grabbed her hand and tugged her toward her mother's magnolias.

"What are you—"

His mouth covered hers while his palms skimmed down her spine to clamp her waist and prevent her escape. As if she wanted to go anywhere.

Her head spun and her hormones rioted. Dear heavens he felt good, tasted good, smelled good. His tongue tangled with hers, coaxing, caressing, and his chest pressed against her sensitive breasts. Her scrubs did nothing to block the intense heat, and reciprocal need blossomed deep inside her.

She had to fight to remember why rubbing against him would be totally inappropriate. Despite the trees, they were in her front yard—which was highly visible from both the house and street.

She wriggled from Roth's arms. When he reached for her she held her hand up in a stop signal as she backed away. "What are you doing? Anyone could see us."

A devilish grin split his face. "It's almost dark, and I did drag you into the bushes for privacy."

"Well, don't do that. Not here. Josh has already seen us kiss once and he's started asking uncomfortable questions. And my father's here tonight."

"Good."

"Good?" He wanted to see the man who'd likely fetch his rifle when he found out she and Roth were sleeping together again?

"I want to see how practice went after I left him at the range today."

"You met him at the range?"

"You knew I was helping him."

"But I didn't know you'd started. You should have warned me. I would have liked to have been there." To run interference.

"No reason for you to be present. This is between him and me."

"But—"

"Piper, your father and I are working out

our issues. Let it go. Your mom's making shrimp scampi, and I'm starving. Unless you want to be the main course, grab the kittens and let's head inside."

'Nuff said. If he kissed her again, she might not make it to dinner. And then her father *would* hunt them down. She grabbed the box of kittens from her backseat. The moment she opened the door to the house the delicious aroma of butter and garlic assailed her senses, but she was more interested in her unsatisfied hunger for the man behind her than her need for food.

And Josh. Poor kid. She was going to break his heart tonight. As if the thought conjured him, he and Sarg raced into the foyer. "Hi, Mom. Hi, Dad. I finished my missed work. Can I pitch at practice tomorrow?"

"A promise is a promise," Roth answered while she was still processing being lumped together as *mom* and *dad*.

"Great! Oh, and, Mom, Grandma and Grandpa are acting weird."

She wanted to ask, "Weird how?" but didn't want to drag Josh into adult matters.

"Cool. You brought the kittens. I was afraid Dr. Monroe would keep them again. Can I feed them?"

"She only kept them last night because of baseball. You can feed them after dinner." Eager to discover the reason behind her parents' behavior, she handed Josh the box and herded everyone toward the kitchen.

Her gaze sought her mother's, but after one quick peek Ann Marie abruptly pivoted to retrieve the serving dish on the stovetop. She carried it to the table. Piper noticed her mother's flushed cheeks as she passed. Flushed from the heat of cooking? Or something else?

Then she looked at her father. His expression seemed a bit…smug? "Hi, Mom, Dad. What's up?"

Her father's eyes flicked to her mother and a crooked smile twitched then he nodded at the island. "My percentages."

Roth braced one hand on Piper's hip and grabbed the piece of paper. Her skin ignited at the contact.

"Way to go, Chie—Mr. Hamilton."

"If you hadn't been such a show-off, I wouldn't have stayed at the range," her father complained with his eyes on the hand at her waist. Piper prepared for an explosion.

"Just trying to provide a little incentive."

"It worked. And you might as well call me Lou."

Call him Lou? Piper's head swung like a spectator's at a tennis match. Her father and Roth were teasing each other—despite Roth's proximity to her? Something was very wrong with this picture. Her entire family had accepted him. How different that was from the past.

Or was it? Would he still leave her? Leave them? The thought niggled like a splinter.

Her mother shooed them toward the table. "I hope you don't mind eating in the kitchen, Roth. Josh has his science project spread out in the dining room."

Roth pulled out Piper's chair, a common courtesy, but she couldn't remember the last time someone had done that for her. Had her last date? That had been over a year ago, so she couldn't recall.

"Piper, please pour the wine."

She filled Josh's glass with white grape juice, then poured Chardonnay for the adults. When she reached Roth's he covered the rim with his palm. "I'll have grape juice."

She searched his face. "You don't like wine?"

"I don't drink alcohol."

"At all?" Not that she had a problem with that. "Is it because of your dad?" Josh asked.

"That's right."

Piper filled Roth's glass with juice. "I thought you went out for beer with the fathers after practice last night."

"I went for the company, not the booze. But please don't abstain on my account. I have no problem with the rest of you having wine as long as you're sober when you operate a vehicle."

"Cool, fill me up, Mom," Josh said.

Piper shot him a level look.

"And of legal age, brat." Roth had a scowl on his face but laughter in his eyes.

Her father lifted his glass as if offering a toast. "Hear that, Ann Marie? If I drink too much, I'll have to spend the night."

Piper did a double take. Her father never drank to excess, and he'd never spent the night in this house.

Ann Marie grabbed the wine bottle and moved it out of Lou's reach. "Then I'm limiting you to one glass."

"Spoilsport."

What was going on? Piper hadn't heard her parents tease each other like this in...since long before she left for Florida. Piper tried to catch her mother's attention, but she looked everywhere except at Piper.

Throughout the meal her father talked to

Roth, Josh and Piper, but his gaze never left Ann Marie.

Josh was right, Piper decided. Her folks were acting strange but in a very good way.

She held her bad news until after the brownies à la mode had been consumed. "Josh. I heard from Sarg's owners today."

Her son's expression fell. "They want him back?"

"Actually, no. Sarg's original owner died two months ago and her son inherited the dog. He was taking Sarg to a no-kill shelter when Sarg escaped."

Josh's eyes filled with hope. "We can't send him to a shelter, Mom. We just can't."

"We can't keep him, Josh. Roth can't continue to carry him around in the patrol car, and like we discussed before, it's not fair to lock Sarg in the house all day."

Roth put a hand on Josh's shoulder and squeezed. "She's right. If I have to put someone in the back of the car, Sarg would be in the way."

Josh's lips quivered. "But I don't want to give him up. I love him. And he loves me. And he loves Dad. If we send him to a shelter, he might never get another family."

Piper's eyes burned. She'd known he'd react this way. "I'm sorry, Josh. We'll have to find Sarg a permanent home. Maybe someone local will adopt him and let you visit."

Silence, broken only by Josh's sniffles as he bravely tried not to cry, filled the room.

Her father slapped his hand on the table, making Piper jump. "No, you're not. You're not giving the boy's dog away."

"Daddy, I called and got several estimates on fencing in the backyard today. All are beyond my budget."

"I'll take him then. There's nobody but me rambling around in that house all day. It's too damned quiet."

"Lou, you never let Piper and me have pets. You swore they were smelly, expensive and damaged a house."

"Well, I was wrong. Seems I was wrong about a lot of things." His gaze flicked to Roth. "But I'm seeing the error of my ways. And now I want that damned dog. So there." He tossed his napkin on the table and folded his arms, acting more like an eleven-year-old than the one sitting across the table from him.

So there? Her father's behavior startled a

laugh out of Piper. She slapped a hand over her mouth. He glared at her.

"Daddy, you don't know anything about caring for a dog, and they are expensive."

"You can give me a family discount at the clinic, and this old dog can learn new tricks. Ask Roth."

Roth's eyebrows arced up. "This is a family argument. Leave me out of it."

"You're his family." Lou pointed to Josh. "That puts you square in the middle of ours. Tell these women I can handle the dog. Hell, might even help me rebuild strength in my left arm and hand if I have to yank on his leash."

"Lou is definitely learning new tricks. And Sarg is extremely well behaved. He'd be a great beginner's dog."

Neither of the men was helping the cause.

"That's it then. I'm taking Sarg. We can even maintain the same deal Roth has with Josh now. I'll keep the dog during the day and Josh can have him evenings and weekends. I'll bring both of 'em home from school."

That would limit Josh's exposure to Roth— something Piper had yearned for weeks ago, but now she liked that her son had such a good role model.

Across the table her mother stiffened. "Now

wait just one minute. You're assuming I want to keep the dog every night."

"You aren't fooling me, Ann Marie. You'd miss Sarg as much as Josh would. Don't think I didn't see you slipping him food under the table."

Her mother fidgeted with her napkin. "You can't drop by every day."

"Why the hell not? I think about you every day. I might was well see you."

The kitchen fell silent.

Ann Marie looked totally flustered. "You could have said something."

"You wouldn't have listened."

"I might have."

Josh rolled his eyes. "See, Mom. I told you they were being freaky."

As fascinated as Piper was by the discussion, she wanted out of this very private argument. "Josh, why don't you show Roth and me your science project before you feed the kittens? Excuse us, please."

Piper rose, leaving her parents to their verbal fencing. She made a point of closing the dining room door, and thankfully, it muted the harsh whispers that launched immediately.

But if she wasn't mistaken, it appeared her parents were finally communicating.

* * *

Ann Marie sprang from the table. "Now look what you've done. You've run everybody off. What has gotten into you tonight, Lou? First kissing me like that, then promising Josh you'll take his dog, then—" Her throat constricted with hope, fear and…who knows what? "Then saying you think about me every day."

"I do. Have ever since you packed your gear and moved out."

"That was twelve years ago! And we were having trouble before that."

He stood in front of her. "So maybe I'm a little slow. Or maybe…maybe I had too much pride to admit I'd made a mistake."

During their marriage he'd never apologized and never admitted he was wrong about anything. "What kind of mistake?"

"Sending Piper away." He looked away before turning to her with such raw emotion in his eyes that it stole her breath. "Letting you move out."

Her legs felt a little shaky. "What brought on this change of heart?"

"The stroke. Losing my job. But mostly seeing the pity in your eyes."

"It wasn't pity, you dolt. It was sympathy. I

hated seeing you lose the one thing that mattered more to you than anything or anybody else—your job."

"You think that mattered more to me than you or Piper?"

"I always knew I came in second, then after Piper was born, third. And then after Josh came home—" She couldn't say more without bawling like a baby.

A scowl buckled his forehead. "And here all this time I've been thinking you were too smart for me and you could have done better than marrying some hick lawman. But what you're saying is just plain dumb, woman."

Too smart for him? Could have done better? Dumb? *Dumb?*

She focused on the latter because it was easier to wrap her brain around and anger didn't make her cry. "Are you calling me stupid?"

"No." He sighed and rubbed his hand over his face. "From the moment you opened that office after Piper started school it was clear you would be a success. And all those big-time real estate agents started sniffing around, trying to lure you to work for them out of town."

He shook his head. "I never should have taken you away from the city. You loved the art galleries, fancy restaurants and all the other stuff.

"You should have married a doctor or a lawyer or somebody who could give you those things. Somebody who could have banked money to pay for his daughter's education instead of counting on his wife to do it. No matter how many promotions I got, that wasn't ever going to be me."

Dear heaven, she hadn't had a clue. "Oh, for pity's sake, Lou. Why didn't you tell me my success bothered you?"

"It didn't. I loved seeing you do well. It made you happy. But—"

"But what?"

"You shouldn't have had to buy everything for yourself. It's a husband's job to provide for his wife."

She stared at him. "What century are you living in? Because I swear, you sound like my great granddaddy. I never expected you to *provide* for me other than to love me and to be there whether I made the sale or lost it. To desire me whether I put on my makeup or didn't.

"And the things I bought were tangible rewards for making difficult sales. As for Piper's college fund… I knew we'd never be able to get enough financial aid to cover it all—especially if she ended up going to vet school.

"I wanted her to have options so she could choose, whether it was college or falling for a rookie cop directing traffic on Western Boulevard. Do you know how many times I had to drive by you that day before you noticed me?"

"I'm not blind. I noticed the first time. Hard to miss a hot blonde in a red convertible. If you hadn't passed me your phone number, I would have tracked you down—I had your plate number memorized."

Flabbergasted, she gaped at him. "Thirty-two years and you never told me that."

"You didn't need to know."

"Yes, I did. A woman always needs to know when a man wants her."

"I did want you." He huffed out a breath then looked at her, his gaze sober and steady. "And I still do."

"Is that the wine talking?"

"You only let me have one glass. Listen, I know we have stuff to work out. But I miss you, Ann Marie. I miss holding you when I go to sleep and smelling your perfume in the bathroom."

She wanted to believe…and yet she was afraid to let herself. "Are you sure you don't mean you miss me doing your laundry and cooking your meals?"

"That, too," he said with a self-deprecating grin that turned her to mush. "You spoiled me. I didn't realize how much until you were gone."

"I did it because I enjoyed taking care of you."

"I hate living in our house without you. And I hate having to make up excuses to stop by. I love Josh, but he's not the one I come to see most of the time."

She needed to breathe, but her heart was so full it was hard to get air into her lungs. "You're right. We have things to work out. A lot of things. But... I think I might like to try."

"Hallelujah, woman. Now come here." He reached for her. Ann Marie met him halfway.

"Interesting dinner, huh?" Piper said to cover her nervousness as she walked Roth to his truck.

Still getting tongue-tied and jittery around him after everything they'd been through was ridiculous.

He stopped between the trees and his truck, hooked his thumbs in his front pockets and rocked on his heels, looking every bit the rebel he had once been. "Come home with me."

Piper stumbled. "I can't have my car parked outside of your apartment this late at night."

"Ride with me. I'll get you home before sunrise. Like I used to."

A heady cocktail of excitement and temptation rushed through her. She was an adult now. Too old to be running off with her lover. "I can't sneak out anymore, Roth. I have responsibilities. Josh—"

"Your mother can watch him."

She ached to say yes, to go to his apartment, his bed, the special place he created when he made love to her and erased her doubts about his past and their future.

The front door opened and her father stepped onto the porch—her mother close behind. Then Piper noticed the overnight bag in her father's right hand and her mother's hand in his left. They strolled down the driveway.

Her mother seemed nervous and excited. "I'm going to your father's for a bit. Don't wait up."

Her mother was making a booty call? Stunned, Piper didn't know what to say.

Her mom's smile faltered. "Unless you need me here?"

"No. Go ahead. Have…fun?"

Her father tugged on her mother's hand. "Let's go, Ann Marie. The kids will be fine."

"I left Josh feeding the kittens. When he's done don't forget his science project. I picked up a movie at the library on the solar system for research."

"Ann Marie, Piper knows about Josh's homework."

"Thanks, Mom." Piper had been trying to get her parents reunited for years. Had Roth's reappearance accomplished what she'd failed to do?

Moments later her father's taillights disappeared around the corner.

Piper looked at Roth, disappointment weighing her down. "I'm sorry."

"I think we have a movie to watch."

"You don't have to stay. And you know we can't—"

"Piper, it's been a good night. I'm not ready for it to end—even if it doesn't end with you in my bed."

"Okay, but I have been up since four, and even when I'm not tired shows about the creation of the universe put me to sleep. Don't say you haven't been warned."

"Then I'd better get this before we go inside." He kissed her long and slow and deep.

She didn't want the night to end either. Or the week. Or the month. Or the—

Oh, Lord. She wasn't in danger of falling in love with Roth again. She'd already done it. In only two weeks. Apparently her mother wasn't the only one going a little crazy tonight.

Chapter Seventeen

Roth couldn't name a time he'd been more comfortable.

Or more *un*comfortable.

Considering he'd lain neck deep in swamp water for hours without swatting at the whining mosquitoes or snakes slithering past, that was saying something.

Josh sat to Roth's left on the sofa, happily munching popcorn and hanging on every word the narrator droned about asteroid showers, black holes and supernovas. Normally, Roth liked astronomy. He'd earned his navigator's certification early on in the Corps and could plot a trail into or out of enemy territory using stars or electronics. But tonight he was distracted by the woman on his right.

As predicted, Piper had fallen asleep a half hour into the movie. Her warm body nestled into the crook of his shoulder and her hair draped his chest, his thigh.

He wanted her—a fact his thickening anatomy couldn't hide. He hoped his son didn't notice. More than that, Roth wanted *this*— nights in front of the television with family.

Because it felt normal. Normal had never been a part of his life, especially not his childhood. Normal had been what other people had. He'd lived in a war zone before and after he'd left Quincey, never knowing why, when or where the next explosion would hit. Even with SWAT one call could send him into a volatile situation.

He craved more nights like this so bad he could taste them. But he was who he was. Seth Sterling's son. He had his father's temper, the genetic tendency toward alcoholism and, as Piper had pointed out, the ability to kill without conscience.

No. Not without conscience. He respected every life he'd taken. But he had justified them. Kill a deer to feed his family. Shoot one insurgent to save a dozen or a hundred other lives.

Take out one criminal to save hostages. He'd had reasons for what he did. But his actions could certainly not be considered the norm by any stretch of the imagination. And though he might argue to the contrary, that was who he was. A killing machine.

Piper and Josh deserved normal. And Seth's return jeopardized Roth's chance at ever giving it to them.

The soundtrack played and credits rolled. Josh stood and stretched. He looked at his mom and grinned. "Happens every time."

"Tomorrow's a school day and your turn on the pitching mound. What's your bedtime?" Roth asked as quietly as he could.

"I'm supposed to be in bed by nine."

"It's past that now. Can you take the dog out and get yourself to bed so we don't have to wake your mom?"

The kid looked insulted. "I'm eleven. Of course I can."

"Then good night, buddy. I'll let myself out in a while." He extended his left fist.

"Okay." Josh bumped knuckles with him, but hesitated rather than leave the room. "You like my mom. Right?"

The simple query reminded Roth of a

minefield—one wrong step and disaster could strike. "Right."

"And you like me?"

"Affirmative."

"Good. I like you, too. And I'm glad you're my dad. See you tomorrow." Josh wandered off.

The pressure in Roth's chest eased when he heard the door open. This father thing wasn't easy. He needed a manual or at least a briefing. He glanced at Piper. He didn't know how she did it, but she'd claimed she'd learned by trial and error. He'd have to do the same. And he had to believe he could do it despite the lack of training and preparation. That was the biggest hurdle.

Josh and Sarg reentered and footsteps sounded on the stairs, then the ceiling above. A toilet flushed. Water ran. Eventually the house fell silent except for the music still coming from the DVD.

He should leave. But he was reluctant to risk waking Piper or to let her go. He enjoyed holding her, feeling her slight weight pressed to his side, hearing the soothing whisper of her breathing.

Having her so peaceful and trusting against him now filled a void inside him that he hadn't previously noticed. He couldn't recall when he'd felt this good. This satisfied. This complete. And he and Piper hadn't even had sex.

Using the remote Josh had abandoned, Roth turned off the electronics. He didn't want to go to his empty apartment. Maybe he should kick off his shoes and sleep with Piper for a few minutes. Here on the sofa. Hands to himself—not an easy goal, but doable. If he gave it one hundred percent.

Sounded like a plan. A good one.

He relaxed into the cushions, tipping his head back and getting comfortable. He was almost asleep when Piper stirred, her face nuzzling his chest and his libido. She sighed, her breath warming his skin through the fabric of his shirt.

In the dim light from the kitchen he saw a smile flit across her lips as if she were dreaming. Then she stiffened and her eyes opened. She bolted upright.

She swiveled in each direction, searching the room. "Where's Josh?"

The slight rasp in her voice threatened his no-hands goal. "Bed."

"How long have I been asleep?"

"Half hour."

"I'm sorry."

"I'm not." She looked so damned sexy with her sleepy eyes and flushed face that he couldn't resist reaching for her, tugging her closer and covering her mouth with his.

Her resistance lasted all of five seconds then she sagged into him, her soft breast pressing his side and her arm snaking around his neck. The awkward twist of her body couldn't be comfortable, and the minimal contact sure as hell wasn't enough for him.

Her fingers clasped his nape and her short nails grazed his skin. A shudder rumbled through him. He grabbed her waist, lifted her and swung her into his lap. Her knees flanked him and her sweet bottom settled on his thighs. He cupped her rear and slid her closer to the part of him straining toward her.

He fisted his hand in the strands of her hair, holding her close. Their tongues dueled, the slick contact accelerating his heart rate into the danger zone.

The message that she wanted him came across loud and clear in the fingers kneading his shoulders, and in the way she shifted her hips against him, rubbing her sweet, hot center against his hard-on. Her "mmm" filled his mouth and desire detonated inside him, igniting a fire he wasn't sure he could contain.

He snapped his head back. He wanted Piper. Wanted the right to spend the night in her bed. But in Quincey that meant marriage. And he wasn't ready to condemn her to life with him yet...or himself to life in Quincey. Not with the time bomb of his father lurking on the horizon. One month. He had one month to soak up all he could of her. One month to solidify his position before the hell of his father's presence threatened everything.

Her lips feathered over his neck. His control wavered.

"Piper."

"Hmm?" Her teeth nipped him, rocking him to the core.

"Babe. I can't believe I'm saying this, but we need to—" Her tongue traced his ear. He tightened his grip on her waist and pushed her butt back to his knees. "Stop."

"Stop? Why?"

Good question. And in a minute he'd remember the answer. But not if she kept tracing his lips with her fingertips.

Marines do the right thing—even when nobody's looking.

He captured those wandering fingers. He

wouldn't take advantage of her lust-and sleep-fogged brain. "Josh is upstairs. Will he come down again?"

The sexual tension drained from her body, leaving her muscles lax. A grimace of disappointment wrinkled her face. "He might."

Her hard nipples tented the fabric of her shirt right in front of his face. He wanted them in his hands, his mouth, his— *Cool it, Sterling.* "As much as I want to be inside you right now, that interruption might be more than any of us can handle."

"Yes." She climbed off his lap.

He held her hand, reluctant, even without the promise of sex, to let her go. And that was saying something since his erection was about to blow his zipper like a brick of C-4.

"I'd love to stay, sleep right here and hold you all night. But my truck parked outside all night is in-your-face obvious."

Indecision chased across her face. "I want you to stay."

"Even though it guarantees gossip?"

"Yes. For once I don't care what Quincey's big mouths have to say. I'm tired of living my life in fear of them."

"They need to get used to seeing us together."

Her breath caught. "They do?"

The lump returned to his throat. "Yeah, they do. I have no idea what kind of hell my father will generate. But no matter what, you and Josh are part of my life now. And I'll do right by you. Think you can handle that?"

Her lips quivered but she nodded. "I can handle it."

"Then come here." He stretched out on the sofa. She lay beside him, spoon-fashion with his groin tucked into the warm crevice of her bottom.

It was going to be one long night. And he would enjoy every torturous second of it. Because one of these days the memories might be all he had to carry him through.

Roth's phone rang midkiss, interrupting his enjoyment of Piper's soft lips and the feel of her lace-covered breast in his palm. He was damned tempted to ignore the summons. But being chief meant he couldn't.

He reluctantly released her. The desire glazing her blue eyes and the sight of her bra peeking from beneath the shirt he'd unbuttoned almost made him say to hell with it.

He grabbed his cell and checked the number. Lou Hamilton. "Sterling."

"You got that newfangled camera working on your patrol car yet?"

Yet another long-overdue upgrade he'd been assigned to oversee. "Yes."

"Then haul your ass out to Johnson's tobacco barns on Sycamore Road. No lights or sirens. I'll be waiting." Lou disconnected.

Did he know something about the vandals? Had he spotted them in action?

He drank in another look at Piper, at her disheveled clothing, tangled hair and swollen lips. This had been their first night alone in the three days, and five since he'd made love to her.

"I have to go."

"What's wrong?"

He wanted to tell her, but for the same reasons he'd sworn Lou to silence, he couldn't. "Work related."

"But it's Saturday night. You're off duty."

"Babe, I want to stay. But I can't." He wished they'd skipped dinner and gone straight to bed. By now he'd have been sexually sated and happy to have a peanut butter and jelly sandwich. But he'd promised her a date. And the steak had been good, her company even better.

He expected her to get peeved. Instead, she

flashed him a rueful smile. "Welcome to parenthood. You never know when you'll get a moment alone."

He planted a kiss on her forehead and inhaled a lungful of her scent. He didn't dare risk touching her lips or he might forget his duty. Then he remembered he'd picked her up so her car wouldn't be parked outside all night.

He grabbed his belt, holster and weapon and buckled them on. "Do you mind waiting here? I'll try to wrap this up quickly."

Her gaze fixed on his gun and the passion turned to worry. "Take your time. Be safe. I'll be sleeping in your bed."

Alone. Damn. "Keep it warm for me."

He raced toward the farm. When he neared the driveway he killed the lights and let the waning full moon guide him. He slowed by Lou's parked truck and followed the man's pointing finger. He eased around the side of the barn. Flashlights—three of them—gave away their owners' locations. Then someone lit a match and touched it to something combustible.

Roth turned on the camera then hit the headlights. The bright beam caught three boys red-handed. They froze, stared at him wide-eyed, then ran. But not before he recognized them from his team. He hit the siren, bailed from the car and chased after the one who'd started the fire—Robbie Weaver.

"Quincey Police. Stop. Now. Robbie Weaver." When the kid refused to slow, Roth sprinted faster, grabbed the boy's jacket and swung him around. Robbie struggled, elbowed Roth in the ribs and kicked him in the shin. Pain shot up Roth's leg, pissing him off. Add assaulting an officer to the charges.

Reminding himself the perp was a boy, Roth tried to be careful. Within seconds he had Robbie cuffed and facedown on the ground. "Given your behavior on the team, I should have suspected you."

Across the field Roth saw Lou corralling the other two. Lou had them by their collars dragging them along. That left hand seemed to be gripping just fine.

Roth glanced to check the status of the fire. The blaze at the base of a metal building had grown to about two feet high. He yanked Robbie to his feet, marched him to the patrol car and put him in the back. "Sit still. Shut up. And don't do anything stupid. I have the entire takedown on tape so don't bother to make up stories."

Roth grabbed the fire extinguisher from the trunk and put out the fire. He returned to the car at the same time as Lou. Two visibly shaken boys stared at Roth.

He studied the older man's labored breaths, but didn't insult him by asking if he was okay. Lou would speak up if he wasn't.

"These two are singing like canaries. Better get them to the station and call the parents and juvenile authorities. You have the ring-leader in your car."

"I figured as much. Thanks for your help."

"No. Thank *you*. I didn't want you here. And I sure as shooting didn't want you near Piper or Josh. But you might be exactly what Quincey needs."

A twinge of guilt pinched Roth. "I hope you feel the same after Seth hits town."

"It'll be different this time. Folks respect you. That means they'll keep an eye on him and look out for your mama."

"I hope so."

As much as he hated doing it, Roth cuffed the boys for their own safety. He had a long night ahead with no idea when he'd get back to Piper.

Chapter Eighteen

Roth checked his G-Shock watch and waited. He'd asked the ALE guys to meet him on the south side of town on a rarely used road rather than have them drive down Main Street and have one of the locals tip off Ronnie Craig.

He hadn't dared to have the agents come through the station since Butch White was part of the good-ole-boy network, and Roth had spotted his deputy having lunch with Craig a couple of times.

A black Crown Vic came into view. *Subtle, guys. You'll blend right in.* The car rolled to a halt beside him. The driver's window lowered, revealing two agents.

"Sterling?" the driver asked.

Roth nodded. "Stone?" The agent confirmed.

"One mile south I dropped a small pine branch in the road marking the driveway on your left. Go a hundred yards and take the right fork. The still is exactly a quarter mile beyond that in an old kudzu-covered silo."

"You've done recon lately?"

"Before sunrise this morning."

"Four hours ago, give or take. The equipment should still be there unless you scared them off."

Cocky bastard. "I was a Marine sniper, Agent Stone, so I guarantee I went unseen. If anybody tips them off it will be you two."

"You can tail us in, but stay out of the way until we need you. Where's your car?"

Roth pointed, knowing the agents wouldn't easily see it behind the branches he'd used for camo. Nor would they see tire tracks, which he'd covered. Stone gave him a blank stare then drove off.

Roth removed the covering then followed. Once they reached the site he deliberately hung back watching for runners. The black vehicle coasted to a stop and the agents sprang into action, circling the silo and calling out identification. Roth's blood pumped. He hadn't been part of a takedown in a while.

He scanned the property, noticing a set of tires showing beneath a camouflage tarp hanging from a lean-to. The vehicle hadn't been here this morning. Roth blocked it with his cruiser then drew his weapon and climbed from the cab.

He squatted, checking below the fabric for feet. None. He eased around the tarp and found a twenty-year-old sedan with an open trunk and an empty passenger compartment. Two cases of moonshine packaged in mason jars and a list of names beside the boxes told the story.

Before he could head for the passenger side to check the registration he heard a commotion. He stepped out of the lean-to. Butch White with his hands behind his head led the pack across the dirt clearing, followed by Ronnie Craig and the agents. White spotted Roth.

Well, well, Roth might have found the reason Deputy White had been passed over for promotion.

"What in the hell are you doing?" White bellowed.

"Looking at a trunk full of unstamped liquor."

"This guy claims he's one of your deputies and he was investigating a call," Stone said.

"There was no call and he's off duty today." White glared at Roth then spit in the dirt.

Roth held his gaze unblinking as he approached the group. "White, you're on administrative leave until further notice."

"You sonofabitch. You're gonna need me when your murdering daddy comes to town. He's out."

Out? Roth tried to conceal his surprise, but White must have picked up on it. "That's right. Seth was released six weeks early. Guess I forgot to give you the message from the parole board."

Roth battled to control the fury. He'd like nothing better than to punch that smirk off White's face, but abusing a detainee—even one who'd made his life difficult in every way possible—wasn't worth losing his job or self-respect.

Six weeks early. He hadn't had enough time with Piper. It had been eight days since he'd returned from arresting the boys to find her warm and waiting in his bed. She'd soothed away the disgust of having to file charges against Josh's friends. And while he'd spent every available moment with Piper since then, he wasn't ready for his father to arrive and ruin everything. *Focus*.

"The sedan behind the tarp wasn't here this morning. The trunk was open and there are twenty-eight jars of clear liquid in the back and a list of names with dollar amounts beside them. You might also want Forensics to check any of the money you find on Craig and see if Deputy White has left behind evidence."

"We're on it," Stone said.

ALE would normally turn the case over to the local law enforcement after the arrests had been made. As much as Roth would love to be responsible for prosecuting Craig, that wouldn't be best in this case. Roth waited until Craig and White were locked in the ALE agents' car to join Stone.

"As much as I hate to give up this one, you need to process this through the county sheriff's office rather than the Quincey P.D. Aside from the obvious conflict of interest, White has loyal followers on the force. I'd hate for evidence to get compromised. Craig's been operating that still since I was a kid. It's time someone shut him down permanently and I'd hate to lose this chance due to a legal loophole."

"Done. And thanks for the tip. Craig has

enough barrels of shine and mash to make this stick."

Roth left the agents to their work. He had more urgent matters to take care of. First he had to verify his father's release. And then he had to see Piper and Josh.

Time had run out on Situation Normal.

Excitement and anticipation bubbled inside Piper. She'd seen Roth turn into his apartment complex as the last morning patient was leaving the clinic and decided to surprise him with lunch.

They'd been struggling all week to find time together. With her mother spending most nights with Piper's father, there had been little intimate time. Maybe after she and Roth finished lunch… Her pulse rate kicked up.

She knocked. Moments later the door abruptly opened. Roth wore sweats riding low on his hips and a white sleeveless T-shirt that revealed his bulging biceps. His skin gleamed, and he smelled of fresh sweat. He must have been working out with the weights he had in his second bedroom. He looked so sexy and male her body immediately began humming with need.

"I brought lunch." She lifted the plastic bag.

He tugged her inside, shut the panel and backed her against it. His lips and body came down on hers before she could interpret his odd expression. Guess he was glad to see her, too. Or happy she'd brought food.

He devoured her mouth in a teeth-grinding, tongue-lashing assault on her senses. The bag slipped from her fingers. Her heart raced to catch up with the wild beat of his beneath her palm. His hands cradled her head, sweeping over her French braid, which he quickly unraveled, then his fingers fisted in the strands.

He broke the kiss and whipped her top over her head, then he found and loosened the drawstring at her waist. The drag of his knuckles against her belly gave her goose bumps and her abdominal muscles contracted. He was a man on a mission—a mission to get both of them naked—then he cupped her breasts, caressing, tweaking and ratcheting up her response at warp speed while his mouth worked magic on the tendons of her neck. Her knees nearly buckled when his teeth grazed her skin.

Swift and sure, his slightly abrasive palms skimmed her torso, her hips and over her bottom, her belly, finding each erogenous zone and activating it to the max. His mouth returned to hers in a fierce kiss. He spliced his fingers between her folds, found her center and stroked her. Desire sensitized her skin. A whimper escaped from her mouth into his.

She trembled from the intensity of his silent, single-minded lovemaking, and tried to match him caress for caress but the molten pressure building inside her distracted her.

His supple flesh felt so good, and she loved the way his muscles rippled beneath her touch. Then she wrapped her fingers around his erection, savoring the satiny strength. She stroked his length, traced the swollen head with her thumb. His sharp intake of breath and a slick drop rewarded her efforts.

His hands splayed over her buttocks and he lifted her. She wrapped her legs around his hips and her arms around his shoulders, loving the hot fusion of their bodies. His damp skin clung to hers.

He covered the distance to his bedroom in swift, long strides and lowered her to the bed. In seconds he'd dealt with protection and followed her. He drove into her, hard and fast again and again.

Hooking his hands beneath her knees he lifted her hips for even deeper penetration, forcing the air from her lungs. She'd missed this, missed him. Being a family with him and Josh was great, but being the sole focus of Roth's passionate, undivided attention was divine.

She dug her heels into the mattress and arched to meet him as her release welled. She squeezed him with her internal muscles, holding him tight, letting him go, loving the guttural sounds she forced from him. He captured her tight and aching-for-him nipple and rolled it between his fingers. With his other he found her center, circled, stroked, pushing her to the edge. Her climax hit hard and fast, magnified by each slam of his body into hers. She rode the aftershocks until, muscles straining, he growled and stilled.

Wow. Panting for breath, she melted into the sheets and tried to gather her scattered wits. She hadn't been expecting *that*. Making love had never been that feral, that driven, that exciting for her.

Roth withdrew and lay on his back beside her. When he didn't pull her onto his chest the way he usually did, she rolled to her side. Something wasn't right.

His body remained tense. The harsh set of his face, the thin line of his lips and the pleat wrinkling his brow did not belong on the face of a man who'd made love with a woman he cared about. He stared at the ceiling, seemingly unaware of her presence.

Uneasiness chilled her skin. Had her surprise visit been unwelcome? "Roth?"

His eyes cut her way. Cold eyes. Hard eyes. A frisson swept her. Who was this man?

She nervously dampened her swollen lips. "What's wrong?"

"ALE arrested Butch White and Ronnie Craig for manufacturing and distributing moonshine this morning."

She gasped. Butch had been like an uncle to her. "Does my father know?"

"I called him."

She knew the deputy had been a thorn in Roth's side, but that didn't seem to be reason enough for this distance. "And?"

"White intercepted a call for me from the parole board two weeks ago. He neglected to mention my father was released from prison three days ago. Early. Some bullshit about overcrowding and good behavior. I tried phoning my mother and her line's been disconnected. She's probably with the bastard."

She wasn't crazy about Seth's return—not after the hell he'd put Roth and his mother through. And the man had killed her uncle. But…

Piper rose on an elbow. "Remember how much you hated it when my father always expected the worst of you? Your father has done his time. You have to give him a chance."

His eyes turned lethal. "He'll only get one."

The hatred in his voice made the back of her neck prickle. It reminded her of the man she'd feared he had become—the one who could kill without qualms.

And then she remembered an animal was its most fierce and most frightening when it was afraid. Roth was afraid for his mother.

Roth saw the trepidation on Piper's face and wanted to kick himself. Damn. He was no better than his father.

"I'm sorry. Apologizing doesn't undo or excuse my actions, but I need you to know my lousy behavior is not your fault."

Her face relaxed a little. "I didn't think it was…unless you didn't appreciate me stopping by without an invitation."

"It's not you, babe. Don't ever believe that. I lost my cool when the parole board confirmed White's bombshell. I came home to try to work out my frustration with the weights. I should have sent you away until I was fit to be around. I had no right to jump you like that."

"Did you hear me say no?"

"I didn't give you a chance."

"Do we need to go look for your mother tonight?"

How like her to put others first. She was a nurturer to her core. "No. They'll come to us. Did I hurt you?"

"Of course not. Making love like that was…*intense*. But I kinda liked it. Until the end when you shut me out."

He'd shut her out because he'd realized that nothing, not even burn-his-brains-to-cinders sex, changed the fact that he was Seth's son, and the physical way he'd had to work out his anger reinforced that point. He'd given the weights one hell of a pounding before she'd arrived.

He pulled her into his arms and inhaled a big gulp of her. He stroked her hair, letting the rhythmic action calm him.

"Roth, I'll be there for you if you'll let me. I want to help."

An unfamiliar sense of yearning swamped him. He'd never counted on anyone but his fellow Marines or SWAT officers and only then because his life depended on them.

He wanted to count on Piper.

Holding her, making love to her hadn't sated his hunger the way he'd expected—it had only made him want her more. How could he walk away from her again?

In all his travels nothing had changed except his age and the mileage on his bones. He still loved Piper.

Loved her. The urge to run charged through him. But Gus's words stopped him. Roth couldn't keep running from who he was. He had to face it. Deal with it. Accept it. He could not let his father determine his fate. If he wanted Piper, he had to stay and fight for her.

But did his feelings matter? Would Piper still love him after she encountered his father and discovered true evil?

"So...have you missed me?" Josh asked around a mouthful of French fries.

Roth caught Piper's smile out of the corner of his eye as he looked across the diner's booth at their son. He squeezed her hand beneath the table.

A month ago he never would have believed he'd miss spending time with a kid, but Roth's afternoons without Josh had lacked something.

"I see you almost every day," he said, deadpan.

Josh rolled his eyes. "That's for dinner an' homework an' baseball an' stuff. I meant carpool."

"I miss you and Sarg. How's riding with your grandpa working out?"

"Good. But Sarg hogs the window seat in Grandpa's truck. I have to sit in the middle."

"Did you finish your chores for Mr. Doyle this morning?"

"Yep. Grandpa says he'll be ready to take me hunting this fall—if I take a safety course this summer."

"Good plan." Despite yesterday's nuclear meltdown in the bedroom, today had been good. He'd joined Piper and Josh for his lunch break after Piper finished her Saturday-morning shift at the clinic. How many more days like this did he have?

As if he'd tempted fate with his question, a moving van rolled down Main Street. Roth, along with every customer in the diner, turned to watch the truck's progress.

They didn't get many newcomers moving

to town. And they were only expecting one set. His parents.

The glare on the windshield kept him from seeing the driver, but there was no mistaking the face leering through the open passenger window. His father's.

Seth spotted Roth and waved—not a friendly gesture, more of an in-your-face one that lit a fire in Roth's chest. He fought the urge to drag the bastard from the truck and beat the living crap out of him in retaliation for all the blows Roth's mother had taken.

His father's lips moved, but Roth couldn't make out the words, and the truck stopped. His mother leaned forward and waved. Somehow he had to convince her to get rid of her no-good husband.

"Who's that?" Josh asked.

"My parents."

Piper squeezed his hand. "Roth—"

"I have to go." He pulled his hand free, rose, slowly, deliberately, holding on to his control with an iron grip. The truck drove away.

"Let me come with you," Piper offered despite the anxiety clear on her face.

That was his Piper. Brave. "No. This is between me and them."

"Lot of nerve coming here, the murdering bastard," Hal Smith from the hardware store snarled as Roth dropped money on the table. "We don't want him here."

Hal's cronies grumbled agreement—a sentiment seemingly shared by all the diners.

Their lynch-mob mind-set forced Roth to do the one thing he'd never expected. He had to defend his father, the man he detested more than anyone.

"I don't want him here, either, Mr. Smith, but until he violates his parole there's not a damn thing any of us can *legally* do about it."

"You arrested kids and Deputy White, but you're gonna let Seth Sterling, a murdering bastard, be?"

"Yes. I am. Until he breaks the law he has as much right to be here as you." And he didn't doubt his father would screw up. "As for the arrests, I took care of the vandalism and moonshine problems. You want to complain about that? Your store sustained damage when those boys set fires in trash cans."

Red-faced, Hal swiveled toward the counter.

Roth strode from the diner and climbed into his patrol car. He drove to his old house and caught up with the moving van as it turned into the driveway.

He met his mother as she stepped from the cab. There was no hug—they'd never had that kind of relationship.

"For your own safety don't let him into the house. Divorce him. Take out a restraining order. I'll protect you."

"Roth, he's my husband, and I meant it when I vowed for 'better or worse, till death do us part.'"

"I don't want it to be *your* death."

She smiled. "It won't be. He's changed. I know it deep in my heart."

"People don't change."

"You did. You went from a long-haired rebel to chief of police." Her obvious pride couldn't hide her stubborn refusal to accept reality, and that confirmed what Lou had told him. Roth's mother had refused help.

His father appeared from the rear of the truck, planting himself between Roth and the cruiser. Seth must have taken advantage of the prison's gym. His rangy body had muscles that hadn't been there before. Roth still had him by four inches and twenty pounds.

"What do you want, boy?"

"I want you gone. From Quincey. From her life."

The smirk returned. "I have every right to be here, and there's nothing you can do about it."

The fact that the law supported the statement pissed Roth off more. He closed the distance until only inches separated him and his father. He loomed over Seth. "I will be watching. If you lay one hand on her or even so much as jaywalk, I'll be all over you. Understand?"

His father laughed. "What are you gonna do? Arrest me? She won't let you."

Cocky sonofabitch. It took a conscious effort not to ball his fists and let loose on that vile, leering face. But he would not stoop to his father's level.

He might be his father's son, but he was not an animal. "Test me and find out."

He handed his mother a business card with his cell and the station numbers on it. "You call me. For anything. Anytime. Day or night."

"I won't need to call. But thank you, Roth."

He hoped she was right. But he didn't believe it for one second.

Chapter Nineteen

Despite the urge to linger, Ann Marie climbed from the bed she and Lou had bought together thirty-two years ago. If she didn't have an appointment scheduled...well, she might have spent the entire afternoon in bed with the man. Shameless, for a woman of her age. But wonderful.

"We have to do something to help Piper and Roth. Between me spending time here and Josh sleeping in the room beside Piper's those two aren't getting much time alone."

"If you're talking about what I think you're talking about, I don't want to think about it."

"You wanted to think about it a few minutes ago."

Shaking his head, Lou pulled on his pants. "What plan are you concocting now, woman?"

"Did you know the Pughs are selling their house and moving to a retirement community in Raleigh? They want to be near their grandchildren."

"No. I didn't know. But what's that got to do with Piper?"

"The Pughs live at the end of this street. The house has four bedrooms and a huge fenced yard, and they renovated last year."

He looked at her blankly.

The man could be so obtuse sometimes. "Their house is perfect for Piper and Roth. They'd be close by if I moved back in here."

"*If?* Damn straight you're moving in. I'm too old and life's too short to waste time traipsing all over town to see my wife."

"Lou, we live four miles apart."

"Apart's apart. But there's a hole in your plan."

Her good mood wavered. She'd planned this perfectly. There were no flaws in her plan. "What hole?"

"I've come to respect Roth and I'm enjoying our range time. But I get the feeling he's preparing me to return to my old job."

"Why would he do that?"

"You're the one who said Piper thinks he'll leave once his momma's squared away."

"How do you feel about returning to work—if the town council would take you back?"

"Mixed." He buttoned his shirt—successfully, she noticed. "A lot happened right under my nose and I missed it."

"You mean Butch."

"I knew he was buying stuff he shouldn't have been able to afford on his salary, but I never questioned where he was getting the money."

"Why would you?"

"Because I worked with the man for twenty years, Ann Marie. I should have known he was up to no good."

"You trusted him and you thought the best of him. You are a very trusting soul, Lou. That's one of the things I love about you."

He fixed his gaze on her. "You love me?"

"I never stopped. Not even when I hated you a little bit."

He took her in his arms and kissed her so tenderly tears sprang to her eyes.

"I don't want my job back. I'm fifty-five. I

put in my thirty years. I think it's time I retired and spent time with my wife, daughter
and grandkid. If there's one thing that stroke
taught me, it's that our days are numbered."

"I agree. I don't want to retire, but I want
to cut back and maybe take on an associate."

"If we can keep Piper and Roth together
and in Quincey, then maybe we'll have more
young'uns around."

"Then you'll help?"

"Tell me what you want me to do."

Happiness swelled inside Ann Marie until
she thought she might burst. "I'm going to show
Roth the Pughs' house. Piper loves it here. All
we have to do is convince Roth to stay."

"I'll speak to Gus. He might have some
clout with Roth." Then Lou frowned. "If I'd
listened to Gus twelve years ago—"

"Hush. What's done is done. You did what
you thought was best. And Roth is a better
man for it—better for Piper and Josh and our
town. That's what counts."

Roth didn't want to be here. He'd rather be
with Piper or dropping by his parents' house
unannounced as he'd done each of the past
three days. Had his mother learned how to
use the cell phone Piper had insisted he buy

her? Had she reconsidered his offer to set her up in a home of her own near his in Charlotte? If he couldn't get rid of his father, he'd relocate his mother.

But Ann Marie had been harassing him to look at this house since Sunday. The best way to stop her calls was to get this out of the way.

She threw open another door. "This is the room their grandson used when he visited."

Roth entered without interest and stopped in his tracks. One wall had been covered in a mural of the planets.

Ann Marie crossed the large space and closed the curtains, blocking out the sun, then she returned to his side and turned off the lights. Constellations—correctly formatted— glowed on the ceiling.

Josh would love this room. But for Roth to give it to him he would have to stay here and live in his father's shadow. Not going to happen. He pivoted and headed for the stairs.

As he made his way through the den he couldn't help noticing what he'd ignored during his cursory walk-through. The rest of the house had been decorated in the same colors Piper had chosen for her own house.

He could picture himself, Piper and Josh

watching movies in this room, sharing meals in the large kitchen or cooking on the brick patio out back.

"The fenced yard is big enough for Sarg."

"Ann Marie, this house is for sale, not for rent, and I've told you I'm not ready to list my Charlotte property yet." He didn't have the stomach to stand here and keep evading the truth. "I have to go."

"Lou and I are reconciling."

Her words halted him in the foyer. "Congratulations."

"I never thought we would because he did some things I considered unforgivable, but now I understand that he believed he was doing the right thing. And the love...well, it's still there."

"Why are you telling me this?"

"We can't undo the past, but we lost a lot of years because of it. I refuse to let it cost us our future. I'm hoping you do the same.

"Please don't hurt her again, Roth. And please don't take Piper and Josh from us."

Her pleas made him uncomfortable. "I have to get to baseball practice."

He retreated to his patrol car. But as the brick two-story faded in his rearview mirror emptiness welled inside him. Piper would love that house. She and Josh and Sarg could be happy there.

Without him.

No, damn it. He wouldn't walk away from Piper again. He wanted her. Needed her.

But could he be the man Piper—and Josh—needed him to be?

He'd conquered his demons, hadn't he? Caged them. Controlled them. Over the past twelve years he had deliberately put himself in situations where he had to master his weaknesses or die. And he was still here, which meant he'd succeeded.

He loved Piper and he wanted a life with her and Josh. But not here. And she had to have feelings for him, too.

The only way to have her in his life was to convince her to move away with him. Not to Charlotte. Somewhere close enough to keep an eye on his parents and visit hers but far enough away to escape the cloud that hung over him here.

He had friends in the Raleigh Police Department. He'd make a few calls and find out if they had any suitable positions available.

Then maybe he could keep Piper and Josh in his life by keeping them away from Seth.

* * *

The moment they stepped from the woods Piper recognized the smooth boulder along the river's edge.

Roth had refused to tell her where he was taking her when he'd picked her up after work. All he'd said was that Josh would be spending the weekend with her parents. They had two days to revel in each other with no boy, dog or kittens to watch.

And he'd brought her here. "This is where we made love the first time." The evening breeze whipping around them and adding a nip to the air might make it a little too cold for history to repeat itself.

Roth squeezed her hand. "It's more than that. This is where my grandfather proposed to my grandmother. I never knew her. She died when my mom was still in school. But my grandfather loved her until his last breath. He was a romantic like you." He touched her nose with a fingertip and Piper nearly melted.

"You never told me that. I thought this was some random piece of Roth land where you thought we wouldn't get caught."

His slow, tender smile sent warmth through her. He led her out to the edge of the rock. Water flowed lazily past. "This is also where

I discovered you were more important to me than winning a few bucks off my buddies. I realized I'd fallen in love with you the first time. Right here."

Her heart bumped wildly. "The first time?"

"You still get to me, Piper. You make my heart race and my palms sweat and you wreak havoc on my control. I love you. I don't know if I ever stopped."

Happiness trapped the air in her lungs. "I love you, too."

"Marry me. Let's build a life together. You, me and Josh. I spoke to a buddy who works with the Raleigh Police Department and there's an opening. It's close enough for me to keep an eye on my parents and for us to visit yours, but far enough away to escape the stench of my father. I don't want Josh growing up in that shadow of shame."

Her bubble deflated slightly. "You want to leave Quin—"

The chimes of Roth's cell phone interrupted her. The softness in his face vanished. "That's my mother's ringtone." He took the call. "Mom?"

The sound of crying reached Piper. Before her eyes Roth became that cold, calm—

deadly calm—man she'd first seen the other night, and she knew this romantic evening wouldn't end well.

"Mom?" Roth repeated. "Talk to me."

"Roth. He's drunk. You were right. He hasn't changed. Please come. He's ranting and I'm afraid." The broken words, interspersed with gasps, filled him with fury.

"Where are you now?"

"In the front yard. I snuck out. Ohmigod. Here he comes."

"Stay on the phone. I'm less than a mile away." He raced for his truck. Piper kept pace beside him. Good. He couldn't leave her here, not with sunset approaching. They climbed in the truck and out of the corner of his eye he saw her dialing on her cell phone.

"June, this is Piper. There's a domestic disturbance out at the Sterling place. Roth is keeping his mom on the phone while we drive over there, but you need to send officers now."

He drove with as much speed as he dared. "Mom. Are you okay?"

He heard a gasp then the line went silent.

"Damn it. We were disconnected."

Moments later he raced up the driveway

but stopped a hundred yards from the house. He left the engine running and looked into Piper's fear-filled eyes. "Take the truck and get the hell out of here."

"I'm not leaving you, Roth."

"Piper—"

"No."

He couldn't waste time arguing, but the idea of her being injured ripped him in two. "Then stay in the truck and keep your head down. Promise me."

"I will."

He pulled his gun from the glove compartment and his Dragon Skin vest from behind his seat and shrugged on the body armor.

The yard offered no cover. He made it halfway across the lawn before the screen door slammed open. His father stepped out, using Roth's mother as a shield. Seth's arm was around her neck. He held a pistol to her head while a trickle of blood ran from her mouth. Roth reined in the rage. He couldn't afford a mistake.

He aimed the gun at his father. "Quincey P.D. Drop your weapon."

"Why? So you can shoot me? You won't do it. You didn't have the nerve when you were a snot-nosed brat and you don't have the guts now." Seth's hands weren't steady. His words were slightly slurred.

Since it was impossible to rationalize with a drunk, Roth had to figure out a way to get his mother out.

"Let her go. Your beef's with me."

"You think I didn't know you were trying to get her to leave me? You think I didn't call your Charlotte department and find out you'd taken a leave of absence? Or hear you promising to buy Eloise a place in Charlotte? *Come live near me, Mama,* you said. I heard every word."

Another vehicle sounded on the gravel driveway, but Roth didn't take his eyes off his target.

"Make him stay back," Seth yelled, maneuvering behind a thick porch column. He shifted left, then right, weaving a little, exposing a shoulder on one side then the other. "Or he'll end up like his brother."

His brother. Lou. Another civilian. Roth hoped the man had the sense to stay back.

A second vehicle raced up the road. Roth recognized the engine sound of a deputy's cruiser. The blip of a siren confirmed it. "Drop your weapon," Aycock's voice said over the speaker.

Aycock and Lou. Neither had the accuracy to take a shot at that range.

"Think you have me outnumbered," Roth's father sneered. "Maybe you do. But I'll get off at least one shot." The muzzle of his pistol dug into Eloise's temple and she sobbed.

Roth itched to pull the trigger. He had the skill and the weapon required for a kill shot. No one would blame him and his mother would be safe. Permanently.

Kill only what needs killing.

The sadistic bastard deserved killing.

Roth stepped forward. "C'mon, old man. You've built up a few muscles in the prison gym. Come down here and let's fight this out man-to-man. No guns." He took one hand off his weapon and curled his fingers in invitation.

Roth saw the moment Seth considered the challenge.

And the moment he rejected it. But pride was still his weakness. Roth could work with that.

"What's the matter, Seth? You afraid to pick on someone your own size? You prefer to beat on a woman or a child? Someone who won't fight back."

If Seth dropped his guard, Roth could take the shot. Right now the damned post was in the way. "I thought you were a tough guy. But you're hiding behind a woman."

He ignored his mother's whimper. He couldn't afford to be distracted.

"Didn't take you long to fall off the wagon, did it? I shut down Craig's still. Where'd you get your booze?"

"None of your business."

That's right. Shift her a little more to the left. Bingo.

The shot rang out and Piper screamed and ducked. When she peered over the dashboard Seth lay on the porch floor propped against the house. Red spread from his shoulder. Eloise stood as if in shock.

Piper watched Roth and Deputy Aycock storm the porch. Horror chilled her. The side door of the pickup abruptly opened, startling another cry from her.

"You all right, baby girl?" her father asked.

Piper looked at the house, at Aycock handcuffing Seth, and Roth, his face devoid of emotion, stiffly holding his mother as she sobbed.

"He shot his own father."

"Didn't have much choice."

Two more cars screeched in. State troopers.

They sprinted to the house and started firing questions. Roth's level, unemotional voice carried across the evening air. How could he shoot his own father and feel nothing?

"Get me out of here."

"Piper, you're a witness—"

"I'll give a statement later. I want to go."

"Let me clear it."

Her father walked toward the group as she unbuckled her seat belt. It was only then that she noticed how badly she was shaking. An ambulance siren whined in the distance.

If Roth could shoot his own father without emotion, was he capable of feeling anything at all? Remorse? Love?

Roth's gaze met Piper's across the distance. He strode toward her. She jumped from the truck. "Piper—"

"Is it true? You're on leave from Charlotte's department?"

"Yes."

"You never intended to stay."

"I came here to convince my mother to leave that bastard. But then you happened. I love you, Piper. I want a life with you and Josh." His eyes looked sincere. But she couldn't trust what she saw.

Pain burned through her like acid. She'd

been fooled by him. Again. "I don't believe you. And I could never love a man who'd take a job—my father's job—under false pretenses, deceive an entire town and shoot his own father."

She hiccuped. "You're not the man I thought you were. That man wouldn't make a woman and an innocent boy love him knowing he was leaving them. Go back to Charlotte, Roth. There's nothing for you here."

She forced her shaking legs to carry her to her father's truck.

Chapter Twenty

"All right, baby girl. You've made the man suffer enough."

Piper looked up from the kitten curled in her lap and spotted her father, wearing his old uniform, in the doorway. Sarg lifted his head from the floor beside her, but didn't dislodge the three kittens sleeping on him.

"Why aren't you angry with Roth? He befriended you under false pretenses."

"Despite what I did to him, he helped me get my shot and my job back. Not that I plan on keeping it once Roth's cleared. That should come through sometime today."

"Daddy, even if it does, he's leaving Quincey.

And he probably helped you only because he didn't want to leave the department in the lurch."

Her father sat beside her on the sofa. "A man's gotta do whatever it takes to protect his family. Sometimes it's not the right thing. I lived that mistake twelve years ago, and I almost lost all of you because I was too blind to see beyond my own plan. And I know you understand because you gave up everything you loved to protect your baby."

She couldn't deny that. "Roth tried to kill his father. And afterward...it was as if he felt nothing."

"Piper, I've seen that boy shoot. At that distance he can empty an entire clip into the same damned hole. If he'd wanted Seth dead, Eloise would be a widow. And nobody would have faulted Roth for it. If I'd been him, I would've killed the bastard."

His vehemence surprised her. He took her hand. "Roth's job has taken him places most men aren't strong enough to go, let alone come back from."

He bowed his head and his jaw worked. Piper waited. And then his gaze met hers. The pain, regret and sadness in his eyes settled like a weight on her chest.

"If I'd had Roth's guts and composure seventeen years ago, my baby brother wouldn't be dead. But I didn't. I stood by—frozen with fear—and let Sterling kill Edgar."

Piper felt his agony. "That's why we never talked about him."

"I'm the reason he became a cop. I let him down. When he needed me I wasn't there for him. I couldn't take the shot. And if you think Roth doesn't feel anything, then you're wrong. He loves his mama enough to come to a town he hated where everyone expected him to be like his no-good daddy. That's love, Piper. The question is, do you love him enough to accept what he's done in the line of duty? It's made him who he is. He can't undo it."

He patted her hand and rose. "I wish I were half the man Roth is."

Piper stared after her father and the realization sank in that she'd let Roth down when he needed her the most. He'd been through hell and she hadn't been there for him.

Karma was a bitch.

A week of administrative leave while the State Bureau of Investigation completed their inquiry gave a man too much time to think.

Roth paced his apartment. He should be writing his resignation letter and packing to return to Charlotte and the job he loved instead of waiting for the phone to ring. He'd achieved his goal of separating his parents permanently. A felon on probation who'd committed assault, was caught with a weapon and threatened a police officer wouldn't be released.

Instead of satisfaction, there was a gaping hole in his soul. Even though Piper loved him, he was losing her. She'd refused to see him this week and wouldn't let him see Josh. Roth had gone to Lou, but Lou had insisted she needed time to think.

Being benched gave Roth a ringside seat to Quincey in action. Lou was acting as interim chief. One of the baseball parents had stepped in as coach, and the townsfolk had gathered around his mother, taking her food, offering emotional support. A local high-powered attorney had offered to handle his mother's divorce pro bono. She had agreed.

Quincey at its finest. This was why Piper refused to leave.

The phone rang. He dove for it. But the number on the screen wasn't Piper's. "Sterling."

"Chief? This is Mayor Snodgrass. You've

been cleared to return to work. Come down to the station and pick up your badge and gun."

Could he take Lou's job a second time? No. But he might be able to talk the town council into letting him take Butch White's place. "I'm on my way."

But first, he had to make a call to Ann Marie.

And once he finished at the station, he was going after Piper.

A knock on the door interrupted Piper's preparations. She dropped her mascara on the counter.

Eager to get rid of whoever it was so she could look for Roth, she answered. Roth stood on the mat. Her body went on lockdown. Her lungs and heart ceased functioning for a dizzying moment.

"I was on my way to see you."

"Why?"

"To apologize. This week has been hard on you. And I wasn't there for you when you needed me. All I could think about was that you could have killed your father."

"Yes."

"But you didn't."

"No."

"Why, Roth? You hated him. Even my father says he would have if he'd been in your shoes."

Roth exhaled. "May I come in?"

"Of course." She stepped out of the way.

Sarg raced into the room, demanding his share of attention, which Roth gave. Then he met her gaze. "I tried to give your father his job back. He refused to take it. He says he'd like to spend his retirement spoiling his grandkids. Plural. Is there something you haven't told me?"

Piper gaped. Was that why he'd come? She tried to hide her disappointment. "No. I'm not pregnant."

"I'd like the chance to give him what he wants. I love you, Piper, and I love Josh. I want to stay in Quincey and make a home with you. If you can look me in the eye and tell me you don't feel the same, then I'll leave you alone."

The love, yearning and—fear?—in those dark eyes was impossible to miss. Her heart soared, but she tamped the emotion. "I love you, too. So much it terrifies me. But I won't be your anchor. We'll go to Charlotte with you. Or Raleigh. If you need to leave Quincey to be happy, Josh and I will adapt. Being with you is what matters."

Roth wrapped her in his arms. Then his lips brushed hers in the most tender kiss she'd ever experienced.

He lifted his head. "You're not my anchor, Piper. You're my safe harbor. You have no idea how many times over the past dozen years you've been in my head."

Hope flickered to life. "But you hate it here."

"This past week has given me an opportunity to see a different side of our citizens. We're a lot like a military unit. We take care of our own. And there's nowhere else I'd rather be than here with you and Josh and any other family we might have."

Happiness made her feel light and giddy. "I'd like that, too."

"I've asked your mother to put in an offer on a house down the street from your father's. I think you and Josh will love it. There's room for all of us and room to grow—if we need it."

He dropped to one knee and took her hands in his. "Marry me, Piper, and let me spend the next fifty years making up for the ones we lost."

Tears burned trails down her cheeks. "I will marry you, but there's nothing to make up for. You're here now, and that's all that matters."

* * * * *

Get 2 Free Books,
Plus 2 Free Gifts—
just for trying the Reader Service!

Get 2 Free Books,
Plus 2 Free Gifts—
just for trying the
Reader Service!

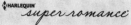

Get 2 Free Books,
Plus 2 Free Gifts—
just for trying the Reader Service!

HARLEQUIN
HEARTWARMING™

Get 2 Free Books,
<u>Plus</u> 2 Free Gifts –
just for trying the Reader Service!